LOVE ME NOT

EDEN EMORY

NOTE

This is a work of fiction. Names, characters, business, events and incidents are the products of the author's imagination. Any resemblance to actual persons, living or dead, or actual events is purely coincidental.
Before moving forward, please note that the themes in this book can be dark and trigger some people. The themes can include but are not limited to; emotional abusive grandparents and aunt, parental death, accident, grief, slut shaming, attempted murder, abusive parent, violence.

If you need help, please reach out to the resources below.

National Suicide Prevention Lifeline
1-800-273-8255
https://suicidepreventionlifeline.org/

National Domestic Violence Hotline
1-800-799-7233
https://www.thehotline.org/

Also by Eden Emory

Elle Mae

Blood Bound Series:

Contract Bound: A Lesbian Vampire Romance

Lost Clause

Blood Royale:

Eternal Captive: A Dark Enemies-to-Lovers Sapphic Vampire Romance

Divine Decption

Winterfell Academy Series:

The Price of Silence: Winterfell Academy Book 1

The Price of Silence: Winterfell Academy Book 2

The Price of Silence: Winterfell Academy Book 3

The Price of Silence: Winterfell Academy Book 4

The Price Of Silence: Winterfell Academy Book 5

Winterfell Series Box Set

Short and Smutty:

The Sweetest Sacrifice: An Erotic Demon Romance

Nevermore: A Deal with a Demon

Stolen Demon Brides:

Taken to the Deadlands

Taken to the Shadow Realm

Taken to the Demon Court

Eden Emory

The Ties That Bind Us

Don't Stop me

Don't Leave Me

Don't Forget Me

Don't Hate Me

Two of a Kind

Hide n' Seek

Queer Meet Cute Anthology

Pétale Auction

Love Me Not

Patreon Only

Wicked corruption: An FF Mafia Romance

Watch Me

Tales of the Stolen Demon Brides

LOVE ME
not
AMAZON BESTSELLER
EDEN EMORY

Chapter 1
Juliette

A mask was a heavy burden, especially when it was my only way into New York's hottest queer BDSM club.

It had taken a good portion of my bus money to get a car to the place. They chose an out-of-the-way, quiet house with an unassuming neighborhood. It's better for privacy that way.

After all, they catered to some of the most high-level and sensitive people—or at least that was the rumor.

They boasted about how good their privacy and security were in the club, and it did seem that way. I didn't even get the address to the place until an hour before I was supposed to arrive.

I wouldn't be surprised if there were some super-secret government officials inside. Or maybe they veered to the more *illegal* side of things.

Either way, the promise of privacy was a plus for me.

From the outside, you'd never know the devious things that took place inside.

The cool air brushed across my skin, reminding me that I

was just there, motionless, looking up at the place with a wide gaping mouth. Could I make it any more obvious I'd never been here before? I pulled my coat closer, debating whether or not it was a good idea to go in. I still had time.

Maybe I could just turn back. Forget I'd ever come. But that would be a waste of the money I spent to get here. And who knew if the auction was the real deal? Or if anyone would even want me?

I took it all in. The night sky, glittering with stars. The carefully trimmed lawn. The gold gate surrounding the entire property. The house itself reaching high up into the sky, looking more like some rich tycoon's mansion than a sex club.

There were lights shining from the inside, but they seemed dim. Either that or they had special films to block out any prying eyes. The latter seemed more likely.

There wasn't anyone outside besides the guard at the door and myself. Only then did I realize he'd been staring at me. Probably as long as I'd been standing there.

Cars were parked on the road leading up to the house, but they were all empty.

What I was here for was all too obvious. If the black studded mask wasn't enough, then my five-year-old bright-red pumps and lacy black dress would paint the full picture.

I didn't have anything appropriate to wear to the club—or the funds to purchase it—so I put together what I had and hoped it would be enough.

Hell, if the auction didn't work out, coming to Club Pétale would be one of the worst financial decisions I made. But for once in my life, I wanted to do something for *me*. Auction and possible money aside, there was another reason I decided to partake in this auction. I wanted to be selfish.

That's what this night was for. *Me*. I had been working too long for other people. For everyone else. But not tonight.

I walked the rest of the way to the entrance with my shoulders back, pausing to look up at the guard with my best smile.

He just stared at me, looking me up and down before motioning for me to try the door.

Phase one: done.

"Thank you," I said earnestly and pushed open the door.

My jaw dropped at what was inside. The whole place reeked of money and elegance, but in a twisted, sexy way. The large blown-up pictures on the walls of various depraved sexual acts had my skin flushing immediately. And just beyond, the people were dressed—or I should say in various forms of *undress*—in sensual blacks, reds, feathers, leather, and everything else you could think of.

There was tasteful music playing in the background and light chatter, but everything was very behaved. Not a rager or a dark dungeon like my spiraling mind had told me it'd be like.

"Holy shit," I whispered, unable to fully comprehend what I was seeing. Immediately, I felt at home. All the nerves from before melting away.

"It's great, isn't it?"

My eyes fell to a girl dressed in an all-red latex suit that went all the way from her neck to her fingers and toes. She had a small mask on her face, her dark hair falling to her waist.

Then I saw the iPad in her hands.

"I don't know what I imagined, but this is better," I said, unable to keep the nervous excitement out of my voice. My decision was cemented then.

I'm doing this. No going back. I was meant to be here tonight.

I would walk home if I needed to. This was going to be a good night. *My* night.

"Wait until you see the private rooms. Name?" she asked, then tacked on. "Alias. Not your real name."

I flushed. She already knew how unprepared I was. Maybe she saw me waiting outside.

"Julie H." It was the only name I could think of when filling out the form and it was similar to mine. I assumed it would be easy to get used to it, but even hearing me say it out loud made me feel weird.

"No matches," she said as she used a stylus to type in my name. She looked me up and down, and I could see the moment of realization on her face. "Oh! You're here for the auction!"

My fingers grasped at the lace, suddenly nervous. Not too sexy for an auction, but I guess fitting for something more... elegant?

"Am I... dressed okay for it?" I asked.

She gave me a warm smile. "You're perfect."

I floundered for a response.

"And... You're sure I'll get the money? Like, this is not some type of trafficking scheme?" I don't know why it came out as a whisper, but it had the hostess giggling.

"Yes. We get a cut, of course, but most will be yours. Don't be so nervous," she said. "It's a single night with you. You fill out your preferences and hard noes and then you get bid on. Super easy."

Something akin to hope had its claws around my heart. I needed money more than I needed food at the moment. Between the debt from my parents' accident and my brother's tuition money, I was drowning. I had yet to be assigned a new family to nanny, but I knew it wouldn't pay much.

I just need enough to get by until then and maybe a bit extra to cover the hospital bills.

"How much do you think I can get?"

A part of me still wanted to run. Turn back and forget I

ever came. But I needed this. And the thought of someone worshipping me and me alone tonight had my skin tingling.

She shrugged.

"Up to them, but bidding starts at a hundred thousand."

I almost fainted right there on the spot.

I came here for a reason and was secretly hoping to meet someone to have a good night with. In other words, I came to get fucked. Thoroughly. But getting some money on top of that? It was almost too good to be true.

"Please show me the way."

I looked up at the empty stage and a nervous shudder went up my back.

It was empty, but I could hear the buzz of excitement working its way through the people behind the thick velvet curtain.

The room hadn't filled up with patrons yet, so they were giving us time to look around and get a feel of the place before just putting us in the spotlight. The girls who had signed up were sitting in the seats and rows next to me. Less than ten, most of them looking just as nervous as I felt, but I tried not to let it show.

I forced the well-worn smile on my face, no matter how I felt inside.

"Is this your first time here?" I asked the brunette girl beside me. She was wearing a pink mask, her bangs popping out above it.

She jumped slightly, as if she wasn't prepared for me to talk to her.

"Oh, um... Yeah, is it that obvious?" I could hear the anxiety weaved into her voice and immediately regretted it.

"Me too," I said quickly, shooting her another smile. "Juliette." I extended my hand but flinched when I realized I'd given her my real name.

She looked around and dropped her voice to a whisper. "Pearl."

I let out a sigh of relief. The last thing I wanted was to be kicked out of the auction for breaking the rules.

"I'm nervous," I admitted. "I'm afraid no one will buy me." I let out a laugh, but it sounded a bit manic even to my ears.

This got a real smile from Pearl. "Me too. How humiliating would it be to just stand up there with no bids?"

"Now, now, relax. Club Pétale would never let that happen," a girl said as she walked across the stage and sat down right on the edge of it to speak to us. "After all, we have a reputation to uphold, don't we?"

She had silver-dyed hair that was slicked back and shaven on the sides. Her face glittered with multiple piercings and her skin was covered in tattoos. They peeked out of her deep purple silk button-up that had the first few buttons undone and the sleeves rolled up. I could see a few leather straps underneath that were mostly hidden by the clothing.

She gave us a sultry grin.

"I'm Sloan," she said, looking each one of us in the eyes. "I'm in charge of memberships here, but since this auction was my idea, my hard-ass of a boss decided to put me in charge of it—"

There was a throat clearing off to the side of the stage. My eyes shot to the sound and my breath caught in my throat as an older woman with honey eyes and matching hair stared at the girl in front of us with a hardened look.

It had fear racing up my spine. She looked like she was going to kill someone.

"Speak of the devil," Sloan muttered, never losing her smile.

"I don't pay you to bad-mouth me."

"You pay me?" Sloan asked, her gaze shifting to her boss, whose edges of her lips tilted before she turned.

"Finish up. Bidders are getting antsy."

"That's Ax," Sloan explained as the other woman disappeared behind the curtain. "She's the boss, and though she seems like she has a stick up her ass, we promise your experience here is of the utmost importance."

Another girl with dark, curly hair and light umber skin pulled up to my side.

"This is my insanely beautiful wife, Lillian. She, along with Nyx, who's waiting for you backstage, is going to make sure you're comfortable. Lil will be in charge of taking pictures, so if you're not okay with that, please tell her so."

I looked up at her and she automatically gave me a warm smile.

"Let's get everyone back before it starts, hm? I think Ax wants to say a few words."

Ax. The scary one.

"Alright then, we will finish this back there."

They showed us through the small back area where there were extra seats, a couch, water, fruit, and other snacks.

"If you need to change, you can do so over there," the girl I came to know as Nyx said as she handed me a water. She had long brown hair with the ends dyed a deep purple with pink at the very end. She had a kind smile that made me like her immediately. "We have extra clothes and shoes in case you're uncomfortable. I will also be the one to see you to your room after you have signed your contract and your bidding has concluded."

"Speaking of contracts, you will sign one now and one after the bidder's bid is accepted and the funds are transferred," the scary one said as she addressed our group. "You will get a chance to back out at every step. After the bidding, we will ask if you're comfortable continuing with your bidder, and there are call buttons in the rooms to alert us if you need help at any time. Nothing is more important than your safety."

When her eyes fell to Nyx, I saw them soften slightly. *I wonder how they ever ended up together.* The scarier one seemed a bit too harsh for someone like Nyx, but maybe it was different behind closed doors. The thought had me flushing, and I turned my eyes to the floor as I wondered what would be happening to me behind closed doors tonight.

"Alright," she said when no one spoke up. "Shall we get this started?"

Maybe I should back out.

I stood by the edge of the curtain as Ax and Sloan gave their speech to the bidders.

I really hadn't fully thought it through. After all, from the time I arrived at the club to the time of the auction, only an hour had passed—if that.

I wanted to do it for the money, of course... But was I really okay with being bid off to a stranger?

Likely a rich one... Obviously queer... Who's also into BDSM... All of it is kind of a plus. And they did say I could back out at any point.

So, if I wasn't really feeling my bidder, I could just... walk away. But Lucas was counting on me.

It was okay for me to live like I had, but I needed to do

something for them. It wasn't just every day that an opportunity like this fell on my lap.

"And now, welcome our first lady of the night—Julie H.!"

Shit. I looked at Nyx, who nodded and motioned for me to walk on stage. *Here goes nothing.*

I rolled my shoulders and kept my head high before walking out and onto the stage. All lights were on me, but I could still make out the crowd. The small room that had been empty was now packed with masked people sitting down, each of them holding a paddle.

"Our first beauty is a charismatic and down-to-earth sub who loves *lots* of praise and is—*ooh*—open to exploring exhibitionism." I couldn't see Sloan from where I was standing, but the playfulness in her voice had me smiling.

I did a little twirl for the audience, earning a few chuckles. They spurred me on, and suddenly, I was playing with the audience. I winked at a few in the front, blew them a kiss, and even started to raise my dress a little to give them a peek at what was hiding beneath.

"Since this is her first ever auction, we will start at one hundred thousand!"

There was a terrifying moment where I truly believed no one was going to purchase me, that I was doomed for embarrassment.

But then one paddle raised.

"One-fifty!"

"One seventy-five!"

"Any take for two hundred?"

"I'll do you one better—three hundred!"

"Four!"

Oh my gosh. I couldn't conceal the shock on my face. *Are people really buying me for this much?* It was going to make all my dreams come true. It was going to change my life.

"Let's keep it going!"

"Five hundred!"

"Six!"

I blew them some more kisses and waved at the ones bidding. *This is really happening, isn't it?*

And then, someone stood up. I couldn't make out their face with the light, but their voice captivated me.

"One million."

Silence fell. Then Sloan, seeming really far away, hit something that sounded like a gavel.

"Sold to bidder number forty-two for one million dollars!"

I couldn't even get a look at her before I was rushed off the stage by Nyx.

"You fucking go, girl!" she whispered to me. "Come with me to sign the paperwork. The bidder will meet you in the room. I'll take you there."

I was in a haze the entire time Nyx was walking me through the paperwork. I heard her, but her voice sounded a thousand miles away and none of it was clicking.

How is this even real? Did someone really purchase me for a million dollars?

Nyx was gentle as she coached me through it, and then, with even more gentleness, she took me through the club.

Before I knew it, I was left in a dim room with a fuzzy carpet and a large four-poster bed alone and forced to come to terms with what I'd just done.

With shaky legs, I went to sit on the edge of the bed, unsure what else to do. But I didn't have much time to dwell.

There was a knock on the door, then silence.

Oh, shit! I'm supposed to answer.

"Come in."

The woman who pushed inside was almost as tall as the

doorframe. Her body was lithe, her hair black and gelled back. She wore an all-black suit with a deep red shirt underneath and a matching satin mask. Her ears had multiple piercings on them, and when she closed the door behind her, I caught the edges of a tattoo on her chest.

But something stood out to me even more.

She's so fucking hot! Holy shit!

"I know it's against the rules, but are you okay if I take my mask off? You can keep yours on if you want."

"Feel free," I said after a moment.

She immediately undid her mask, and I was hit with her fully uncovered face. I didn't think she could get even more attractive. I was wrong.

Her skin was unblemished, her eyes hooded and filled with the kind of need no one had ever looked at me with in my entire life. She looked to be slightly older than me, but it was more about the air around her than anything else.

There was no hesitancy in her movements. No second guessing. She knew what she wanted and she was in control.

She dropped the mask on the floor and stalked toward me, the sound of each step winding me up further and further. When she got to me, I expected to have to look up at her, but she got down on her knees.

My breath got caught in my throat.

"Can I touch you?" she asked.

I couldn't find my voice, so I nodded.

Her hands started on the bed before they came to rest on my thighs. Heat flushed through me immediately.

Hot *and* respectful? I couldn't wait for her to fuck the life out of me.

"No degradation, no pain play, no anal, no water play. Is there anything else on your *hard no* list?"

"I am open to trying other things," I said slowly. "But I want discussion on it first. Consent."

Her eyes ran down my body. "If I'm not getting enthusiastic consent from you, darling, I won't do it."

"Do you have anything you particularly like?"

Her hand trailed up to my hand, then up my arm.

"Already trying to please me? I didn't know I had such a perfect little surprise waiting for me here tonight."

Heat stemmed from wherever her fingers touched. My breath hitched, and I froze as she moved them up to my exposed collarbone.

"I want you to feel good," she murmured. "I'm not sure if you'll get to touch me tonight. But you..."

She licked her lips.

"Then..." I spread my legs. "Please, touch me."

She let out a shaky breath, and her hands were suddenly at my ankles, slowly moving up, taking the dress along.

"How do you feel about titles, Angel?"

My head spun when she finally got the dress to my knees and laid an open-mouthed kiss on my kneecap.

"I'll call you whatever you want if you keep calling me *that*." I don't know what it was about the pet name. Maybe it was the way she said it. Maybe it was because I finally felt like I was doing something *good* in my life.

All I knew was that I needed more of it.

"*Sir* will do, Angel."

"Sir," I breathed out and spread my legs further for her.

"Pull your dress up for me, Angel. I don't like my hands full during my meals."

I picked it up from her and opened my mouth to say something in return, but I was cut off when her face was buried between my legs.

I wasn't wearing underwear, and that was a fact I was now thrilled about.

Her right hand came around my ass, holding me in place, as the other grabbed my thigh and forced it to stay wide.

"Oh God," I cried and tried to remain sitting, but I found myself falling to the soft bed, keeping the dress up as her tongue ravaged me. She started with deep, long licks before teasing my clit and going back and forth between it and my entrance.

When her teeth grazed the sensitive bundle of nerves, I all but lost it.

It seemed so unfair. There I was, getting my pussy eaten for a million fucking dollars. But a voice in my mind told me I deserved this. I deserved to win. For the hot woman to want me bad enough she'd get on their knees and all but beg to taste me.

It made me feel powerful. Important. *Desired.*

"Sir, please. Just like that."

"You beg so sweetly," she groaned and pulled away just to meet my gaze. Her thumb replaced her mouth and rubbed hard circles over my clit.

My body arched.

"Fucking perfect, Angel. Do you see how well you respond to me?"

Jesus. Her praise went straight to my head.

"I've never wanted to please anyone more. No one's ever made me feel this way."

It was true. It sounded so cliché and overdone, but if I was on the verge of coming with so little stimulation, I was almost worried about what the rest of the night held.

"Your smell is mouthwatering. Your sounds are majestic. And your fucking taste? *It's divine.*"

I couldn't breathe. Even her words were attacking me in such a way that they rendered me helpless against her.

"I want to taste," I breathed.

"My perfect little angel," she murmured. She kept her thumb on my clit, never slowing her pace, and then used her other hand to slowly push two fingers inside me.

Only then did I realize that she hadn't even been inside me yet.

I expected her to just pump in and out a few times, but she was a woman on a mission. She set a pace that had my hips lifting, her thumb never stopping, and when she finally hooked her fingers—

"Yes, sir. Please don't stop. Please please plea—"

I came with a cry, my eyes fluttering shut as the first orgasm in over a year came rushing at me. It had my entire body in its claws, rendering me completely useless as it assaulted me.

Her fingers continued to coax it out of me, extending it way further than I'd ever felt before.

Just as it was over, she was climbing over me, her fingers brushing against my lips. Again asking for permission.

I opened my eyes before opening my mouth for her. I might not have thought my taste was *divine*, but right now it seemed like it was her favorite meal. How rude would I be if I didn't act like it was the most goddamn delicious thing I'd ever had? Especially when she put so much work into it.

I sucked her fingers and licked them clean.

"How long has it been since you came like that?" she asked, pulling her fingers out.

"A year," I said, not hesitating.

"You're so fucking perfect." She grabbed my chin lightly. "I want to come like that every time, do you hear me?"

Self-consciousness reared its ugly head.

"I don't know if I can—"

She covered my mouth with her hand.

"You will, Angel. You know why?"

I shook my head.

"Because I told you so. And tonight, your pleasure is mine. You want to satisfy me, right?"

I nodded enthusiastically, and she pulled her hand away, letting me speak.

"More than anything."

She sent me a dazzling smile.

"Then be a good little angel and do that again for me. Give me a show. Next time I want to hear you scream at the top of your lungs. Okay?"

I nodded and took a deep breath.

"We'll take a break after the fifth one."

I jerked my head up in shock, but she was already there, burying herself between my legs. Her fingers entering me, her mouth on my clit.

I fell back onto the bed, unable to do anything but take it all.

Multiple orgasms. One million dollars. And a hot, masc woman willing to do anything to get me off.

This had to be a fucking dream.

But at least for now, I'd let myself have this. I deserved this.

Even if only for one night.

I'd deal with everything else tomorrow.

Chapter 2
Lux

I'd never have thought a million dollars would place me close to the possible love of my life, but I'd always known one thing to be true.

Money does buy happiness.

In this specific case, it bought me a single night with the girl of my dreams.

Soft skin. Silky blonde hair. Pouty red lips.

She was a knockout.

The cherry on top? The way she *responded* to me. The way our bodies fit together perfectly.

I couldn't get enough of her.

I wanted more and more and only stopped because I saw my little angel getting worn out.

I wanted to break every rule. I had already done it by taking off my mask, so what was one more?

But I knew the rules were there not just for my sake, but for hers. She never took off the mask, meaning she didn't want to be known.

Which meant that if I gave her my name, it might put her in an uncomfortable position thinking I wanted hers.

I did. I wanted everything. Her name. Where she lived. What other dark, dirty fantasies she had that we hadn't gotten to.

And goddamn it, I wish I'd let her touch me.

I might have wanted others to before, when I was neglected and horny, but I *craved* her like she was some type of fucking super drug.

Her soft moans filtered through my mind over and over again. My body seized with a need for her. I could still feel her skin against mine. Could still taste her sweetness on the tip of my tongue.

If only I had the time to chase her. Rules were for the club; they couldn't dictate what we did when we weren't there.

I imagined bumping into her on the street. Or maybe if she worked in a service job, I could show up wherever she worked as a customer.

The fantasy of going to a random coffee shop and her being the barista was tantalizing. I pictured myself stopping at one on my way to work. Not the regular one I went to, but a random one that was just there when I was suddenly craving coffee. I would decide to get out of the car and get it. I would be standing there, moving up to the front of the line, and when I looked down, my little angel would be there. Waiting for me.

I would be breathless, and she would recognize me immediately, a blush coating her face.

I wouldn't pressure her, but I would plan to go there every day before work until she finally wrote her number on my cup.

But that was a silly daydream. Because, one, I never got coffee outside. And two, having time to even stand in line was laughable.

Going to the club set me back hours. Normally, in the dead of night, I would be able to finally get some peace and quiet and get some stuff done. The rest of my company wasn't working. Everyone was asleep in the house. And finally, I had uninterrupted thinking time to myself.

But I decided that I needed to get laid instead.

And drop one million fucking dollars.

I wasn't mad about the money. It was a small drop in a large pool that I had collected for myself over the years. And if I was being honest, I wasn't even mad that I had a pile of work waiting for me. I was still more frustrated with the fact that I had no time to do what I really wanted to do.

Find out who my angel truly was.

Because I had bigger things to take care of. Like many things in my life, I had to leave her behind too. *Love.* I almost scoffed at myself for such a ridiculous thought.

Someone like me, falling in love?

But that was the first thing I thought when I met her. It was what plagued my mind when I woke up every morning. Getting laid had been the plan. They invited me to go to the auction, and I thought it would be a good idea to at least have some mediocre sex. I never expected to pay one million dollars, but as soon as I saw her walk across the stage, I knew I couldn't bear anyone else having the chance to take her from me.

Which was why I had a message on my computer screen ready to be sent to an information broker, Mia. One I promised myself I wouldn't use again because of just how crazy she was.

But I needed to know. I didn't know how much longer I could hang on with her plaguing my mind.

"Lux? Is your internet breaking up again? This is why we need you in the offic—"

I cleared my throat; I had totally forgotten I was on a call with Dominic. I hadn't listened to at least the last 20 minutes.

My mind started drifting as he was going on about some possible reconstruction of the main floor and offices and how it would affect productivity.

I think he also mentioned that they were overcharging us? I had no fucking clue. Something you'd think as CEO I'd be worried about.

"I'm here," I said. "I'll look over the contracts when I get in tomorrow."

Tomorrow, yes. That was the plan. What I should be focusing on instead of daydreaming about my one-night stand.

"What? You're coming in so early? What about Bella—"

As if she heard it, there was a loud thud outside my office. Then another. It sounded like she somehow knew exactly where I was and was throwing it directly at my back. The only thing protecting me was the wall that separated my office from the backyard.

She better not be playing target practice with the statues again.

"I have the nanny coming tomorrow," I said, rushing the words out.

"It's only been a week since you fired the last one. Are you sure—"

"I'm sure," I answered with a huff. I was already standing, trying to get out of the meeting as fast as possible. "She's trying to run them off. And it's working, so I threatened to sue the nanny company. They said they're sending me their best."

I had work piling up. A lot of the stuff was hard to do at home, especially with Bella needing me all the time. I didn't blame her after what she'd been through. I just didn't know how to help, even though I desperately wanted to.

It wasn't just my duty. I loved her. And her mother.

He let out a chuckle.

"Best of luck. I'll see you then."

"See you."

I set down the phone with a sigh and stared back at the message on my computer, pausing for just a moment to try to think about the consequences of what I was about to do.

And then there was another thump.

I pushed my chair back and made my way out through the quiet house. My shoes squeaked against the marble floors. I had bought this house a few years back after realizing that it wasn't reasonable for me to be living in some random apartment when I had the money to build my own.

So that's what I did. But it felt a little lonely. The only thing brightening up the place was an eight-year-old with a shit-ton of grief and no outlet for it.

When I finally reached the open living room, I paused, taking in the sight in front of me.

Both Bella's personal chef and driver were standing by the large open sliding door, peeking out at the little girl. They were not nannies, something they had warned me about, but they also seemed to have warmed up to Bella, so they took it upon themselves to step in while I was finding a new one.

I appreciated them.

They stiffened when they heard me walk up, both turning their heads to look at me. I saw a mix of panic and exasperation on their faces.

"I tried to offer her snacks, but she threw them at me," the chef murmured, the evidence of her action splattered all over her apron. I noticed a few red splashes on her thick black hoodie. Usually, she was pretty good about not getting it on her clothes, being a professional and all, but she must've been hurrying to try and meet Bella's needs.

"Send your stuff over with mine to the cleaners," I told her.

She stood straight, her ears turning red. "No need, sir."

"Then you send it yourself and send me the bill. No negotiating."

I looked at her driver.

"I even offered to take her to Adventureland," she said with a shrug.

With a sigh, I looked out to the backyard. Bella was now on her iPad, acting as if she hadn't just been throwing rocks at my office wall.

"The nanny's coming soon," I informed them, unable to take my eyes off the pouting eight-year-old.

I felt a pang of grief when I saw her. It was inevitable. When she was born, I thought she looked more like that useless piece of shit Lily married. It annoyed me that she went through nine months of pain, high blood pressure, and an emergency C-section for her to come out looking like him.

It was insulting. Just like their entire relationship had been. She loved him unconditionally. Didn't matter that he didn't have a job or provide for them.

She said he was a good dad. She overlooked it when he'd come home late. When he'd miss important events. I didn't even go to family events anymore because of my vile mother, but I heard enough to know he wouldn't go to them either, leaving both of them to fend for themselves.

But as she spent more time with me, the more I could see my beloved sister in her.

Especially in her temper.

My sister was sweet and took a lot of shit from everyone for the sake of love, but when you got her angry—*oh boy*. I distinctly remember hiding out in my closet one day after school when she got mad at me for tearing up her homework.

In my defense, I thought it was a love letter from the boy who bullied her.

I saw that same girl now in Bella.

"That's good," the chef said with a sigh. "I love that little girl to death, but I'm not cut out for babysitting."

"Me neither," the driver muttered. Her hair was in a mess, her bangs pushed up and to the side after running her hands through it one too many times. "The only experience I have is babysitting my baby cousins once in seventh grade."

"At least you have experience."

The truth was that I was allergic to kids. I had never wanted them. Never had a maternal bone in my body. I always wanted love. Yearned for it. But kids? They were a whole different ball game.

You had to carry the child for nine—if not ten—months, your bones literally shifting in place, gaining up to sixty pounds sometimes, only to go through the most traumatic experience of your life before having to take care of a living, breathing thing that literally can't do anything on their own.

Not to mention, relying on a partner becoming a good parent.

But then Bella came into my life. I definitely wasn't her first choice of guardian, but my sister had put it in her will that she would go to me. She even had all the paperwork drawn up. All I had to do was sign.

And I couldn't leave her. I might not have been close to her before, but there was no way I would leave her in the hands of my mother.

I wanted to be the aunt she needed, but I never wanted this. I never prepared for this. It had never crossed my mind. To me, my sister would live forever, and I would die way before her death even became a topic.

Bella deserved someone better than me. More prepared. More maternal. More structured. Someone who could go on a field trip and would know what to say at parent-teacher conferences. Someone who knew how to address her and do her hair in the morning instead of leaving her to do it herself.

Someone who was definitely *not* me.

I watched how she tapped angrily on her iPad, her lips still in a pout. She had the same dark brown hair as my sister's husband, but her eyes were the beautiful hazel of my sister. She was still in the T-shirt and puffy tutu skirt she had picked out this morning, though now it was pretty dirty. Just more evidence that she was actually digging in the dirt for rocks to throw at my wall.

With a click of my tongue, I turned on my heels and headed back to my office. I sat down at my desk, my hands gripping the sides of my chair.

This one has to work. I don't have any other options. I'm running out of time—

The thumping against my back wall started again. She started with just a single rock, then paused when I didn't immediately come back out before throwing another. And another. And another.

Tomorrow. Just wait till tomo—

Then I heard a crash somewhere. It sounded like something shattering.

Again, my mind went back to the message I wanted to send the information broker. I could just do this one thing for myself.

Just like my trip to the club, I needed *something*. Anything to take my mind off the stress of the real world. It wasn't what I should be spending my time on, but it was just some information, right?

I wouldn't act on it... Or at least that was what I promised myself.

I just wanted to find out who she was. That was all.

Maybe where she worked.

Maybe when she went to the club.

Anything.

I took out my phone.

Maybe if I pay her extra, she can get my angel's phone number—

Another crash brought me back to reality and I quickly shoved my phone back into my pocket before I got any more ideas.

Chapter 3
Juliette

I stepped out of the bathroom to boisterous laughter. Cursing, I tried to step back in.

Maybe they haven't seen me. Maybe I still have time to go back and pretend I'm still taking a very, very long—

But of course, dreams were just that. *Dreams.*

"Julie? You're home? Come eat with us!"

Shit. I quickly took the towel off my wet hair and hung the damp fabric before shutting the door with a soft click. I really didn't feel like talking to anyone.

You would think that getting someone to bid one million on me and spending the night getting railed into oblivion would make me feel super carefree and just wash all my worries away.

But actually, the additional money only added to my stress. Instead of making all my problems vanish, it tripled them instead.

The shared bathroom was adjacent to the living room and right in the line of sight of the dining room. Not an ideal living situation, but the only thing I could afford. I was offered one of

the rooms with a private bathroom, but that was an additional two hundred I was not willing to spend.

I mean, I would much rather have dinner at least three nights a week than a bathroom inside my room.

I headed back to my room to change before meeting my roommates. I hadn't heard them over the water and the mental math in my head. They often congregated in the living-dining room, and while I normally would have loved to hang out with them, the pressure of the money in my bank account was too much.

"I didn't hear you come in," I said with a smile as I joined them at the dining room table.

Harmony was at the head, her black hair pulled into a messy bun, wearing a hoodie from her college. Erin had her nose in a book but lifted her head to give me a smile, and April was the closest to me and gave me a shy smile as she brought her bowl closer to scoop some of the slop into her mouth.

Harmony was the loud one, but she was also the most caring. She mothered us to death and often cooked when she had time, though it usually was some questionable mush of ingredients. Luckily, it had never tasted bad.

She passed me a small bowl of rice and motioned for me to pour a heaping pile of sauce and meat onto it.

My stomach gave me away, growling at the smell.

"Beef and tomatoes," April whispered. April was the shyer one. She wasn't one to typically initiate a conversation, but if we were all together, she'd usually join.

She worked at a small boutique on one of the walking streets at the park. This was quite far away from where she worked, but, like me, she couldn't afford much.

She didn't talk much about herself or her family—or anything really—so all I knew about her was that she worked at a small boutique that sold handmade soap she would some-times bring back for me.

"Not half bad this time," Erin muttered.

Erin was a student, and I believed she was getting her master's, though I wasn't completely sure. When we hung out and talked, we didn't really get too personal. She was also the most sarcastic of the group, so it was hard to actually tell when she was telling the truth.

At first, she rubbed me the wrong way because I took every-thing she said a little bit too seriously. But after a while, I real-ized she was actually pretty sweet and looked out for us. Whenever her school had free food or any of those small gift bags they handed out, she'd bring us back some.

I remembered more than one time when she snuck us into her school for free food at some event. It was fun pretending to be in college, even though I never had a chance to go myself.

Even community college was too expensive for me, so expe-riencing that meant more to me than she probably realized.

With a smile, I took a large bite of the food.

"How'd the *thing* go?" Harmony asked. "You know, the *sex cl—*"

"Oh my God," I interrupted with an eye roll. "Is this really what you want to talk about right now?"

Anything but that. But her gaze told me that she wasn't going to let it go that easily. That was the thing with Harmony. She loved to gossip, and if she smelled something juicy, she would not back off until you spilled everything.

"Yeah, Harmony, not the place. I'm eating." Erin's tone was sarcastic, though her gaze was locked on me and her expression was dead serious, telling me she was also waiting for me to give them all the dirty details.

I told my roommates a lot. Sometimes more than they told me. I couldn't help it—I liked them, and more often than not, if

I felt comfortable around a person, I would share too much. They were the closest things I had to friends.

We watched movies, we painted our nails together, and had most of our meals together as well. So sometimes it really did feel like we were good friends or maybe even family.

But I hadn't told them about the money.

That felt too... private. And if I was being honest, I hadn't really come to terms with it either. I couldn't believe what I had done. And I felt maybe even a bit... ashamed.

Most of it felt like an unbelievable dream that I wasn't sure actually happened until I looked at my bank statement.

Flashes of that night kept coming back to haunt me.

Her tongue on my skin. The way her hands felt as they roamed over my body. The things she said.

She had made me feel so much more than anyone else ever had.

She was caring. Attentive. The perfect partner.

I was nervous the entire time. I felt bad because I didn't even reciprocate. I wanted to touch her and taste her so badly, but she took over from the start and barely let me up for air.

Yeah, we took a break every five orgasms or so, but after a while, those breaks blurred together. Even if they lasted five, ten, twenty minutes, it still felt like only a moment before we were back at it.

And then she just up and left me.

Not much aftercare besides a few soft words, and she was gone. She looked at me right before she left. Lingering at the door as if she wanted to say something. As if she was trying to decide something.

But in the end, she left, and I stayed there, decompressing on the bed, trying desperately not to fall asleep. I barely made it home, and as soon as I did, I crashed out on my bed.

We did everything we were meant to do there. She bid. She paid the money. I received it. We fucked. And that was it.

Still... I knew that if I had met her on a different occasion, I might try to start something more with her.

There was an instant connection between us that I'd never felt with anyone else in my life. I was never one for a one-night stand. I mean, I had a few over the years, but I preferred long-term relationships.

But this was different. I wanted to know more about her, but I stopped myself from asking. It was in the club rules that we had to stay anonymous. That was the whole purpose of it. I didn't want to know her, and she didn't want to know me.

She took her mask off for me, though. She broke the rules, and she didn't even look like she cared.

Which led me to fantasizing about going back to the club just to find her.

I mean, she'd have to come back, right? You wouldn't just spend a million dollars to fuck someone and never go there again, right?

"That good, huh?"

I couldn't help the heat that ran up my skin. There was no hiding my blush, so I didn't even attempt to as my face reddened.

"Oh, fuck, did you actually do something there?" Erin asked, leaning in with her eyebrows raised, the small silver ring on top of her right one reminding me a little bit too much of one of the club workers.

"I don't kiss and tell," I forced out.

Harmony slammed her fork down, causing me to jump.

"You so do, you *whore*! Tell us everything!"

I couldn't help but laugh. That was Harmony. Maybe someone who didn't know her would get offended by what she called us, but I knew she didn't mean it like that.

"It was a *very good* one-night stand," I replied and took another bite, leaving them hanging before I continued. "But that's all I'm telling you."

Harmony let out a squeal and grabbed Erin and April's arms, shaking them violently.

Even Erin cracked a smile.

"So you're going back, right?" April asked in a soft voice.

I turned to answer her just as my phone started vibrating in my pocket.

I fished it out, and my heart stopped when I realized it was my boss. I answered quickly, her voice filtering through the speakers immediately.

"Juliette, I need you to take up a job *now*. It's important."

My resignation was currently folded up in my purse, ready to be handed in tomorrow. I had originally thought going to the auction would only give me a couple thousand, maybe a few hundred thousand. No way in hell would it have been enough to quit my job.

But then she paid a million fucking dollars.

The money would be enough for me to not only pay for Lucas's college but also give me some time to move on with my life. Move closer to him and my aunt. Give me the time to find a job, maybe in a school or a daycare.

The most important part was to pay off my parents' medical debt and Lucas's college, though. And now I could.

At least that was what my mental math told me. I meant to double-check on paper after my shower, but then I was summoned to the dining room. And I definitely hadn't expected my boss to give me another job so soon.

I was in between positions now—something I would usually complain about, but that gave me enough time to think.

I bit my tongue, not knowing what to do.

"Is there no one else?" I asked in a small voice. I didn't like rejecting her or the families. It made me feel bad.

"We've been through almost all of them," she admitted with a sigh. "Can you please help with this?"

"I don't know... I was going to take a break—"

"It's a rich family," she added quickly. "Twice your usual pay, and I'll add an additional ten percent to your bonus."

Damn. Even if I was going to leave, that was pretty good in comparison to what I usually got paid, and working could probably help me get my head on straight, my shit together, and figure out what to do with the money.

"Let me think about it, okay?"

"Get back to me tonight, please."

We hung up and I leaned back into my chair with a sigh.

"Another nannying job?" Harmony asked, and I nodded.

My hand itched for another bite of the food, but my stomach was in knots and my head had started to hurt.

"Let me go do some math," I said as I stood.

"Uh-oh. She's doing math, everyone!"

I shot Erin a half-hearted glare as the others snickered. It wasn't a secret that I was shit at math. I liked to blame it on the fact that I didn't go to college, but in reality, I hadn't paid attention to algebra or geometry or literally any math class I'd ever had since I started going to school.

"Come back to finish your dinner before it gets cold!" Harmony called after me.

"Will come back in a bit! Just give me a second!"

"It'll probably take at least an hour," Erin teased. "Might as well put it in the microwave so she can heat it up later."

I pushed into my room and shut the door behind me, leaning against it with a sigh. The room was barely big enough for a twin bed and a small desk off to the side where my five-year-old computer was. As soon as I got myself together, I sat down on the rickety chair and pulled up my bank statement, the calculator, and my calendar.

I added up the huge medical debt left from my parents' accident, all four years of Lucas's schooling, and how much it would take to move my entire life.

I didn't know what school he would choose. I had to do a quick search and see what the average cost of tuition was per year, and the number was high. I even added a twenty percent buffer on his yearly tuition after realizing that he would need textbooks and clothes and a place to live.

The money in my bank account was good... But after actually putting everything to paper, it started to feel like it wasn't enough.

The more I added, and even without factoring in any of my monthly expenses, the more I realized quitting now probably wasn't my best bet.

Fuck.

Maybe it would last me a few months—a year even—but after that I would be stuck in the same situation. I would be back to working to make ends meet, and if Lucas needed anything else while he was in college, I would not be able to help him or myself.

I can always go back to the club...

I put a stop to that thought. It's not that I wouldn't like to, but I wasn't sure if I wanted to go back and find myself in a room with someone other than... her.

I needed the job. No matter how much I didn't want it, there was no denying that I still needed it.

One more job. Just one more that would hopefully last me a while so I could save up. Get away from my overcontrolling boss who paid me literally pennies on the dollar. Then I could go.

I dialed my boss again, and she picked up on the second ring.

Just one more job, and that's it.

"I'll take it."

Chapter 4
Lux

Any minute. She'll be here any minute now, and then I can finally have a bit of my peace back.

I looked at the hands on my watch as it counted down the seconds. Bella was in the backyard again, this time thoroughly ignoring me. It was better this way.

Today was the day that I finally got a new nanny.

I had decided not to sue the nanny company because they assured me this was the right one.

And it wasn't like the other nannies were horrible—I mean, if I was being painfully honest, they weren't that great—but Bella wasn't the easiest to deal with.

She didn't want any of them. Hell, sometimes it felt like she barely even wanted me. She would try everything in her power to get them to quit.

But we couldn't do that anymore.

I didn't like the rift between us, but I needed my time. I had a company and businesses to run. I needed to make money. For both of us. And I couldn't do that if I was forced to be around her twenty-four seven.

Nor did I think she liked it very much. *Me.* Didn't like *me* very much.

I tried to tell myself that it wasn't dislike. That maybe she was just placed in a situation that she didn't know how to handle, and this was her way of expressing her feelings. But I needed someone who could be here to help her through that.

To help *us* through that.

At this point, I needed someone who was more than just a babysitter, and I hoped that whatever person they were sending me would be the answer.

My phone was already blowing up. More messages about when I was coming in and if I could attend in-person meetings and events. It wasn't just Dominic, but every other person who had heard the rumor that I was coming in today.

Though Dominic specifically had been bugging me for the exact time when I'd be in the office. I had about 10 messages from him alone.

He acted like he cared about me and Bella and pushed me to stay home, but I knew he was struggling inside. He was a good man. He tried to shield me from most of what he was dealing with over there, but it still got to me.

The employees were asking. So were the contractors, the board members, everyone. Each day that I was gone, the rumors got worse and worse, and their confidence in me lowered by the minute.

It wasn't just because I was usually the person who was in the office every single day. They had heard about the accident, and to them, that made me a very unstable CEO.

I didn't want them to think that I was some struggling, grieving woman. It had already been hard enough to maintain my position. I needed to prove that I was still capable.

I had more than enough shares if the board decided they wanted to do some funny shit, but in order to protect my position, I needed to fucking be there. There were just too many things that could slip by right under my nose.

If this nanny doesn't work...

I didn't even want to go there. I was out of options.

When I heard the car driving over the gravel out front, I was up and marching to the door.

My hand was around the knob, opening it before she'd even gotten out of the vehicle. She was sitting in a beat-up, old car, grabbing her things from the passenger seat, and I watched as she turned to the rearview mirror to quickly fix her hair and check her makeup.

I was still watching as she got out of the car, her face hidden by the curtain of shiny blonde hair. She was wearing a light pink sundress with one of those soft fabric tops that hugged her breasts. The rest of it had a small pattern that I couldn't make out from where I was standing. The dress was long enough to cover most of her legs, except for a small portion at the end. It was enough to call my attention there and to her white tennis shoes.

I was sure it was meant to be cute, girly... But my mind immediately went to the gutter. Specifically to my night with my own blonde beauty. To her legs that looked so similar to these wrapped around my shoulders. I remember trailing kisses from her hip to her knee and down to her ankle.

She rounded the car, her head down as she looked in her large tote bag, not looking up until she got to the steps.

Alarm bells started ringing in the back of my head. Suddenly, the girl in front of me morphed into the girl I had spent the night with. *My angel.* The same lithe fingers. That same slender neck. Those beautiful blonde locks.

Actually, she really does look like—

My breath caught in my throat and my grip tightened on the door, my fingers aching as I applied a bit too much pressure.

The world turned on its side and slowed down to the millisecond. All the noise from the background lowered until it was nothing but a hum. She turned to look at me, and I immediately knew she was the angel I met at the club.

The mask had obscured a little bit of her face, but not enough for me not to know who she was right away. Those large blue eyes that were once pleading for me to put her out of her misery were now looking straight at me. Wide-eyed and just as shocked as I was.

The same ones that had looked at me with a devotion I'd never seen before. Like she trusted me more than I'd ever even trusted myself.

I watched as her large smile quickly dropped when she realized who I was too. The realization was daunting for both of us, and suddenly my mind was working a million miles an hour.

Shit. Shit. Shit. Not good.

Without warning, I slammed the door shut before she even got up the stairs.

I wanted to meet her again. That was all I'd been thinking about. I had to, somehow.

But if I'd known that all those thoughts would manifest into this very awkward moment, I would take it all back.

Meeting at a coffee shop was one thing. Her, the girl I fucked at a queer BDSM club, being my new nanny? *No fucking way.*

"What did I just do?" I said with a light groan and leaned my head against the cool wood of the door. I focused on my breathing because at that moment it was the only thing that I could do.

Please. Please tell me this is a bad dream.

But I knew it wasn't, because I could still hear her outside, climbing the steps with a slight bit of hesitancy.

Maybe if I don't answer I can pretend she's not here?

Just then my phone gave a few quick buzzes, letting me know that I actually did need to get her inside because she was undoubtedly Bella's new nanny.

Maybe she's just here because she's stalking you.

I scoffed at the unlikeliness of it. No, this had to be the universe fucking with me. There was no possible way. Especially when I had just hired a fucking information broker to find her.

The doorbell rang throughout the foyer. *Fuck.*

I wondered how long I could keep her out there before she walked away. She would probably stand out there for a few moments before calling her boss, who would then call me. I wasn't sure that she would leave, though. She didn't seem like the quitting type.

Two more vibrations.

"Fuck it."

I opened the door and gazed at the woman who threatened to turn my life upside down right in the eyes.

She was even more breathtaking in the daylight. Her hair had that sun-kissed golden sheen to it. Her makeup was light but complemented her large eyes and button nose. I saw the few freckles on her face, which were barely noticeable. One right under her left eye, one by her nose, and another by her lips.

And the dress. I forced my eyes to stay on hers instead of roaming her body the way I wanted.

There was no denying that she knew who I was too, especially since I had been stupid enough to take off my mask. Now I wish that I'd actually abided by the club rules. I never thought something as simple as showing my face would fuck me over so badly.

Because I thought I'd never fucking see her again.

But I could play it off like I had no clue who she was. The power was in her hands because, at the end of the day, she was the one who could decide whether to accept the little game I was going to play or call me out right away—and probably leave then.

But the sad truth was that I needed her.

At least for the day.

Tomorrow, I could figure out what I wanted to do about my one-night stand and million-dollar purchase invading my life.

"Hi, I'm Juliette Hayes, Bella's new nanny."

And there goes the last bit of hope that I had that she was some type of stalker.

I opened the door and motioned for her to come in.

"I'm Lux. Nice to meet you, but come on in. I have places to be."

Chapter 5
Juliette

*L*ux.

Beautiful, fierce, dangerous-looking Lux stood right in front of me, looking every bit as delicious as she had the night we spent together. Though this time her voice was tinged with anger and not at all like the honey-coated praises she gave me when we were in bed.

Am I that easy to forget?

I mean, I was wearing a mask, but it barely covered my face. I was having a hard time believing that she didn't recognize me, especially with how intimate she became with my body. Even if she hadn't seen my whole face, she would recognize everything else, right?

No, there was no doubt that she recognized me. Because, even if she had never taken off her mask, I would've recognized her.

But as she held the door open for me, her posture gave nothing away. She acted like this was the first time she was seeing me. Like I truly was some stranger that she had just randomly hired to look after her kid.

She looked taller than she did at the club, standing at least a foot over me as she looked through me with those deep brown eyes like I was nothing.

Maybe it was because she was on her knees between my legs most of the time we were together. Or crawling on top of me. Or behind me, her head buried in the crook between my neck and my shoulder, teasing me as she brought me to orgasm over and ove—

Enough.

It was bad enough that she was suddenly my new boss. I didn't need to make it worse by replaying everything that happened that night at the club. I could pretend not to know who she was too. It was probably better this way.

But I made a mental note to immediately call my boss as soon as I was off. I knew this job was too good to be true.

A rich family with additional pay and a bonus? That should've tipped me off right away. But I had been too blinded by the stress of having money only to realize that it would actually be gone in no time if I didn't work at all.

I didn't know what was more surprising. That I'd meet her again so soon after she fucked me better than anyone ever had or that she had a child.

Lux did *not* seem like the motherly type. Hers was more of a *Don't fuck with me* vibe than a *Come on, baby, let me get you a juice and a snack* vibe. I couldn't even imagine her changing diapers, let alone taking care of a child well enough for her to last until the age of eight.

Since the job was so last minute, I didn't get to study the file like I normally would have. I actually just glanced at it before I got out of the car and noted that I would be taking care of an eight-year-old named Bella, who had gone through almost every single nanny in our agency. Which meant trouble for me for sure.

But there was a bigger problem than the eight-year-old. There was no way I'd be able to see this job through with her being my boss. No matter how much I still wanted to, I couldn't spend my days thinking about fucking her. There were some lines I wouldn't cross.

I was a professional, after all, which was why I was so highly rated—and recommended—at my agency and why I was able to keep up this job for so long.

Selfishly, I let my eyes drift down her lean, suited figure. Heat ran through me at the small bit of tattoo peeking out of her cleavage. Back in the club, I had gotten a lot closer to that tattoo. She had never fully undressed, but she had unbuttoned her shirt enough for me to get a good glance at the way it worked its way down from her chest to her stomach.

I fantasized about licking it. About following that trail down and seeing just how far it went.

She cleared her throat, forcing my eyes back to her face.

"Done checking me out?"

Holy shit.

My face heated and I let out a panicked laugh. *Yeah, this is definitely a different side of the girl who made me come enough times that I forgot my own name.*

"Just curious about the tattoo," I lied. "Beautiful house."

I walked in, looking around at the massive space in front of me. Never in my life had I lived in anything so magnificent. Crown moldings, shiny marble flooring, black leather sofas that matched the black tables and other furniture splashed all around.

She had a very specific style. Dark, sleek, elegant—much like her as a human being. It fit her well, and it almost seemed a little bit too intimate to walk into it. Like I was seeing a part of her that strangers never would.

Strangers. That includes me, the girl she fucked once at a BDSM club.

The house was large and open, giving me a perfect view into the kitchen and backyard. I took it all in, noting that even with a child, everything was pristine.

"Bella is in the back," she said, shutting the door behind us and walking past me. I took it as a cue to follow her. "Her chef is out at the store. She'll be back later. Her driver's number is on the fridge, but for today, please stay here."

I let out a little hum of agreement, not really expecting *this* level of richness when my boss warned me about them.

If she had a million dollars for a single night with you, it's no wonder her house looks like this.

Maybe that's how she managed to raise a child. By throwing money at her. Buying her people to take care of her instead.

I bit my tongue trying to stop the rude thoughts from swirling through my mind.

There was nothing wrong with having the means to give all this to a child. If I did, I'd also want to give my kid everything I could. A chef to make them nutritious meals. A private school to make sure they got the best education. All the beautiful clothes money could buy.

But this still felt a bit crazy.

The backyard was a mix of neatly cut grass, an outside lounge area with its own fireplace, a circular pool and jacuzzi to the right, and, if I squinted, I could make out a fountain off in the distance and a few statues around it.

I would say the whole property was at least two acres. I think there was even a tennis court off to the back left, though I couldn't be sure as thick trees covered the perimeter.

"There she is," she said as we came to a stop at the wide-open French doors.

Bella was sitting on the ground with an iPad in hand. She was tapping at it angrily, a pout on her face. She looked up at us with a glare.

She had chocolatey brown hair and eyes that were just a few shades lighter than Lux's. While she didn't look overwhelmingly like her, I could see a bit of the resemblance in the way she scowled.

The same scowl Lux had met me with at the door.

Bella was wearing a mid-length denim dress that had quite a few dirt stains on it already, even if it was only early morning. She was clutching her iPad tightly, like she was afraid I'd take it from her.

And her hair... It was down, brushed but a bit frizzy, and I spied a knot off to the side. Maybe it was from playing too hard, but I knew one of the first things I'd help her with would be hairstyles she could play in.

"I have to leave soon, Bella," Lux told her. "This is your new nanny. Give this one a break, will you?"

My skin heated at her words. They were so simple, but in my delusion, it felt like she was saying it because she had a soft spot for me.

"Hello, Bella," I said as I walked toward her. "My name is Juliette and I'm here to hang out with you today."

When I sat down on the grass next to her, she snatched her iPad away, holding it close to her chest. Maybe one too many nannies really had tried to take it from her.

I wasn't a fan of iPads either, but I wasn't about to get in there and just take it. It could be something important to her. I didn't know what her habits were or what she used it for.

Plus, right now I was just some random stranger coming into her house. I didn't have a right to take away what was hers, even if she was a kid. She still had feelings and wants and needs, and I would respect them.

Though I would make sure to try and introduce her to some other hobbies in hopes of distracting her from the thing.

"Just today?" Bella asked. "Does that mean you're already fired?"

A small, badly concealed chuckle made its way to my ears before it turned into a cough, and I tried not to full-on glare at Lux.

It seemed Bella and Lux had a bit more in common than the scowl. But that was okay. I could be chill. This wasn't the first time a kid had an attitude problem.

"Nope." I gave her my best smile. "You're stuck with me until your mom says so."

Her face twisted, and she was up and running back to the house with an angry growl before I could stop her, even leaving her iPad on the ground. Her suddenness took me by surprise, and I twisted around to see her run past Lux, who looked at her with a pained expression.

When she looked at me, her face had hardened again.

Fuck. Am I in trouble?

"That's a new record. You lasted what? Two minutes?"

Panic seized my throat, and I rushed to her. *No, no, no, there's no way she just fired me like that.*

I was starting to realize why my boss had called me and asked me to take this. I knew families like this, ones who would go through lists of nannies and none of them would work for them. Most times, it was definitely an issue with the family, not the nanny, but this one seemed... complicated in a different way, somehow.

"I'm sorry. I don't understand why—"

Lux crossed her arms over her chest, her glare deepening. I hated that look on her face. I hated doing something wrong. Especially when it came to her.

I wanted—no, I *needed*—to make it right. Not just for the

sake of the kid, but for her. I wanted her to look at me with those eyes again. The ones filled with satisfaction. The ones that looked at me like I could do no wrong.

It hurt to see it changed so suddenly.

"Did your agency not give you the file or did you just choose not to read it?"

When I didn't answer right away, she turned around with a huff, shaking her head. She was leading me back into the kitchen and, no doubt, to the front door if I didn't stop her in time.

Shit. I needed to fix this. My mind ran through the numbers again, reminding me that I still needed this job.

"I needed you today. I can't believe they fucked up this bad again."

"I'm sorry, just tell me what I did wrong and I—"

She turned around, her eyes ablaze with anger. I hated it. I didn't want to see this angry side of her. It hurt, but her next words hurt me even more.

"Her mother died in a car accident two months ago," she growled. "I'm her aunt."

Oh. I deflated a bit. *Shit.* I knew all too well what it felt like to lose your parents. Granted, I wasn't as young as Bella was when it happened, but it hurt nonetheless. And this was way too fresh.

Damn, I feel like an asshole. I'm being an asshole.

Last-minute or not, I should've read that file front to back before getting out of the car.

"I'm so sorry, I—"

"You're fired."

She tried to turn away from me, but I caught her suit jacket —and the grimace when she looked at where we were connected.

"Please, let me just try again," I begged. "I'm good at what I do. I'm one of the top nannies at my agency. You can ask them if you don't believe me, but I have a list of references and other families you can talk to. I promise I am the nanny you need, and I can help."

There was a pause as if maybe she was actually considering what I was saying. Her eyes looked down from my eyes to my lips and then to where I still held her suit jacket.

"That's left to be seen," she said before tugging her clothes from my grip.

She turned back around, but this time, I scrambled to get in front of her and childishly held my arms out so she couldn't move.

"I need this job," I confessed, trying to add every bit of desperation I could to my voice. "Please let me try again."

Her nostrils flared, anger lit up her face, and before I knew it, she was advancing on me fast and pushing me against the countertop. The hard stone dug into my back painfully, but none of that mattered because suddenly she was as close as I wanted her to be.

Stupid hope came alive in my chest.

"What happened to the million dollars then, huh?"

My heart dropped to my stomach.

Chapter 6
Lux

"**S**o you do know me."

As if I could forget you.

I let out a scoff, my hand coming to trace the neckline of her dress. *I shouldn't be touching the nanny.* But my hand had a mind of its own. I wanted my little angel back. I wanted her more than I'd wanted anyone else in my life.

And she was right there. Tempting me with what I couldn't have.

Maybe this was the universe getting back at me. Or teaching me a lesson by dangling everything I ever wanted right in front of me and watching as I struggled to keep my hands to myself.

"*Biblically,*" I spat. "The real question is why the fuck are you trying to infiltrate my life? Was my million dollars not enough for you? You have to get on my payroll as well? Or maybe you're secretly in love with me."

Okay, fine, maybe I shouldn't have said that.

Her face twisted, her breathing deepened. There was a beautiful bit of red spreading over her face and neck.

I didn't care about the million dollars. I didn't give a single shit about it. Yeah, I thought it was a little weird that she was still taking this nanny job after getting all that money, but I wasn't mad about it.

Whatever else was going on in her life had made it so she was right here with me again.

"I'm on the agency's payroll. Get it right."

Oh, the little kitten has claws.

I was excited about this development. Our time in the club hadn't given me enough of her. She'd been running rampant through my mind ever since, but in my fantasies, she was still the submissive, perfect little angel.

Apparently, she could bite back. And it made me want her even more.

I cursed myself for it.

Regardless, she was back in my life. Reward or punishment, and for how long, was yet to be seen.

With all that in mind, was it even appropriate to keep her as a nanny?

My brain told me it was an immediate no. That I should throw her out and make good on my promise to sue the shitty nanny agency that just couldn't seem to get it right. Nothing good would come out of this obvious conflict of interest.

Plus, how would I be able to keep things professional?

She's the last chance Bella has. I have. We have.

Her breath hitched as I placed my hands on the counter on either side of her. Closing in. Fuck. I couldn't stop myself. All I could think about was hoisting her up on the cool marble, ripping her panties off, and feasting on her cunt like I'd done back in the club.

Is she wet for me right now?

The look on her face was deceiving. She was angry. Obviously, with my comments, I expected nothing less.

But there was also that blush.

The one that made me want to tease her even more. The one that told me she was probably enjoying this a little bit more than she should.

I knew she wanted me too. She didn't have to say it; it was written all over her. It made it worse.

"I'm keeping your shitty company in business." My voice lowered. "Do you know how many nannies I've been through? You were supposed to be my last chance, so you can imagine my surprise when, out of all the people in the world, *you* show up at my doorstep."

She puffed up at that before placing her hand on my chest and giving me a slight push. The warmth of her hand seeped into my skin and had shivers bursting out from where she touched me. I wanted to lean into it.

Instead, I let her push me away.

"I'm qualified," she said, even more annoyed, like she took it personally. "Just because we met under unusual circumstances—"

"A sex club? No, not unusual at all."

She raised a brow at me. There was that attitude again. My hands itched to push up her dress. Maybe even put her over my knee and *really* punish her for those words.

"Is that judgment I hear? From the same person who spent a million dollars to get laid? What? Couldn't get anyone to do it willingly?"

As angry as I was, her little comeback was funny to me.

"I don't care what you do in your free time," I replied. "Nor should my *extracurriculars* be of any concern to you."

She let out a scoff and shook her head.

"You're unbelievable," she murmured, then turned to me with a glare. "Listen, I said I needed this job. Again, I have references. I'm good at it. I'm sorry I messed up with Bella, but I know I can do this."

Her eyes never wavered from mine, that determination shining through like a beacon.

I should shut her down. I wanted to. It was the best thing to do in this scenario.

I bit my inner cheek and took another step back, which was a mistake. It allowed me to really look at her, finally taking in the sinful dress she was wearing. I wanted to stop myself, but I couldn't.

How can something so flowery and girly look so delectable on her?

It hugged her breasts and hips but fanned out, showing me the outline of her body. A body I knew so well. It would be so easy to push the thin fabric up, reach into her panties, slip my fingers into her—

"Maybe it's you who's secretly in love with me," she said as she stepped past me with a smirk. "Try and keep it professional, hm?"

Her quip had shock and arousal shooting through me, and desire made me lightheaded. My traitor hand moved on its own again, meaning to grab her hip, but I shoved it in my pocket and grabbed my phone instead. The pile of messages brought me back to reality.

Right. I need her. I could figure out what to do with her *after* work. I couldn't waste any more time, not after I had promised them I would be there today.

There was a light shuffle that made me turn to the hallway leading to Bella's room, and I was surprised to see her standing at the corner. *Eavesdropping.* If she were anyone else, I would be annoyed. I just hoped she hadn't seen anything... compromising. By the look on her face, I didn't think so.

"Are you firing her?" Bella asked, a frown on her face. "I can't hear from here."

"Then why don't you come closer and find out for yourself?"

The slight curiosity that lit Bella's face had hope shining in my chest. It gave me a little peek at who she had been before the accident.

Just for now. I'll figure out something better soon. I promise. I tried to convey it with my gaze, but when she got to me, she looked up at Juliette like she was an intruder. I wouldn't be surprised if she had been like this with all the nannies.

Juliette leaned down to her level, something only a few nannies had done before. She didn't have to give me her references. It was clear to me, even if she hadn't looked at the file, that she had been around a lot of kids.

"I apologize, Bella. I really didn't know, and that's totally my bad. Can you forgive me?"

Bella's cheeks puffed out and she looked up at me for reassurance.

I gave her a short nod.

"People make mistakes," I said, sending Juliette a look. "No matter how thoroughly you try to prepare them."

Juliette's face twitched at the obvious slight.

"Yeah, I mean, you're obviously not my mom," Bella added. "All the other ones could tell. Why not this one?" She leaned closer to me. "I think this one should be fired."

I was desperately trying to keep a straight face. Bella had been around me long enough to become a very cutthroat eight-year-old.

"We will do a trial run," Juliette said with a clap of her hands. She sent Bella a smile that didn't convey her feelings at the situation. "How about this: you give me one day. One day where we can do *anything* you want, and if you're still unhappy, I'll just quit. How about that?"

My heart jumped in my chest. *She should quit now. That would be the best-case scenario for all of us.*

But something inside me hoped that she would still be here when I came back from work. Actually, something inside me hoped for a lot more than that, but I couldn't let myself recklessly go there.

Professional, remember?

Bella gave her a hesitant look.

"Adventureland?" she asked.

Juliette looked at me. Bella had never wanted to go to Adventureland, so I knew she was just trying to push the boundaries. Because of everything that had happened, she had been going to school on and off, and she didn't need to go today. Technically, she could do whatever she wanted.

"If you want."

Bella pouted. "Gardening?"

"I love to garden," Juliette replied.

Bella's frown deepened. I could see what she was trying to do, and it was hard to keep the smile from my face now.

"Running?"

Juliette shifted her feet to show Bella her tennis shoes. "All set and ready."

"Swimming?" she asked. "You don't have a bathing suit."

"No, but I can watch you."

"That's not fun," Bella shot back with a frown. "You won't have fun."

Juliette gave her a smile. "What are you talking about? I get to spend the day with the coolest kid in New York. I'd say that's pretty fun to me."

Bella tried not to show it, but her face lit up at the compliment.

"Well..." She hesitated for only a second. "Then I guess I can start by showing you my cartwheels. I can do them one-handed."

Juliette stood and held out her hand for Bella as she said, "That's so cool! I can't wait to see it."

Bella looked at her hand critically before taking off to the backyard. When I looked back at Juliette, she was wearing a satisfied smile. One that had my heart skipping a beat in my chest.

"Told you I could do it."

I straightened and put my phone back in my pocket. "Awesome. Then I'll be off. You have my number if you need anything. At least I hope your good-for-nothing agency gave you that."

Her sheepish look told me they didn't.

I held out my hand, silently asking for her phone. When she took it out, it was, of course, covered in a bulky, pink phone case. When she unlocked it for me and handed it to me, I noticed her wallpaper was a photo of her and a teenager.

They seemed close. Their faces were smooshed together, smiling widely at the camera. Juliette looked maybe a couple of years younger in it, and I almost asked her about it.

I wanted to, but I had to keep this professional. So I put my number in and gave it back.

Her lips twitched at the contact name.

"*Lux Sterling*. I thought you'd go with something else."

"Like what?"

She shrugged. "Since you're so convinced I'm in love with you, maybe *Secret crush* or *Most handsome woman on the planet*."

I was annoyed at how well she knew me even after just a single night together, especially one where we didn't really talk. If this were any other situation, I would definitely add my number under something cute and flirty. Maybe *The only woman who knows how to make me come.*

But this is not any other situation, is it?

"*Sir* will also do."

I bit my tongue so I wouldn't add, *As you well know,* and was more than pleased when her cheeks reddened again.

"Juliette! Look!"

Bella's call was the thing I needed to snap me back to reality. *Right, no flirting with the nanny.*

"Text me if there's anything."

"We will be fine," she assured me. I nodded and turned to leave, but her voice stopped me.

"Lux."

My name slipping from her lips had a shiver running up my spine, and I had to suppress it as I turned to her.

"I'm sorry," she said. "For getting it wrong. For not being prepared and... for your loss."

A sudden wave of grief hit me like a truck. It felt especially worse because it looked like she actually cared.

So I just nodded and walked out of the house.

Chapter 7
Juliette

Bella was like any other eight-year-old.

She loved to play—with her toys and her food. Loved to get dirty and run around. She had a give-no-fucks attitude that I absolutely loved. Honestly, she was a really good kid.

But it was obvious that she was extremely lonely.

"One more time, then you have to change into something clean and take a water break, okay?" I said as she stood in front of me, panting.

Even through all of the playing, she still respected me as the one in charge, something that shocked me based on her earlier attitude toward me. Maybe it was less about her pushing the nannies away and more about how those nannies had treated her.

"I know I can make it. Just one last chance!" She took off running to the far side of the yard before I could say anything else.

I looked at the stopwatch on my phone. She was nowhere

near the ten second mark, making the trip to the end and back in about thirty. Forty if she was tired.

I paused it, letting her catch up a bit before starting it again.

"You're better than the others," Gina, who I came to know as her personal chef, said from behind me. I looked up to see her holding some finger food and water with cucumbers in it.

"I'm not doing anything," I replied, giving her a smile. "Just letting her play."

"Maybe I should say that I think she likes you more." She handed me a glass of water. It was cool, the condensation already wetting my skin.

"Thank you," I said and took a sip of what was probably the most refreshing water I'd ever had. *Rich people.*

I still couldn't get over it. I had worked for some wealthier families, but no one this rich. I knew that the size of the property itself was a testament to how much money she had. Surrounding us were multimillion-dollar houses, but hers was nothing like them, which meant she had opted to build this thing from the ground up.

That made me wonder what she did to make this kind of money, so I decided to look her up when I got home. The file probably didn't have anything about her specifically, so I'd try Google and maybe LinkedIn.

A smile pulled at my lips as Bella made her way back toward us. I had yet to help her put her hair back in braids. so her hair still whipped around her as she ran. Her smile was so wide it looked like it might be making her cheeks hurt.

"Food!"

Gina laughed and lowered the tray so Bella could come in and grab two handfuls of snacks.

"Time?" she asked me, already shoving them into her mouth.

I picked up my phone and showed her. "Closer! Twenty-six!"

She let out an exaggerated moan and fell to the ground. A chuckle escaped my lips. She spread out in the grass, her fingers grasping the blades and her eyes locked on the sky. Her chest rose and fell as she tried to catch her breath, and slowly she started to calm down.

"I have to say, I think you're the best kid I've ever had the pleasure to nanny."

She tore her eyes from the sky to send me a suspicious look. "Are you lying?"

I brought my hand up to my forehead in a salute-like gesture.

"Scout's honor."

She gave me a black stare.

"What's that mean?"

Gina laughed. "She's just promising you it's true."

"Okay!" With that, Bella pushed herself up from the grass, and she was off again, racing to the far end of the backyard. I noted the fresh grass stains against the back of her dress.

"Water, Bella!"

"When I come back!"

Gina and I were silent for a beat. I was just about to turn to her and offer her a seat when she spoke.

"I think it's because no one mentions her mom," she said. I turned to look up at her. "Like everyone tiptoes around it. Almost like she never existed."

I pursed my lips. That wasn't uncommon. People had done the same when my parents died. No one talked about them, and that angered me. I loved them. I missed them. They deserved to be talked about and remembered. They had made a difference to me.

But now that I was an adult, I understood this side a little bit more. I mean, how would anyone look at such an innocent young child and bring up the fact that their parents were just brutally ripped from them and their life turned upside down?

"Grief is hard. To be honest, I'm not sure how to navigate this." All I knew was what I had experienced myself, but I had been a teenager, while Bella was barely entering her childhood.

"I think she's just lonely and misses them." Gina's voice was soft. "We've been trying. There's only so much any of us can do. But you two seemed to hit it off right away. I think you'll be good for her."

"I hope," I murmured and forced a smile to my face as Bella reached us again.

"Hydrate, Bella," I told her, handing her the glass from Gina's tray. "Then you have one last round. Remember what you promised?"

She gave me a pout.

"Homework, *ugh.*"

"That's right," I said. "You, me, and that English assignment you've been putting off."

English, math, history. Because of what happened, Bella hadn't been going to school, but she still had to do her homework—by herself. And what eight-year-old wants to do that? So, of course, there was quite a pile of it for us to do before she had to go to school the next day.

"Two more times?" she bargained.

I restarted the stopwatch.

"If you can make it under twenty, I'll give you *three* more times."

And she was off once more, giggling as she ran.

"I don't know how you did it." Lux's voice came from behind us, causing me to jump as I looked up from my Kindle. My eyes fell to the pile of blankets on the couch across from me. I was on the other couch, the fireplace roaring between us.

After a full day of play and homework, Bella knocked out at seven before Lux came home. But she hadn't wanted to go to her room and instead camped out on the outside couch until she fell asleep.

The night air was a little bit chilly, so I made sure to bundle her up with the blankets and sit as close to the fireplace as possible, but I hadn't expected Lux to take so long getting home. Bella had already been asleep for an hour and a half.

"She tried to wait up, but she was exhausted," I said as I started to pack up my stuff. "We finished English, and I tried to get some math in, but she hates that even more. It's due Wednesday, though, so we will try again tomorrow."

When I glanced back at Lux, she was staring at me. I paused for a second. The tiredness in her eyes was obvious, her suit slightly disheveled, strands of her black hair sticking out.

"Busy day, huh?"

She let out a sigh and sat down on the couch, running a hand through her hair, pushing it back and out of her face. I found myself entranced by the sight of her.

It was easy to forget everything when she wasn't there during the day, but everything started slowly coming back to me with her nearness.

"First day back at work in weeks," she replied. "I wasn't lying before. I can't tell you how many nannies I've been through. This seems like... a miracle."

Seems like Bella isn't the only one who's had it hard.

She leaned her head back on the couch, and my eyes immediately fell to the column of her throat. I swallowed thickly.

Such a perfect, sinful sight. When Lux had stepped into

the room that night, I thought she was drop-dead gorgeous. Sexy in a sophisticated, sharp way. And now, seeing her here, her shirt slightly undone, her hair tousled, it was almost too much.

"She's a great kid." I forced the words out through a very dry throat. "Misses you. And... them." I kept my voice lower at the end.

"You can go," she said without looking at me, her voice devoid of any emotion.

Shit. I guess I didn't pass the trial run.

I grabbed my bag and moved to leave. I could turn back and beg her again, but there was no use if she had already made up her mind.

"Tomorrow, seven sharp. It's her first day back to school after a while," she said, her voice following me. "Drop-off is at seven forty-five."

I turned around, unable to stop the smile from spreading across my face. Lux had turned her head to the side, finally meeting my gaze, exhaustion clearly weighing her down.

"I'll see you then, *sir*."

Chapter 8
Lux

I grumbled as I watched the minutes tick by on my phone.

Not a single call or text from anyone.

I had ordered her private chef to text me if anything happened, but she had been radio silent all day. I was tempted to look at the cameras, but I didn't want to be *that* person.

Taking in Bella had made me a special kind of paranoid. I was worried about if she was getting enough to eat, if she was happy, if she had done well at school, if she was getting along with the nanny, and the driver, and the chef.

More importantly, I knew I had to work, but my mind kept wandering back to them. I wanted to be there with them to make sure everything went okay.

This was part of the process. I needed to let go. I knew that.

But knowing it didn't stop me from worrying. I had thought through it all and knew that I didn't need to worry. That, even if somehow my angel turned out to be the worst nanny in the history of the planet, the chef and the driver would have my back.

They told me that every time I hired a new nanny and

things went particularly nasty. They would text me updates, and usually that meant I needed to leave work early, but this was the first time in forever that I was still at work. It had already been more than three hours.

Dominic said something else, and I nodded, unable to take my eyes off my phone.

Nothing? Is there really nothing to update me on?

"So you agree to invest the three million in a manure farm?"

My head snapped up, my gaze meeting his. His lips were pulled into a smirk. He was sitting on a chair a few feet away, his body turned to me as he spoke, which meant that he had been watching me for some time.

"Sorry," I mumbled and turned my phone screen down. "New nanny."

He looked at the screen showing month after month of revenue for one of our smaller products and slowly shut his laptop. I should have been listening, and I mentally kicked myself for worrying so much.

The whole point of getting a nanny was so I could be here and be present, yet somehow, I was ruining it.

"Issues again?" he asked with a raised brow. "I thought this one was the best they had."

"The best they had actually dropped out," I said as I turned my phone back over to check. Though a little devilish voice in the back of my mind had a hard time believing my little angel was anything but their best.

Nothing.

"Yikes." He leaned back in his chair. "Well, you better get home and deal with it—"

"You're right, I should get home." I stood quickly, grabbing my laptop and phone. He was giving me the perfect excuse to take my leave, and of course I was going to take it. What was the point of being at the office if I wasn't listening and kept worrying the entire time?

I was about to run out the door when my phone vibrated with a message from a number I hadn't saved.

When I opened it, there was a picture of Bella at the dining table, a large pencil in one hand while the other rested on her forehead. She was glaring at a piece of paper in front of her and had probably the biggest pout I'd ever seen. But Juliette?

She was *smiling*. A big, unrestrained smile. Something I knew that likely annoyed Bella even more. I couldn't stop looking at her, even when I knew I should. I let myself, for one selfish moment, just stare at the beautiful girl on my phone.

The words that followed it made my heart stop.

UNKNOWN

Homework time :)

She's okay. Had her lunch and dinner will be soon.

Take your time.

How did she know I was worried about her?

Because Juliette was made for me.

Shit. I couldn't keep having these thoughts.

Still, my mind went back to our time in the room. I had needed her then in an entirely different way, and she had delivered. Now I needed her for something else, and she still exceeded my expectations.

Swallowing the knot in my throat, I sat back down at the desk. *She's got this.* It was still hard to tear my mind away from them, but seeing the picture of them together and Bella actually doing something productive had hope blossoming in my chest. It was enough for me to pull myself away from my anxiety spiral and pay attention to what Dominic was actually saying.

"Sorry," I said with a sigh. "My mind's all over the place. I'm not going home. We can continue."

"Are you sure?" he asked as he slowly lowered himself back into the chair. I didn't tell people much of anything, especially work colleagues, but Dominic was the one exception to the rule.

We had gone to college together, and when I finally got myself up on my own two feet and started my business, he was one of the first people I thought about hiring. Since then, he had never let me down. He had taken up a lot more work after my sister had died to help me manage both the company and Bella.

I don't know when or how I'd ever be able to repay his kindness, but someday I would.

I nodded. "Let's get this done."

I had my phone face up, their image still there. Another message popped up, this time of Bella earlier in the day, running toward the camera, a big smile on her face.

My chest ached at the sight of her smile and the tooth she was missing.

When was the last time she smiled like that?

I'd never seen it. Bella was never playful with me. She was always pouting, whining, or just overall unhappy. There were a few times when she was just... *normal*, but never happy enough to give me a smile *that* big.

"What's got you smiling?"

I definitely *wasn't* smiling, but Dominic had known me long enough to see the smallest changes in my expression and read my emotions.

Deciding not to shut him out, I showed him the one of Bella smiling. His eyebrows raised to his hairline.

"Are you sure that's the same kid?"

This had my lips twitching.

"I think I found the perfect person for Bella," I said and turned the phone back to me, taking in her smiling face.

"I'm happy for you, truly. You need this."

I put my phone away, content that Bella was being taken care of.

Juliette's updates allowed me to focus on my work for another two hours before heading home to find them both on the outside couches. Bella asleep, Juliette watching over her. It was... domestic, and I realized I liked it.

Maybe a bit too much.

Just like I liked her calling me *sir* again a bit too much as well, even though I knew I definitely shouldn't.

I waited until I heard Juliette's car leave to pick up Bella, enjoying the calmness of it all. There weren't many times when I could be with Bella like this. When the world around us slowed down and quieted. When I could just look at her.

It was starting to cool down outside, but the warmth of the fireplace kept the outside lounge area warm. The light lit up her chocolate brown locks, casting a reddish hue on her skin.

She stirred just slightly but then leaned into me, not waking up, even as I shifted her weight in my arms.

I was never going to be a mother, but that didn't mean I wouldn't try to protect Bella with everything I had. And not just because she was my sister's kid.

Because she deserved it. She deserved the world.

Standing there, looking down at her while she was sleeping, just made everything else in the world fall to the background.

She was all that mattered. She was the reason I did all this.

I didn't know how long I stared at her, but when my arm started to get weak, I knew it was time to take her inside.

I took Bella to her room down the hall, careful not to jostle her too much. She curled into me, her small hand gripping my suit. I set her down on her bed, tucking her in and placing her favorite, worn bunny by her side. She grabbed it immediately, and the faint scent of her mother reached my nose.

That bunny had been one of the few things she had insisted on bringing from her house. I pushed her to bring more toys or anything that had sentimental value, but she wouldn't.

Looking at her made my heart ache.

I constantly worried about her. And I wondered if that was how all parents felt about their kids. If they thought about them constantly. If they started counting down the minutes from the time their kid walked outside until they were back inside safely. If the only thing they wanted to talk about was their kid.

That was how it was for me now.

Everything had been hard for her since the accident, so even though Juliette had shown me how capable she was, I had still been worried that Bella would do a one-eighty and reject her.

I was shocked to see her asleep when I got home. She'd only fall asleep in my presence, and even that was a struggle. She liked to go to her room by herself. She didn't like being tucked in. No bedtime routine, no book, not even a game on her iPad. She'd just simply go into her room and go to sleep.

I had reached out to her pediatrician and tried to get her to see a psychologist, but nothing worked. As soon as I tried to put her in front of a professional, she would shut down. They were supposed to help, but instead it always sent us two steps back.

Not to mention she'd always stay up until I got home, which meant she had always refused to sleep when any of her nannies were around, no matter how exhausted she was.

Until now.

But still, having Juliette here was... inappropriate at best. The only thing on my mind today besides Bella was Juliette. Despite the photos and the messages, despite all the things she'd done right, I'd actually come home with the intention to fire her. Not because she didn't blow all other nannies out of the water, but because of how awful it would be for me to keep her here.

I wanted her. The one night we had had only deepened my appetite for her. I thought that I was obsessed before, but having her so close and so unavailable at the same time was too hard for me to handle.

If I kept her here, it would literally only be a matter of time before I fucked up. The temptation was too great.

It might make it easier if she pretended not to notice me or if she showed me she didn't want me the same way I wanted her. But our mutual desire for each other was all too obvious.

It was dangerous, and something happening between me and Bella's nanny would be disastrous, especially if it got messy.

Bella needed stability. She needed someone she could count on. A constant in her life after such a heart-wrenching life change.

I got up as slowly as I could, trying not to wake her. But just as I was going to turn back to the door, her small hand reached out and grabbed my wrist. I turned to her, but her eyes were still closed.

"I changed my mind. Don't fire her, Auntie Lux," she said in the sleepiest voice I'd ever heard.

My heart lodged in my throat.

"Go to sleep, Bella," I cooed, placing her hand back on the bed and covering it with mine.

"I—" She let out a yawn and rolled over. "Like her." The last part came out as more of a mumble.

She's making this hard. Impossible.

All thoughts of firing Juliette were suddenly erased from my mind.

Bella rarely asked for anything or admitted to liking anyone. Not even any of my other staff, let alone someone she'd just met.

Why her? What had Juliette done today that made Bella like her so much? And so quickly?

Whatever the answer, there was no way in hell I'd fire Juliette now.

Which meant one thing and one thing only.

I have to keep my hands off her.

Chapter 9
Juliette

I sat in my beat-up Honda looking up at the mansion Lux Sterling lived in.

I had thought long and hard about if I was going to come back today.

It would be best not to. Especially with what had happened between us. *And what I still want to happen.* When she had me up against the counter, I wanted nothing more than to relive our night right then and there.

It was highly inappropriate, and I was glad I had found the strength to push her away. Fucking my boss was far from what I usually considered morally allowable.

I needed the job. And I felt like her grieving niece needed me too.

I don't know how you did it, Lux said last night. That meant I was doing something right for this little girl.

So I was going to go in there, be the best nanny I could be to Bella, and leave.

No flirting with Lux. No touching. *And definitely no fucking her.*

Just as I was going to force myself out of the car, my phone buzzed with a message from Lucas.

My chest started to warm, and when I opened it, tears sprang to my eyes.

LUCAS

So… This just came in the mail.

It was the first of what I knew would be his many acceptance letters. *Finally.* Things were looking up for us. After our parents' accident, it was just the two of us. We were the only ones we could rely on.

But taking care of a kid while still being a teenager wasn't easy. Our aunt had custody of us—well, him—and there wasn't much I could do except make empty promises, like paying his way to college.

It was what enticed me to go to the auction in the first place. *For him.* I wanted him to have the life that I didn't get to have. I didn't get to go to school. I didn't get to find a good job. I wouldn't be able to create a career for myself.

I was too busy trying to figure out what I was going to do with all the debt that was suddenly in my name. At first, they didn't try and give it to a minor, but once I turned eighteen, suddenly all these bills started showing up.

The ambulance. The life-saving medical treatment that had been given to my parents that ultimately failed. We had waited weeks for them to do everything they could. One would suddenly do better and there was hope, then the other would crash. After playing tug-of-war with their lives, the doctors that promised they would try their best stood in front of seventeen-year-old me and said there was nothing else they could do. Moments later, my aunt was handed a bill, which was then promptly handed to me. An early birthday present from her.

A massive debt that detailed every single insanely expensive treatment that did nothing but prolong my and my brother's pain. I had read it over and over. Fought the insurance company on duplicate and inflated charges. But their grubby little fingers were trying to claw out every single cent I owned and would ever make.

I tried. I went to community college and tried to get my general education done, but after not even a semester, I realized that I was paying a lot for very little and I would have to do it for four years.

That's when it hit me that it would probably be better for me to start saving for Lucas's college fund instead of my own. Seeing that dream come true for him now was more than I could've ever imagined.

I typed back a quick message.

ME

Congrats! You and I have a date at TGIFs tomorrow!

I would officially be telling him I would pay for his college. I didn't really know how I was going to explain it yet, but I would figure something out before then. I really didn't want to tell him the truth.

I tried not to let myself feel any shame about selling myself at an auction, but it was hard. Not just because of society, but my aunt had always been pretty vocal about making sure I stayed a *pure woman.*

Those words always cut a little bit deeper.

I did what I had to do, and I would do it again.

I forgot everything else and focused solely on Lucas and the bright future ahead of him. I couldn't wait to see the look on his face.

LUCAS

Actually, I'm staying over at a friend's place. Can you pick me up from school Friday?

Don't need anything fancy. A congratulatory boba will do.

Disappointment sprouted in my chest, but I was happy he was getting out with someone his own age. It'd been a while since I heard him talk about any friends. After the accident, he had kept to himself. Even more so after we were separated.

ME

You got it!

I would have to ask Lux for the time off, but I could deal with that later. I let myself sit in the warm feelings of pride that swam in my chest. I was almost giddy with it. I couldn't believe that my brother was actually going to make it, and I was going to help him get there.

I let myself have one more lingering moment before I got my stuff together. Time to turn off my sister brain and turn on the nanny brain.

Pushing myself out of the car, I rushed to the house. I had spent a little bit too long in the car and was now worried about the time.

I knocked on the door, but no one came to answer, so after a moment's hesitation, I tried to open the door. Unlocked. Seriously?

I peered in and could hear Lux and Bella in the kitchen before I could see them.

"She's finishing breakfast, come in," Lux said.

"Juliette! I saved you a Mickey pancake."

I pushed into the house with a smile on my face. When I finally turned the corner, I spotted both Lux and Bella at the island countertop. Bella had a plate of half-finished food in front of her, while Lux only had a coffee and an iPad.

Lux's hair fell slightly into her face, missing its usual gel. Her suit had been replaced by a casual sweater and slacks that she somehow made look even sexier.

"This one's for you!"

Bella stabbed her fork into a pancake that looked nothing like the cartoon mouse. Probably because there was a huge bite taken out of it.

"Can you help me eat it? I'm stuffed," I said and patted my belly. "I had a very yummy green smoothie."

Bella made a gagging noise. "Gross!"

She took no time shoving the rest of the pancake into her mouth. I could see that she was still eyeing the sweet treat. Bella was trying to be nice, but I could see how much she actually wanted it. I didn't really have a green smoothie, nor was I one of those who enjoyed it, but I would feel like shit if I took her pancake.

"You're early," Lux noted. When I looked at her, her eyes were already digging into mine.

"I wanted to spend some time learning the morning routine," I replied with a smile. "Plus, I hate being anything other than early. Even being on time stresses me out."

Lux made a noise deep in her throat before turning back to her iPad.

Okay...

"Are we wearing our princess pajamas to school today?" I said to Bella, noticing her wild hair and clothes.

We had time, but not enough to wrestle her into something else if she chose to be difficult.

"No!" It came out as an offended gasp before she started shoving food into her mouth. I couldn't help but smile at her haste.

"How about I do your hair while you finish?" I offered.

Her eyes widened, and she nodded.

"Do you know how to do fishtail braids?"

"Do I know?" I scoffed. "You're looking at the world's best braider. French, fish, double-crossed with a bow, I can do them all!"

Her smile got wider and wider. I took it as my cue to go to her room and nab the brush. There was no spray bottle, but I'd make do with the kitchen sink. I needed to get one and some leave-in conditioner since Lux was severely lacking hair products.

"We're going with a fishtail then?" I asked as I came back and stood behind her, lightly fanning out her hair to see the damage.

"Two, please!"

I started by brushing it a little, but there was a stubborn part that just kept sticking up, so I wet my hands at the kitchen sink. Once I patted the water into the affected spot, it was easier to manipulate her hair into a braid. As crazy as it looked, she didn't have too many knots, which I was grateful for.

"Oh, shoot! I forgot the hair ties," I muttered as I got to the end of one.

"I'll get it," Lux said, standing. I shot her a smile.

"The small clear ones, if you have them. Or maybe a bow. Would you like that?"

I leaned over to see a frown on Bella's face.

"We don't have bows," she replied with a pout.

Ah, I see. Lux wasn't really attuned to little girl needs.

"No problem. Lux can get me what you have, and maybe after school you and I can go on a hair tie and bow shopping spree?"

Lux came back with the hair ties, and once I had Bella's braid done, something else was handed to me.

A shiny black card.

"Use this today," she said, her voice low. I looked up at her, shocked.

"It's a few bows," I whispered. "Not really worthy of a black card."

Lux gave me a look.

"Everything Bella needs is worthy of a black card."

Something in my chest warmed at her declaration. *Maybe I was wrong about Lux.*

The worst part, though, was that it made me want her even more. In my line of work, I saw so many kids whose parents would never say something like that. And she wasn't even the girl's mom.

That single sentence had me rethinking everything and looking at her in a different light.

Shut it down.

Lux turned to the little girl. "Bella, time to go to school. Go get dressed."

Bella gave her aunt the grumpiest look imaginable but still scooted off her chair and headed to her room.

"She's a good kid," I said when Bella left earshot. But when I looked up at her, my heart stopped in my chest.

Her hooded eyes were looking at me with an intensity that caught me off guard.

I'd almost forgotten that she wasn't like every other parent I dealt with. That she was actually someone who had the ability to steal my breath from me with a single look. Who could make my knees weak with just the brush of her hand.

"I allowed you to come back," she reminded me. "For Bella. She likes you."

I swallowed the knot in my throat. *Why do I feel like I'm a kid about to get scolded?*

The need to please Lux was so strong I was already thinking through every little thing I could have possibly done wrong and getting ready to apologize for it.

"Like I mentioned, we went through a lot of nannies. That was because she never liked any of them," she continued. "I don't know what you did, but it saved your job."

I pulled my bottom lip between my teeth. *Bella likes me?* I mean, guessing by the way that she offered me her pancake, I would say that I was on her good side, but I hadn't done anything special, other than treat her like a kid.

"I'm not sure what I did either," I admitted. "But I can assure you my number one goal is to make sure she's happy and taken care of. You can trust that."

"Good," she said. "Can I also trust that nothing will happen between us again?"

My skin heated at her words, and while it shouldn't, disappointment filled me.

"I don't know, can you trust yourself?" I shot back with a

raised brow. "You're the one who pushed me up against the counter."

Her lips pulled into a deep frown.

"A moment of weakness," she said after a moment. Her eyes raked my form, taking in the light blue sweater and lowly white skirt. "Don't wear the sundress again."

I had to look away from her as my heart began pounding in my chest and heat flooded my body, swirling deliciously in my belly.

It made me want to wear it again. Test exactly what it did to her. What she'd want to do to me in it.

"It's work-appropriate," I muttered.

"It's only appropriate if your goal was to get fucked again. Tell me, *Juliette*, was that your intention when you came into my home?"

I gave her an incredulous look.

"Don't act like such a-a—"

"Barbarian? A wanton, needy bitch in heat?"

I had to cover my mouth at the vulgarity of her words. My eyes shot to the hallway connecting us to Bella's room, but there was no sign of her.

"Now that it's out in the open, I can be honest," she said, taking a step closer. Her delicious scent filled my nose. Her body heat sunk into me. I had to crane my neck up to get a good look at her. "I've never needed anyone like I need you. I want to drop everything, whisk you away, and keep you chained up on my bed begging for me to stop as I make you come over and over again. Give you every single pleasure imaginable, like nothing you've ever felt before. Your taste is still so fresh on my tongue, and I've been yearning to get even the slightest hint of it again."

My shaky hand landed on her stomach. I'm not sure if it was to steady myself or create some space so I could breathe, but it did the opposite. Touching her ignited something between us. It was a connection, an undeniable tether between us that reminded me just how good it had been that night.

"Do you see?" She dropped her voice into a whisper. "This can't happen. I can admit how much I want to ravage you , but nothing like that can *ever* happen again. Not when Bella needs you. Can I trust myself? I'm not sure. So I need us to be on the same page. I need you to keep me grounded when all I can think abo—" She exhaled. "Tell me you understand."

I understood all too well. Lux was a better guardian than I realized. She cared more for Bella than she let on. She knew Bella needed me and was willing to put her own desires on the back burner, no matter how strong they were.

But can I trust myself?

After yesterday and this morning, one thing was certain. It wasn't just about the money anymore. Bella needed me, and it hurt my heart to think I'd ever disappoint her.

So there was really only one answer.

"I understand," I said, looking up at her and removing my hand. And then, because I couldn't help myself, I gave her a smile and added, "So you *are* the one in love with me. I knew it. Who would have thought the big bad Lux was so obsessed with little ol' me?"

The tension stayed for a moment before she took a step back and shook her head while letting out a light chuckle. The heaviness between us disappeared, and I felt a weight lift off my shoulders.

The burning need for her was still there, but at least now we were aligned in wanting the best for the girl.

"Juliette! How does this look?"

Bella came running out of her room wearing a light blue cardigan and cream pants. I didn't miss how we were practically matching.

"Beautiful!" I said with a clap of my hands. "We're twins! And it looks so cute with your braids!"

She paused when she got to me, her hand shyly reaching up to feel her braid.

"Get going or you'll be late," Lux ordered.

I took Bella's hand and was just about to take her out when the little girl paused, turned back, and ran to Lux. She flung her arms around her legs, giving her a hug that surprised both of us.

Lux's eyes widened, and then very slowly her hand came to pat Bella's head.

There is something there. It made my chest warm.

Bella ran back to me without looking back at Lux and placed her hand in mine. I sent Lux a small smile before turning away, leaving her in a shocked daze.

I showed Bella outside to where her driver was waiting for us. She was a young woman with a high ponytail, a button-up, and jeans. She smiled at Bella and opened the door for her to climb in.

"Juliette," I introduced myself. She gave me a smile.

"Oh, I know, you've been the talk of the staff. I'm Marci."

"Oh?" I asked with a quirked brow.

"By staff I mean me and Gina," she clarified with a shrug.

I laughed and ducked in to sit next to Bella.

"You got your homework?" I asked once Marci started the car and had us heading to the school.

"Yep!" She opened her backpack to show me the neat folders stacked inside. "All ready."

"Perfect," I said, giving her a smile. "Okay, now tell me, who has a crush on whom?"

Her eyes lit up. "Oh my gosh, you'd never believe it. So, my friend Kinsley, there's this boy in the grade above. They've been best friends for, like, *ever*. I don't really get it because he's gross and still eats his boogers. I mean, that's so first grade, you know? Boys are gross like that—"

I let Bella ramble on, listening to the gossip of her year. It became more obvious that while she knew people and had a few friends, she was pretty lonely with only one semi-close friend. She even admitted to spending a lot of lunch times alone, reading or playing in the jungle gym by herself.

I tried not to outwardly show just how much I felt for her, instead smiling along and chiming in until we pulled up to the school. She grabbed her backpack, hesitating when she opened the door.

"You promise we will get the bows after school?" she asked.

I nodded and gave her my biggest smile.

"Promise!" I said. "Do you want me to go with you?"

She shook her head.

"I know the way." She hesitated for a second, almost taking a step forward before she said a quick bye to Marci, got out, and made her way into the gates.

Was that... Did she want to hug me?

"I see what Gina was saying. She likes you," Marci said as we drove away, pulling me from my stupor. "She had all the others wait at home. It was just her and me."

I frowned as she disappeared inside and we pulled away. I didn't really have experience with grief and loneliness at her age, but I knew the best thing I could do was just be there for her.

"So where can I take you? The mall? A bookstore?" Marci asked.

I met her gaze in the rearview mirror.

"Do you have time for a coffee?" I asked. "I was wondering if I could pick your brain for a bit."

Her eyes lit up. "I thought you'd never ask. I know just the place."

Just the place seemed to be a hip-but-quiet café filled to the brim with plants that only sold overpriced matchas and specialty coffees. There was a small loft upstairs where we chose to sit down and have our chat.

Marci seemed all too excited to share everything she knew about Lux and Bella.

"No, I was hired just for Bella," she said as she swirled the coffee in her hand, the ice slushing together loudly. "Lux likes to drive herself for the most part. A control thing, if you ask me."

I hummed and sipped my matcha.

"How has Bella..." I paused, looking for a word.

"Been coping?" she supplied, and I nodded. She let out a heavy sigh. "Honestly? I don't think she has. I've never seen her cry, though I've seen her throw fits like no one's business. I think it's her way of letting the emotions out. Anger is one of the last stages of grief, right? But the issue is that no one can really help her through it. You've seen Lux, it's like talking to a brick wall."

I chewed the inside of my cheek, not bothering to correct her about the grief stages.

"She's not that bad."

"Because she wants to fuck you," she replied with a grin. "To everyone else, she's like an unfeeling block of ice."

Heat rushed up my neck.

"She does not," I lied, remembering her admission that morning. I could still feel how her words washed over my skin. How she felt when she was close enough to touch.

The promise of it all... but also the threat.

She's right. Bella wouldn't be able to handle it if we had a falling out. And more importantly, I'm here for Bella. *Not to be Lux's new toy.*

"Oh, yeah, *sure*," she said with a snort, and just as she was about to put her cup down, she paused, her eyes going wide. "Oh my God, you want to fuck her too, don't you? I don't know why I didn't see it."

I gave her a glare and sipped my matcha.

"I don't fuck my employers."

She tipped her coffee to me in a mock cheers.

"Does Bella have any hobbies?" I asked.

The driver let out a hum. "She paints on her iPad. Plays a few gardening games. But that's it."

I nodded and let that sink in before standing.

"Take me to the craft store then, will you?"

She hastily got up.

"Now?" she asked. "You have, like, all day."

"After that you can drop me off back home," I said and turned to the stairs that led straight down to the exit.

"Boring!"

I couldn't help the smile that spread across my lips.

Maybe I can last a while at this job after all.

Chapter 10
Juliette

O r not.

After spending all day between the craft store and setting up back at the house, I found myself with Marci back at the school and waiting for Bella.

I even planned exactly where we would get the bows. We'd stop at the big retail chain stores, and then there were a few boutiques that I personally knew of.

But as soon as I saw her walk out of the school gate, I knew none of that was going to happen. The very excited and happy eight-year-old came back a totally different person. Her hair and clothes might have been the same, but everything else had taken a one-eighty. I expected her to run into the car, excited for our shopping together, but she was like a dark cloud on a rainy day when she entered the car.

Even with the obvious change in her demeanor, I still thought I'd give it a go since she had been so excited for it in the morning.

"Are you ready to get your bows?" I asked, trying to get a good look at her face, but she kept dodging me. I waited, but she still didn't look at me, choosing to cross her arms and pull her iPad out from her bag instead. She started up a small game and mumbled something under her breath.

"What was that, sweetie?"

"I don't want stupid bows," she said with a pout.

Oh, no. I knew this too well. If I wasn't careful, we were going to have a tantrum. I just hoped no one said anything today to hurt her or make her think something she loved—like bows—was stupid.

"Really?" I asked and leaned forward to try and get a look at her face again, but she hid it from me. I knew something must have happened at school, but I didn't want to call her out on her behavior. If I did, this might make the whole situation worse. There was never any use trying to get kids to talk about anything if they didn't want to. You had to wait until they were ready.

So that was what I did. I waited.

Marci met my eyes in the rearview, silently asking if we should steer off course. I nodded. We could always go later if Bella wanted.

"Anything interesting happen at school today?" I asked. "Did Carly get in trouble for her obvious cheating?"

Bella didn't take the bait and remained focused on her game, her little fingers tapping the screen a bit harder than necessary.

Okay, then. I took the hint.

The rest of the ride was silent. When we got to the house, she stormed out of the car and went through the door without even waiting for me to get out.

I got out, shooting Marci a look.

"I'll let you know if we decide to go," I said. She nodded and motioned for me to go after Bella.

I rushed up the steps and into the house, but she was

nowhere to be seen. I walked slowly into the living room, trying to see if she was hiding out anywhere, but still nothing. Getting a bit worried now, I beelined to her room, hovering outside when I found the door closed.

Maybe another nanny would just barge in, but not me. She had to come to me. I wouldn't invade her privacy.

I should text Lux. But I stopped myself. I was supposed to be the person Bella trusted and the nanny Lux relied on.

I could figure this out myself. And I wanted them to trust me enough to.

"Bella? Are you in there?" There was no response. "Take your time. If you'd like, I'll be waiting outside for you. I bought us some paint stuff! Maybe we could do it together?"

Silence. *I'll check back later.*

I made good on my promise and headed outside, where I had left the canvas and painting supplies set up for us. Gina had also placed some lemonade and Bella's after-school snacks on the table.

I sat down and started to prep the paint and brushes. I knew at some point Bella would come out; I just didn't know when, so I wanted to make sure everything was ready for her. I had gotten us both some paint-by-numbers-type flower easels that should be easy enough without too much of a headache.

Before I was done readying her paintbrushes, I heard her shuffle her way to the sliding glass door.

She didn't say anything, so I let her look over what I was doing.

"We can eat first or eat while we paint. What do you say?" I asked without looking at her.

"I can do both."

I nodded. "Sure thing. Take a seat, little lady."

I finally looked at her when she was walking up. The frown was etched into her face, making her look so much like her aunt. Technically, she should be doing her homework first, but she had just come from a full day at school—obviously not a good one—and I was giving her an escape.

Besides, homework would still be there later. Maybe it was because I didn't end up going to college, but I didn't put too much emphasis on getting it done at a certain time. As long as it was done, that was all that mattered.

"It's paint-by-number flowers," I said. "I'm not a good painter, so I thought this would be easy enough for me. I heard you do it on your iPad, so maybe you can give me some pointers."

I placed the food on a stool closer to her seat and easel so she could grab it when she wanted. She silently maneuvered herself onto the seat, her eyes scanning over the colors.

"Purple, please."

I sent her a smile and dabbed a good bit of purple on the plate for her. She was looking over the numbers on the canvas, but I could tell that she was mapping it in her mind instead of trying to follow the actual assigned colors. I liked it.

She hesitantly grabbed some finger food before using the other hand to pick up a brush, dipping it in the paint.

"Do you like to paint?" I asked and followed suit, picking purple and matching it to the numbers. It was supposed to be pink, but I agreed with her that purple was prettier.

"It's okay," she muttered.

"I've never been that crafty," I admitted. "I wanted to be, but I always messed it up, and my drawings never came out right."

"I like watercolor," she murmured, smearing her purple a bit too far. "It's pretty."

She let out a huff when she saw it went outside the lines, glaring at it as if that could correct it.

"It's okay," I whispered. "We can fix it later."

She nodded and dipped her brush again, moving on to another purple section. This time, she tried to slow down her movements, but her wrist flicked out ever so slightly.

"The paint's too thick," she growled when she got it wrong again.

"It just takes some practice," I said and pointed to my sad attempt at the painting. I had purposely colored outside the lines too, but that apparently didn't make her feel better. "Maybe switch colors?"

She wiped off the brush on the paper towel I set aside for her and picked yellow next.

I should have seen it coming.

As soon as she made the first stroke, it became obvious that she hadn't wiped it well enough and the purple mixed with the yellow. There was about a two-second delay before she was off the chair and pushing the easel down to the floor.

"Stupid paint! I hate this!"

I put my paintbrush down and got off my seat. Whatever had happened at school had been building up inside her, and I knew it wasn't going to stop there.

"It's so stupid! I don't even like this! I don't know why you had to ruin it like this. I don't want to do it anymore—"

And on and on she went, repeating more or less the same things. I quickly kneeled in front of her, trying to get in her line of sight, but she was too worked up.

"Bella," I said in a calm voice. My hands came to her side, gently rubbing them up and down her arms, trying to ground her. When that didn't work, I gently squeezed her arms up and down, from her shoulders to her wrists, before taking her hands and squeezing them in a slow rhythm. This seemed to work a bit better. "*Bella.*"

Her eyes washed over me, and her rage turned to heavy breathing. That's when I saw the tears building in her eyes.

"Take a deep breath with me, sweetie, okay? Bella, *hey*." I gently touched her cheek to get her attention, but her hand was suddenly up, swatting mine away.

"Don't touch me!"

"Okay." I raised my hands to show her they weren't going near her. "But can you breathe for me? Better yet, help me do something. It's a bit silly, but I promise it works, okay?"

Her breathing was getting quicker, tears falling now.

"Pretend we're blowing out candles," I said as I held up one hand. "I'm holding them here, okay? It's not like one or two; there's a lot of them, so you may need to blow a few times, okay?"

She gave me a shaky nod.

"One, two, three—"

I started blowing softly, and she hesitantly took a breath and blew out the air onto my hand.

"Good job," I said with a smile. "Again. A lot of candles, remember? Think twenty-seven. That's how old I'll be in a few months. Imagine it's me and you with a huge cake and all my candles on there. We have about half to go."

Another exhale, this one longer, and her breathing notably slowed.

"Great! Can you give me one more?"

She nodded, taking a deep breath and blowing them out.

She took a few more deep breaths by herself this time. I was immensely proud of her. Not many children would get it this fast, and I usually had to try more than once, but Bella was special. At times, I felt like she was a little bit too grown-up for her own good, but watching her breakdown made me see the child she actually was.

This time, I reached forward to run my hands down her arms.

"You okay?" I asked.

When she met my gaze, sobs built up in her chest as if she couldn't hold them in anymore.

Oh no. My heart broke for the little girl.

I opened my arms, and she dove into them, her small arms wrapping around my neck and hanging on for dear life. She was shaking with the force that she was using to hold onto me.

"I know, I know. Let it all out."

I rubbed her back as she sobbed against me. When she tried to crawl into my lap, I moved to sit with my legs crossed and pulled her to me. She wrapped her legs around my waist, and I held on tight.

Her tears soaked my sweater, but I didn't let go. Not even when she cried all she could. Not even when she just leaned into me, seeking comfort I'm not sure she'd received since her parents died.

I murmured softly in her ear, telling her I understood. That it was okay to cry. And that I wouldn't leave her.

When I finally looked up to the sliding glass door, I saw Marci and Gina there... and Lux.

She came home early.

I don't know how long she'd been standing there, but it took me by surprise. I didn't move a muscle. Not until Bella was completely relaxed in my arms.

I stared into Lux's eyes the whole time, and I could see she was pissed. At me, at the situation, at... Who knows?

I don't give a shit. This little girl needs me.

Gina and Marci made themselves scarce, sensing the tension.

Small snores came from Bella, making my heart hurt even more for her. *How long has she been holding that in?* She cried so hard, she exhausted herself. I pulled away enough to look at her, noticing her eye bags.

Does she have trouble sleeping?

"I'll take it from here," Lux said, coming out to the patio and carefully grabbing Bella from me.

"It's okay. She'll want me to be here when she wakes up so I can—"

"You can meet me in my office," she replied pointedly, her gaze telling me that I fucked up.

I bit my tongue, watching her as she took Bella to her room. Her facial expression was unreadable.

"Well," I said with an embarrassed smile as I passed my coworkers. "I'm likely getting fired. It was nice working with you. Can you point me in the direction of her office?"

Marci saluted me while Gina gave me a pitiful look before replying, "Take the hallway, second door on the right."

"Good luck," she whispered, and I just nodded.

Lux's office was so obviously hers. Large black bookcases with more knickknacks on them than books. A dark desk with an expensive-looking chair and a closed laptop on top. The windows showed the mess of our painting disaster outside.

I walked up to the desk, my eyes narrowing in on the only picture frame there.

I turned it around, my breath catching when I took in the picture of Lux, baby Bella... and probably her sister. They had the same hair and eye color, though her sister's features were rounder.

The door clicked open and shut, the sound ringing throughout the silent office, and I quickly put the frame back in its position.

"She had a hard day in school and I think it's all finally coming out now. She needed the cry—"

Her hands were on me, turning me around and forcing my butt against the desk. I looked up at her in shock. The anger in her eyes had my heart dropping.

"It's your second day and you're already making her cry?

Even the shittiest one from your agency didn't make her cry. What the fuck did you do?"

"Excuse me?" I asked, my voice raising.

"You heard me. Fuck, I should have fired you when I had the chance."

I cocked my head to the side.

"What happened to Mrs. *Bella Needs You*, huh?" I asked. "Kids cry, Lux. Especially kids whose parents fucking died, and based on what I just saw, I wouldn't be surprised if you've never even hugged the child."

I knew it was the wrong thing to say as soon as the words were out of my mouth.

Her hand was on my jaw, her body pushing into mine, forcing me to lean back into the desk. She fit snugly between my legs, but that wasn't the most damning thing.

It was how hot and bothered I was getting by the position. By the intensity in her stare. And just how woefully inappropriate and wrong it was in this moment.

"Don't you dare judge our relationship," she growled. "You don't know shit."

I swallowed the fight I still had left in me. "You're right. I'm sorry."

The words caught her off guard. Enough to bring her back to herself and realize the situation we were in.

She backed away quickly.

"You're trouble," she whispered. "I can't do this. I'm firing you."

Chapter 11
Lux

Coming home to Bella crying was my worst nightmare. Her teacher had called me, saying that some kids had been picking on her today. She often gave me a heads-up when Bella had a bad day. All of the staff knew about her parents and wanted to make sure she was taken care of, so the communication was constant.

But I'd never expected to see her crying. Nor did I expect to see her hanging onto Juliette like she was afraid she'd be violently pulled away from her.

It hurt me to see it. It hurt even more when I realized I couldn't do anything. That I didn't even know what to do.

I stood there, watching as they blew out imaginary candles, frozen in fear. I'd never felt panic like that in my life except on the day they told me she was mine.

But somehow... Juliette took it all. She calmed her down and sat there with her for over an hour until she cried it all out.

All while I watched, helplessly.

Bella didn't need that. She needed to be happy, playful. She didn't need someone to make her cry like that.

I was blown away by how she handled it, but I couldn't help but think that if I hadn't hired her in the first place, Bella would have never had such an explosive outburst.

"I've been here for two days," she said in a slow, careful voice. "I know you don't want to hear it, but Bella needs to cry like that. She can't just keep it inside."

"A child needs to be happy," I spat back. "She doesn't need to cry. She needs to laugh. Play. She doesn't need to... *remember*."

Juliette's face twisted into a frown. Her kissable, plump lower lip jutted out, inviting me to bite it.

"You know that's not true, right? She went through something terrible. If she keeps it in, it's not good for her."

I ground my teeth together. I didn't want to hear it. I couldn't. I didn't want to think of Bella crying like that again because... I wouldn't know how to handle it. I wasn't like Juliette.

My heart jolted when her hand came to cup my cheek.

Why are you touching me? The words were on the tip of my tongue, but they died when I saw the sincerity in her eyes.

No one's ever looked at me like that.

"Have you taken your time to grieve your sister, Lux?"

It felt like a dagger straight to the heart. Her facial expression and the warmth of her hand were like she was slowly dragging it down my middle, cutting me open and baring my most vulnerable parts to her.

"The fuck is it to you?" I growled, but that didn't stop my throat from threatening to close or my eyes from stinging.

In truth, I hadn't. I had been so consumed with making sure Bella was okay and that my work was taken care of that I pushed all thoughts of my sister away as soon as they popped up.

"Oh, Lux," Juliette whispered.

I gritted my teeth to stop the onslaught of emotions she was pulling from me.

I wanted to lean into her like Bella did. Hold onto her and never let go.

How did she do that? How was she able to render us both into crying messes? How was she able to pull the one thing the both of us wanted to forget out of us and bare it to the universe?

Grief was ugly. Twisted. I'd rather lock everything away in a box and throw away the key than do whatever it was we were doing right now.

So I did the only thing I could think of. The only thing that could stop all these ugly emotions from making their way to the surface. The only thing that would ground me.

I kissed her.

I leaned forward, pressing my lips to hers, but I didn't wait for her to respond. I kissed her like I was suffocating and she was the only oxygen source. Because that's what it felt like in that moment.

I needed her. Needed her to take all the pain away.

Maybe it's not just Bella who needs her after all.

My hands came to her thighs, hoisting her up onto the desk. She let out a gasp, giving me entrance to her mouth. Her hands were digging into my shoulders, pulling me closer, both of us grabbing at each other like we couldn't bear to be separated any longer.

She met my kiss with an equal amount of passion. Her tongue teased my own, like she'd been waiting for this moment.

My hands were traveling up her thighs, and she shuddered against me. I needed to touch her.

I need her. Now.

"Juliette," I whispered against her lips. "Let me feel you."

My hands reached under her sweater, feeling her warm

skin. Her breath hitched when I met her breast, my thumb hesitantly swiping over her quickly erecting nipple.

"Juliette, tell me this is okay."

She pulled away to look up at me, her eyes wide and her face flushed. *So beautiful.* Just like that night, those eyes were begging me to take care of her. Begging me to touch her. To ravage her.

"Lux... It's not okay."

Her words had me crashing back to reality.

She's my nanny. She's here for Bella. Not for me.

I have to stop.

"Right," I said, clearing my throat as I pulled away. "I'm sorry. I—"

Her hands were instantly on my suit jacket, pulling me closer.

"It's not okay... But I don't want to stop. Just this once, Lux. One more time, please?"

There was no way I'd ever be able to deny her. I was a goner from the moment I saw her walk up on stage, and now that she was finally giving me *permission*, I all but fell to my knees right there, ready to kiss her shoes as a show of gratitude.

"Just once," I vowed as I started to push up her skirt. She leaned back on her palms, her hooded eyes watching me as I readied her. "Just a taste."

When her skirt was all the way up to her hips, I gently pushed her chest, laying her down across my desk. She was spread out like a decadent feast just waiting for me to have my fill. Her light pink panties with a small heart sewn into the lace were the sexiest thing I'd ever seen.

She helped me pull up her sweater, baring her bra to me just before she cupped her tits, her thumbs running over her nipples.

Fuck.

"Please, Lux."

I leaned down, pushing my face between her legs and placing a kiss on her clothed cunt, watching her body arch in response.

Gently, I pulled her underwear to the side, flattening my tongue and running it up the length of her folds. I wanted to tease her, take my time, but we were on borrowed time, forced to hide our dirty little secret.

She still tastes fucking delicious.

The moment her sweetness hit my taste buds, I lost all control. My lips fastened around her clit, sucking in long intervals before spearing her with my tongue.

"Oh, fuck," she moaned, her hands flying to my hair and pulling me closer to where she wanted me.

I obliged and flattened my tongue again, eating her out like she deserved. She was truly an angel, and I was nothing but her servant, ready to give her anything she wanted. I might have had her calling me sir, but she was always the one calling the shots. She just might not have realized it yet.

Her control was a leash wrapped so tightly around my neck, it was threatening to cut off my air supply, but I was grateful for it. Grateful for a chance to even just touch her.

I fucked her with my mouth like it was the last time. Because it had to be.

We couldn't do this. We both knew it. We just needed to take the edge off. That's all it was. But then why did my hand slip inside my own pants? Why were my fingers circling my clit before pushing inside? Why was I fucking myself to her moans?

"Lux, Lux, *Lux.*"

Her chanting my name was like music to my ears. It catapulted me further. It had me moving up her body, forgetting about my own orgasm to chase hers.

My lips claimed hers, my wet fingers moving from my cunt to hers, joining our wetness. So sinful, but goddamn it, we melded together so well.

I pumped my fingers into her, curling them, and pulling an orgasm out of her within seconds. Then I pulled away to take a good look at my masterpiece.

Her hair was fanned out all over my desk, her lips open in a breathy moan, her skin flushed. Her sweater was pushed all the way up, her skirt around her waist. My eyes traveled down to see where we were joined.

"Fuck, you'd take my strap so good," I groaned and fit another finger inside her.

"I want it," she moaned. "Give it to me."

"If you're good to me," I murmured, immediately cursing myself for making her a promise I couldn't keep. "You'll be good and come again for me, won't you?"

"Yes!"

Her cunt squeezed around me, giving me a preview of what was to come.

"You're so responsive," I praised. "You were made to get fucked by me."

"My body belongs to you. All of it. I'll do whatever you want."

It was dangerously easy to fall back into the people we had been back at the club. So easy to get lost in how perfect she was for me.

I'd forgotten this was to be our only time together. I should have fought off the orgasm. Should have tried to keep her needy and begging for longer to satiate this insane hunger I had for her.

But I didn't. I did everything in my power to make her come. My thumb was at her clit, my fingers curling inside her. I worked her cunt in every way I knew to make her come even harder than she had that night.

She arched her back, her eyes closing and her mouth opening wide as she came around my fingers, moaning my name in a way that had my cunt pulsing.

So perfect. Why did she have to be my niece's nanny? Why couldn't I have met her again under different circumstances?

When she came down from her orgasm, she sat up, her arms wrapping around my neck and pulling me flush against her. I had no time to move my hand. Her hips jerked against me, telling me the greedy little thing wanted me to fuck her again.

I kissed her back with unrestrained passion, pouring every single fiber of my need for her into it.

I need to get it out. I need to get over her.

Her hands traveled down my body before they made it to my pants.

I need to stop her.

But I couldn't.

I pulled away and leaned my forehead against hers as she unbuckled my pants and slipped her delicate fingers into my folds.

"You're soaked, Lux," she murmured, her bright blue eyes looking up at me. "Is all of this for me?"

"You're just so perfect I can't help myself," I confessed, my hips jerking against her as the heel of her palm brushed against my clit.

"I've been so good to you, haven't I?"

"So good," I forced out. I should have been the one in control, but she was turning me into a mess. She was pulling the leash tighter and tighter. Maybe that was my kink. Being controlled by her. With each rock of her hand, I found myself unraveling further and further until there was nothing I wouldn't do for her.

"Then do I deserve your cum?" she asked, her lips brushing against my exposed collar.

"You do. God, you do." I was coming faster than ever. She was playing me so well. She knew exactly what I wanted to hear. "You've been such a perfect little fuck toy. So willing. So ready. You deserve it all. My orgasm. My cum. I'll reward you with my strap, I promise."

"Make sure you remember that," she whispered. "Now come for me, *sir*."

I couldn't hold back. I came hard, having to lean against her for support. Wave after wave crashed through me. I couldn't do anything but take it. Juliette was whispering things to me, but they just got lost in the madness of it all.

When I finally came down from the high, I pulled back to look at her. My hand was still in her pants, hers in mine. Her cunt fluttered around my fingers.

"Fuck it," I groaned and started to pump my fingers in and out of her again. "One more. One more, then we're done, okay?"

"This is a mistake," she groaned against me.

"The biggest," I admitted, my voice cracking as her heel started to rub against my clit.

"I don't know if I can stop."

"We need to try."

"In a bit," she murmured, quivering against me.

"In a bit," I agreed and captured her lips again with my own.

Chapter 12
Juliette

"You can't be serious." Harmony's arms were crossed in front of her chest, her eyes narrowed at our landlady.

I had been pulled into an emergency meeting as soon as I got home from my thorough fucking with Lux. We said we'd stop, but it was almost impossible to tear ourselves apart from each other, even after a third time.

I could still feel her touch on my skin. The scent of her cologne was woven into my clothing, giving me a whiff of her every time I moved.

I wanted to take them off and wash them immediately to try and forget the massive mistake we had made, but I didn't have the chance because, when I got home, all the lights were on and everyone in the house, plus the landlady, was waiting for me in the living room.

Sensing this was serious, I took a seat next to Harmony, who was in an all-pink matching pajama set, waiting for the news.

When she told us what she had gone there to say, all chaos

broke loose. I had to hold onto Harmony's sleeve to stop her from getting up and getting in the landlady's face.

"There are laws about this," Erin said with a huff. She was wearing an all-black ensemble, her makeup-less face showing just how tired of it all she was.

"I'm giving you girls a week," Patricia said. She was wearing a gaudy fur coat and too-big-for-her-face sunglasses, and her black hair was cut into a bob.

She looked like a wannabe mob wife. and not the cool kind. The kind who liked to show that they were rich. Those who would buy expensive clothing and drive new cars even year but never gave anything back—the stingiest when it came to giving some away or helping out.

But I didn't say anything. I didn't know what to say. I wanted to move out with the money, but every other place in the area or close to Lucas was far too expensive for me to go it alone, especially if I wanted it to last.

Since leaving my aunt's place at the ripe age of seventeen and a half, I had never lived alone. Never had the money to.

Even with money now, I was still panicking.

The money is for Lucas. To pay our debt. Not for something like this.

"Can't your daughter wait?" I asked. "I mean, at least thirty days so we all have enough time to find a place? That's the least you can do, right? Most laws state you have to give us thirty days."

"I didn't know you were all lawyers," she said with a sneer. "You're lucky I'm even giving you a week. There's no more discussion on this. Geez! To think I was nice enough to give you a heads-up. I could have just walked in here and demanded you move right away."

"This is totally illegal," April muttered. "But we don't have enough money to hire a lawyer."

"That's what she's banking on," Harmony said, her voice dripping with disdain. "That we're too poor to fight back. Or too scared to try."

Patricia huffed and turned to leave.

"One week, ladies! Now, if you'll excuse me, I have a wedding to prepare for!"

She left the house, slamming the door as she did. We were left in tense silence for a moment as we all tried to come up with our own version of a plan.

"Who gives their daughter a fucking *house* as a wedding present?" Harmony muttered, kicking the dining room table we were all gathered around.

My mind was already hazy from all the stuff I shouldn't have done with Lux, and I couldn't even begin to think of what I would do next.

"Well, I'm fucked." Erin pulled out her phone. "My job barely pays enough for this place. Though maybe this is my sign to move back in with my parents and save a bit to buy my own."

"In this economy?" Harmony scoffed. "I don't think I'll ever be able to buy my own."

"A girl should have *some* goals, Harmony," Erin said pointedly.

I stood, sending the group a sheepish smile when they looked at me. I had nothing to say, nor did I really have the brain space for it right now.

My Lux-induced buzz had come to a screeching halt, giving me whiplash with just how fast it all turned. All I wanted was to go to bed and think about this tomorrow.

So that's what I would do. There was no use pushing myself to come up with something when I couldn't get my brain to work. And honestly, I'd probably do more harm than good right now.

"Sorry, guys, I'm beat. And I need some time to consider my options."

None of them said anything, all obviously in their own world, desperate to figure out where they would be next week.

"Right, that's fine," Harmony finally said, perking up. Her hand came to rest on my back. "Go get some rest."

"Sleep well, Julie," April added in a low voice. She wasn't looking at me but instead looking at her hands on her lap as she messed with her nails.

"Don't forget, it's Waffle Wednesday tomorrow," Erin reminded. There is a small but forced smile on her face.

"How could I forget?" I gasped. "But I have to be at work early to send off my kid. So could y'all maybe get up at like... *sixish?*"

"Oh, absolutely not," Erin said with a frown. "We'll just save some for you."

"I can get up," April offered, sending me a look. We both knew I wouldn't subject her to the hell of early mornings.

I actually like the early mornings. The quiet when no one was awake and no one could bother me. It was just me, myself, and whatever I had to do, when stress from the world hadn't sunk in yet and I was left to daydream about everything that could be.

"You'd be the only one," Harmony said. "I haven't gotten up that early in years."

I gave them a smile. I knew what their answer would be. "Then after work. Save me some, and maybe we can talk about everyone's plans."

There were a few nods and goodnights as I left. I hurried back to my room, locking myself in it.

Shit.

I sank back against my door, all the energy and breath leaving me.

What the fuck am I supposed to do?

Before I could talk myself out of it, I typed a quick message to Lux. My fingers paused on the keyboard, and I added one thing I knew she'd love.

ME

Sir, just to confirm. I'm not actually fired and should def report for duty tomorrow, right?

My heart hammered in my chest as I waited for a reply. Seconds ticked by before my phone buzzed twice.

LUX STERLING

See you tomorrow, Angel.

I walked into the house one more time on Wednesday morning, not knowing what to expect. How to act.

I mean, we had broken the biggest fucking rule there was. Repeatedly. No matter how good it felt.

Bella was at the island, and Lux was sitting there with her iPad and phone in hand, looking as serious as ever.

When Bella looked up at me, I saw an embarrassed look crossing her face.

"Juliette..."

"Don't worry about it, Bella," I said and rounded the island, smoothing down her hair. "Are you feeling better?"

She smiled, and all the tension went away. Only then did I realize she was probably worried I'd be mad at her for her little outburst. My heart melted at that.

"A lot!" she said with a wide smile. "Can we go get the bows today?"

"Of course!" I reached into my purse, glad I remembered to bring some from my own collection. It was severely lacking in comparison to what a little girl her age needed, but it was something. "We can get some more, but I brought a pink one, a black glittery one—"

Her gasp had warmth expanding in my chest.

"The black glittery one is so cute!"

I let out a chuckle and gave it to her before placing the rest on the counter. As she was looking at it, a brush and water were pushed across the counter to me by Lux.

I looked up at her, my heart skipping a beat when she met my gaze.

Memories of the day before flashed through my mind.

Her tongue against mine. Her hands on my waist. Her fingers inside me. I was so tired, but I had still tossed and turned all night just thinking about it.

God, I want more. I need more.

It was a mistake. I knew it was. I reached out to take the stuff, my fingers brushing across Lux's. Her eyes had a light to them that told me she too was thinking about what happened, and I took a shaky inhale, trying not to show how affected I was by just a simple touch.

Lux retreated slowly, her hand flexing and nails digging into the counter as she stared at me.

Fuck. We were so fucked. Whatever arbitrary rules we'd made to protect Bella and keep this strictly professional had gone straight out the window. But as I took the stuff and began to do Bella's hair as she ate, all I could think about was how much I needed this job.

And not just for the money. That's what was even more dangerous.

"Is it okay if I pick Bella up for lunch today?" I asked Lux.

"Yes!" Bella answered for her, but I kept my eyes on Lux. She put down her iPad, a smile pulling at her lips.

"How about we all go together?" she offered, surprising me. "Where do you want to go, Bella?"

Lunch with Lux? My heart skipped in my chest. It was so normal yet so... intimate. Like something a normal couple would do.

Bella jutted out her lower lip. "Can I have time to think about it?"

"Sure," Lux said and got up. "If that's the case, I'm off so I can catch up on some work and meet you later. Have a good day at school, Bella."

"Bye, Lux!"

I was stuck watching Lux's retreating form with my heart pounding in my chest.

She hadn't fired me, which was a good thing. But I hadn't even begun to bring up the apartment issue and how I'd likely need a few days off to figure it out.

I was going to keep this job for the time being, meaning I would need to be close to here. Which meant moving further away from my aunt's, and there was no telling I'd even be able to get a place in this area.

"Ready to get dressed and go?" I asked Bella.

But she was silent. I leaned forward to look at her, and her smile was gone, a more serious expression taking its place.

"You okay, Bella?"

She peeked at me before her eyes fell to the pink bow in her hands.

"I... Um... I—" She let out a long breath. It was shaky toward the end, and I immediately stopped what I was doing and placed my hands on her shoulders.

"What is it?" I asked in the lightest voice I could manage.

"I... miss my parents." She whispered it as if she didn't want anyone else to hear. As if she were telling me a secret. I immediately felt even worse for her. I had told Lux that she couldn't just push it down this way, and I wasn't going to let her do that either.

"I know," I said, and slowly wrapped my arms around her. She paused for a moment before I felt a few tears fall onto my arms.

I didn't say anything. I didn't move. I barely breathed as I let her decompress in my arms again.

It didn't get past me that it happened right after Lux left. I had a feeling that she was maybe trying to keep it together for her aunt.

"Can I tell you something?"
She nodded.

"I lost my parents too. It's been years, but I still miss them every day." My voice caught at the end, and suddenly I was the one fighting back tears.

I remembered it clearly. The look on the officers' faces as they came to knock on the door. Lucas and I had been alone, and I had no idea what to do when they gave me the news that both our parents had died in an accident. Hit and run. *Probably a drunk driver*, they'd said.

It was inconceivable. I mean, they hadn't even been gone that long, and now they were never coming back.

Everything after that was a blur. Between taking care of my brother, going to the police station, trying to make it work with my aunt, and then also trying to go to school and thinking about college... It had been too much.

So I had no idea how Bella was keeping all this stress and grief inside her small body without feeling like she was going to explode.

Her hands came up to grab my arms, returning my hug.
"I don't want to feel this way. I just want them back."

"I know, sweetie."

She took a deep breath and leaned back into me.

"My mom used to do my hair," she said. "This pink bow, it's like the one she got me for Christmas."

I swallowed the knot in my throat, unsure what to say.

"It's okay to feel this way. The bad feeling inside us—the heaviness—it's because of how much we loved them. Just because some emotions don't feel good doesn't mean we should ignore them. We feel things for a reason, and the more you push it away, the worse it'll get."

"When will it be over?"

I pulled away and started finishing her hair.

"Every person is different," I said. "I still miss mine. But it does hurt less now."

She turned to me, her eyes red from the tears, but I was happy to see that they were not falling anymore.

"I'm sorry about your parents."

I wondered how many times she heard that before to know she had to repeat it.

"I'm sorry about yours." My eyes shot to the clock on the wall. "Do you still feel like going to school? If it's too much, I can have Lux call in sick for you."

She shook her head.

"I feel better now," she said and sent me a smile. "Plus, I want to show off my bow. And if I don't get to school, how can you take me out for lunch?"

I couldn't help but smile back at her.

"You're right. Let's go! Are you ready?"

"Yep!"

She bounded off the chair and ran to the door, all the tears and grief slowly dissipating. Kids were amazing. I knew she was hurting, and I knew most of the time she was putting on a brave face for her aunt, but seeing how well she could bounce back was astonishing.

I took my time in the kitchen, trying to push away my own grief that sprouted after sharing what happened to my own parents.

But that wasn't the only thing.

I took Bella to school, avoiding the look on Marci's face. Maybe she was surprised I didn't get fired. Maybe she could see right through me.

That didn't matter.

Once I was back in the house and alone, I realized that I had no idea how to do this.

The truth was, I didn't want to lose my job. I didn't want to move on.

It wasn't about the money. It was about Lux, but not just about her.

It was Bella.

The real question was, what the fuck was I supposed to do now?

Chapter 13
Lux

This was the biggest fucking mistake I'd ever made in my lifetime, and as a CEO, I had made countless mistakes. I had learned from all of them, and they had made me the person I was.

The *billionaire* I was, to be exact.

I was cutthroat. I knew how to run a business. I knew how to make money.

What I didn't know was how to tear myself from Juliette.

Because no matter what I kept telling myself, no matter how much I tried to stop myself, I always found myself getting closer to her. Touching her. Begging her.

I have never repeated a mistake more than once. Juliette was the exception to that rule.

The worst part was that I could still taste her, no matter how much I tried to get rid of her. No matter how much I tried to remind myself that we weren't supposed to be together. That it was wrong. That Bella needed her. That we couldn't jeopardize Bella's happiness, especially when Bella seemed to be... bonding with her.

I was really trying not to care about her, but desire outweighed my rational mind.

And the damnedest thing was that my brain was trying to convince me it wasn't a mistake at all. It kept reminding me how good we felt together. How right it was. How I knew she was meant for me from the moment I met her in the club bedroom.

She was my angel. Perfectly made for me. Sent to me from wherever she came from.

I would only be working half a day. I had three meetings, multiple emails to send, and at least five project proposals or reports to read, but the entire time I was just waiting until the clock struck eleven-thirty so I could get in my car and meet my niece and her nanny for lunch.

I sat at my desk, my laptop open in front of me, but I wasn't even looking at the words on the screen. Instead, I had a pen in my hand, and I was tapping it against my desk, my eyes trained on the clock.

My laptop pinged with a message from my assistant.

Gilbert asked if he could have an emergency meeting with you in five. Just confirming if you have time. Your calendar is empty.

Quickly, I went into my calendar and blocked off eleven-thirty to two p.m. Then I messaged her back.

> If it's an emergency, he can either ping me or email me. He can even call, but I have other things to do. I don't have time to meet.

And just as I hit Send, the bastard himself messaged me on our company's messaging system.

> There are issues with the numbers on the transparency report. I need to talk about it now. Press is calling us out.

I dropped my head into my hands. They were waiting for me, and I wasn't going to fuck this up. Bella had been so excited about going out to lunch. There was no way I was going to miss it.

There was also no way that I was going to miss my first real meal outside with Juliette.

I pushed my chair back and walked to my door, dragging it open to see Gilbert talking to my assistant about ten feet away from me. Both of them stopped what they were doing to look up at me.

"You have ten minutes," I said, opening my door and motioning for him to come in. "I need to know what the errors were, what you're going to do to fix them, and who I need to fire."

His eyebrow shot to his hairline.

"Fire?" he asked with a shaky voice but hurried into my office.

I shut the door behind him.

Yeah, fire *for jeopardizing my date with Juliette and my niece.*

I didn't mean to act like a woman obsessed, but I couldn't help it. I was getting even more annoyed just looking at him as he floundered to give me an excuse.

"Well, you see, my team triple-checked the numbers before publishing anything, but then this morning I got an email from—"

"What are you doing to fix it?" I asked, crossing my arms over my chest.

"I still have his email pending in my inbox. I didn't want to reply without talking to you—"

"That's it?" I asked. "You want to talk to me about it? No plan?"

Maybe some other day I would've taken pride in watching him squirm under my questioning, but today I had no patience for it. My eyes fell down to my wrist, taking in the time displayed on my watch.

Eleven thirty-six.

"Get this sorted out today," I ordered as I walked past him, grabbing my stuff. "I don't pay you to come ask me how to do your job. Find out what was published incorrectly, fix it, and then get back to the board saying it's been fixed. It's not that hard."

"But Lux—"

"Anything else?" I asked, turning to him, but I was already at the door, my hand ready to pull it open.

He froze under my gaze.

"No, that's all. I'll work on it today."

I gave him a nod and left the office, but not before stopping by my assistant's desk.

"Get me that report," I ordered.

"It's already in your inbox," she replied, her voice low. "It's been there for a few hours, actually."

I felt a flicker of annoyance, but not as strong as the sinking feeling in my stomach as I realized that because of my obsession with the nanny, I had somehow overlooked something that important.

"Thank you. I'll have a look when I get back."

I vowed to get my shit together. I had a company to run, and my time away made them soft. Made *me* soft. I was usually on top of everything and would've never let anything like this slip through.

I should have fired him on the spot. But instead, I was rushing down to my car and out of the parking lot, not even giving him a second thought because all I could think about was meeting my girls.

"Panic attacks are not normal, Bella," Juliette said, giving the girl a look.

Work was far from my mind as I sat down at the diner table, sipping on my hot coffee and looking at Bella and Juliette. Bella had finally decided where she wanted to go, and it was a surprise to all of us. A small diner about thirty minutes away from our house that looked to still be run by a mom and pop and that also happened to have her favorite pie.

The seats inside were covered with an old plaid pattern, and pictures hung on every single wall—many of their family and, of course, their customers throughout the fifty-something years they'd been in business.

In no time, Bella had chowed down on a kid's meal and quickly requested a big piece of pie. The pie was obviously her main goal. It was about as big as her face, and the flavors changed with the season. At the moment, it was cherry.

The diner was quaint, cute even, if I was being generous. I had no idea if she remembered, but we'd been here when she was about four years old and half the size she was now.

When her parents were alive, they had brought us all here for Sunday brunch. I forgot what we were celebrating or if it was just a random meal with the family, but I remembered my sister and her husband sitting in front of me while Bella sat next to me in a booster seat. A seat she didn't need anymore, though sometimes she did still sit on her knees so she could lean on the table and take a huge bite of her pie without any of it falling on her.

I kept watching her, waiting for another outburst, but there was none.

She was sitting next to Juliette and eating her pie as happily as could be.

But I was still left with an uncomfortable feeling.

"So, remind me, what do we do when our chest starts to get tight and we can't breathe?" Juliette asked. I don't know how we got back onto the topic of panic attacks, but it worried me. As if talking about it alone would trigger one.

It scared me to see Bella like that. To see her unable to breathe, crying, and looking to someone for help when I didn't know how to help.

I'd just stood there while Juliette took care of it. Useless.

Apparently, that's what I was now. I couldn't work. I couldn't be a good aunt to Bella. *Fuck,* I couldn't even have a professional relationship with the nanny.

"Call an ambulance," I replied.

Her eyes caught mine, a smile pulling at her lips. I had to stop looking at her, but I couldn't pull my gaze away. Every single time our eyes met, I got flashes of us together in my office, zaps of electricity ran up my spine, and I was left breathless.

And that has nothing to do with a panic attack.

"We blow out candles!" Bella said, pulling my attention back to her.

"Exactly." Juliette patted the top of her head.

Her hair was in one single braid with a bow at the end. The same bow Juliette had brought that morning.

God, why is she so good at this?

I couldn't believe how easily she'd gotten along with Bella. I couldn't even count the number of nannies we'd been through to get here. But somehow, as soon as she showed up, everything changed.

She even messed up on the first day, something that none of the other nannies would have recovered from.

But she did.

Maybe because it was meant to be, I thought, before pushing that delusion out of my head. There it was again, the obsession.

"Oh, yeah, Lux," Juliette said, turning serious. "There's no good time to say this, so here goes. My landlady is ending my lease early, and I need to find a place to stay. I'm going to try to do it over the weekend, but I may need to take some days off here and there for viewings."

My heart stopped.

A sinful thought flashed across my mind. I didn't want to say it out loud. I couldn't. But there had never been a time in my life when it felt like the universe had been more on my side than right now.

We had a spare room. She could stay there. I made sure to keep at least one available just in case and turned the rest into more functional rooms, like a gym.

It was supposed to be for guests, but let's be real, when had

I ever had a fucking guest stay there? I didn't plan on bringing anyone in there anytime soon either.

Plus, having her at home would actually be very beneficial. She could help Bella get ready in the morning and maybe help me set up a nighttime ritual for her that didn't involve her going to her bedroom alone. They would never be late to school or breakfast.

She would always be with us.

Which is dangerous, so you can't go there. You can't have her that close—

"You could stay with us!" Bella blurted out, putting a stop to my spiraling thoughts.

She could. She *so* could, and I wanted her to *so badly*.

"I'm sure Juliette doesn't want to stay at her place of work," I said quickly.

A bit too quickly.

Juliette laughed and leaned against Bella. The sound of it brushed against my skin, heating it. Embarrassment had my ears burning. I was being way too obvious, and Juliette clocked it, hard.

"That's sweet of you, Bella, but I need to find my own place."

Right. Of course. I cleared my throat.

"I mean, if it's an emergency, you can stay with us... for the time being," I said after a pause. "You know, if you don't have a place."

Juliette looked up at me, her thoughts clear on her face.

That would be an epically bad idea, Lux.

I knew it, but what kind of person would I be if I just let her struggle?

I imagined her close, just a door away. I could sneak into her room in the middle of the night. No one would know. We could keep it to ourselves. Our dirty little secret in the dark.

"And it'd be easier for you to be near Bella," I added, shifting in my seat.

"Yeah, we could have sleepovers!" Bella added enthusiastically.

Juliette laughed again, and I could feel the heat working its way up my neck. She knew exactly what I wanted.

Her.

"Thank you, Lux. I'll consider it," she said as she pulled her phone out. "Bella, it's about time we go. Go wash your hands in the bathroom. Don't want to get pie filling all over that pretty dress of yours."

Bella bounded off to the bathroom while Juliette and I got up in silence. I paid the bill at the counter, lost in thought.

"That would be a terrible idea, you know," she finally said.

The worst, honestly.

"Oh, I know." I turned around to look at her. "I'm just doing my job as a concerned employer."

I couldn't help but smile at Juliette's incredulous look.

"Uh-huh, I'm sure that's all you want."

"It is!" I shoved my hands in my pockets to stop myself from touching her but leaned forward, keeping our eye contact.

"What?" she asked with a raised brow and leaned back. I took one more selfish look at her. Today, her hair was pulled back, with small braids on the side of her temples that disappeared behind her ears. The rest of her hair sat in light waves on her shoulders. She was wearing a purple pastel top and a long, white skirt with purple flowers embroidered on it.

I wondered how we looked together. Such polar opposites. I almost never wore anything other than black or deep jewel tones. My hair was black. My eyes were dark.

Juliette was pretty and angelic, not to mention she smelled like fresh flowers. Lilies, I thought.

Her eyes shifted to the side and back to mine. It was quick, but I caught the hesitation in her stare.

"Are you actually considering it?" I asked, teasing heavy in my tone. There was a burst of excitement that shot through me at the thought.

"You offered," she said with a shrug.

"It's my duty to make sure my child's nanny is taken care of," I said, and both of us noticed my slip of the tongue right away.

My child. I'd never called Bella that before. Because she really wasn't; she was my sister's kid. It just came out so easily.

"Right... Or maybe you just want to take advantage of me." She rolled her eyes at me. "Obsessed much?"

She was obviously trying to save me from that slipup. Maybe she saw just how conflicted and panicky I was after saying it. I appreciated her attempt to lighten the mood, but I had too much to unpack with the last sentence.

"I would say you're actually obsessed with me." I crossed my arms. "Here I am, a concerned employer, while you're actually considering moving in with us. Do I need to start locking my door at night to stop you from sneaking into my bed?"

A small smile played on her lips at that. It would likely be me sneaking into her bed at night, and we both knew it.

Obsessed. She was right. There was no other word for it.

I was looking forward to her reply when Bella came running back to us, excited to leave

"Let's go!" she said and grabbed Juliette's hand, pulling her back to the car.

An unnamed emotion started bubbling inside my chest as I watched them together.

I'd never been able to be like that with Bella, neither before nor after the death of her parents. Bella had never been that open or touchy-feely with me. There had always been a space between us, whether physical or emotional, I didn't know. But I knew I was to blame for that.

I wasn't like Juliette. I couldn't talk about my emotions or help Bella deal with hers. I wouldn't know where to start.

The only times she'd get close to me were when she was knocked out and I was transferring her to her bed. Maybe she cuddled against me for a moment because she forgot who I was and why she was stuck with me. And even those moments were short-lived.

My chest burned. Was this... *jealousy?*

I didn't have time for that.

With a sigh, I left the diner and watched as Juliette and Bella got into the driver's car. Mine was waiting on the other end of the parking lot. Just like that, we were going to part ways, and this lunch date would be over.

Just as Juliette was about to duck in, I made the decision to follow her.

"Auntie Lux! What are you doing?" Bella asked, a small frown on her face.

"What? I can't spend time with my niece?'

Bella pouted. "It's just... You've never seen me off to school before."

I could feel Juliette's staring at me, but I couldn't meet her gaze.

"Today is different," I said with a huff. I met Marci's eyes in the rearview mirror. "Drop her off and then drive me back here. I left my car."

"Yes, sir."

The car ride was silent. Obviously, my presence was interrupting their little routine, and neither Bella nor Juliette knew what to say.

Is my presence really that awkward?

When we got there, Juliette got out of the car with Bella and stood outside, watching her go in.

Bella paused for a second to send me a small wave, and my chest felt warm. Even more so when I waved back at her and a small smile was on her lips before she turned and ran inside.

Only when Juliette got back into the car and we were alone did I come to regret my decision. The space suddenly felt too small. Too tight.

I didn't know what to talk to her about. Didn't know where to start.

The driver was already pulling away and heading back to the diner.

"What will you do after this?" Juliette asked casually, as if the tension between us wasn't stifling.

"Work," I said a bit too harshly. I cleared my throat and shifted in my seat. "I have a few meetings. Some with the board. Another with the head of marketing. And then right before I left, someone decided to tell me that they fucked up majorly on one of the transparency reports. After that, I'll be home."

"I know you're some big shot CEO... But what about having dinner with Bella?"

I looked at Juliette, our eyes catching. I hadn't realized I was leaning closer and closer until our faces were almost touching.

"She has Gina," I murmured. "I'll be honest. I'm not much of a cook."

Juliette gave me a look before looking away and shaking her head.

"I mean as company. But that's okay, I'll be there anyway."

I paused at her words. They made me feel uneasy.

"What do you mean?" I asked. "Should I be there?"

Juliette was silent for a moment before she looked at me.

"It would be best for the family to eat together. Good for you and her to bond. I can tell she's been feeling a bit lonely."

My chest twisted. I couldn't remember having dinner with anyone other than for business. I would usually come home late and have no time to eat, so I grabbed something quick and called it a day.

Even back when I was younger and still living with my mother, I would desperately try to skip mealtimes because I never wanted to talk to her. My sister was different. She would go to every single meal.

But she was always the favorite and Mother never lectured her like she did me.

It had shaped the way I saw family dinners, and I'd never thought twice about eating alone after that. But I also never thought about what Bella wanted.

"I'll work on it," I said and pulled out my phone. I had a meeting at five-thirty, so I canceled it.

Dinner it is.

Chapter 14
Juliette

We stared at each other across the table.

All three of us—me, Bella, and Lux. The house was huge, probably the biggest house I'd ever had the pleasure of working in, but suddenly with all of us at the table, and Gina and Marcy no doubt somewhere close by, it felt... crowded.

Not in a bad way, though. I was grateful that Lux showed up, and I knew Bella had to be too, but since I knew this was not the norm, no one really knew what to do or say.

None of us spoke. The sound of our utensils scraping across the plates was the only sound in the room. Most of the meal was already gone, and I knew I had to do something.

"So how was school today?"

Bella lit up, excited that someone was finally asking her a question. I wanted to let Lux take the lead and try to bond with her niece, but maybe she needed a little bit of help.

"So good!" she replied. "Justine complimented me on my bow and everyone was so jealous that I got to go out for lunch. I even missed the first few minutes of math. It was great!"

"We'll work on getting you back sooner next time," Lux said, her voice causing Bella's gaze to snap to her. A frown appeared on her face.

Yeah, Lux didn't seem like the type of person who would be excited to miss part of her class. She was probably one of those who would show up early, sit down, and have all her paperwork and homework out even before the teacher entered the room.

"Let the girl have a little fun!" I smiled, trying to lighten the blow. "Don't you know all the cool kids show up to school late after lunch? It's like a time-honored tradition."

Lux pressed her lips together.

"I never got taken out of school for lunch," she grumbled. "I was always on time too."

I tried my best to keep a straight face. *Yeah, Lux, I figured out as much.*

But the way she said it was a little bit endearing.

The confident, overpowering, workaholic Lux, who clearly ran a tight ship at work and who had a way with words that made your knees go weak... was admitting that she was somewhat of a nerd in school.

"So... you weren't cool," Bella summarized.

There was a long silence before the laugh I was desperately trying to hold in slipped out. Bella joined me, laughing so hard that she needed to lean against me for support.

Lux looked mortified at our reaction.

"I was cool!" she huffed. "I got straight A's and got accepted into an Ivy League school with a scholarship!"

"As if that's what makes people cool," I teased.

Lux's frown deepened.

"Getting into a good school is pretty cool," she muttered.

I leaned forward and touched her hand lightly, lingering for a few seconds. "It's very impressive," I said, but there was still a smile on my lips.

Her being a nerd wasn't even the funniest part anymore. It was her reaction, that little pout when she realized we were making fun of her. The way she was glaring at the plate in front of her, as if it was the one that was teasing her and not us. She even went as far as pushing her food around on her plate.

Slowly, our laughter died down, and we all finished our meal.

"Go put it in the sink," I asked Bella once she was done and already slipping out of her chair.

"We have a person for that," Lux said quickly. "Don't tell me you've been making her do it."

I raised a brow. I knew she probably employed someone to clean the house, but I'd never seen them.

Regardless, in my world, cleaning up after yourself was an important skill to learn. Lux could insist that Bella didn't do the dishes *after* I left. While I was here, she would be doing it, and I would be doing mine as well.

"It's polite," I argued. "And I'm not making her do anything. It's a suggestion."

"I'll take yours too, Juliette," Bella said, then paused to look at Lux. "*Not* yours."

A shocked, exaggerated laugh pushed itself from my mouth at Lux's gaping mouth.

"*Rude,*" Lux muttered under her breath, though all of us could hear it. Bella let out a small *humph* and took her things to the kitchen sink.

Lux leaned back in her chair, watching her niece at the kitchen sink while completely ignoring her aunt.

"I'm gonna go play!" she announced after she was done and ran out to the backyard without casting so much as a glance at us.

It took her maybe about three minutes to wash the dishes, so I knew I would have to go finish it, but at least she tried. And she was finally joking around with Lux. All of it a step in the right direction.

"Be inside in twenty to finish the rest of your math!" I yelled after her before getting up and heading to the sink. *Yep, not washed properly.*

I heard Lux's chair scraping against the floor and listened as she walked toward me, carrying her own plate. I could feel her standing there, so I moved aside so she could put it down.

She didn't move back. She stayed there, hovering over me, my back to her front. I could feel her warmth. She felt good, and we weren't even touching.

I turned my head to look up at her, my lips still quirked into a smile.

"What?" I asked, noticing the frown that was somehow still marring her gorgeous face. "Don't like a bit of teasing with your dinner?"

"If I knew you were going to gang up on me, I would have skipped dinner entirely."

But even as she said it, there was a lightness to her tone. She might have had a frown on her face and a grumble in her voice, but there was a spark in her eyes as she looked out at Bella.

Dinner may have started out rough, but it was a success in my book.

"She just wants people around," I said, turning around to look at her. "She's lonely. You having dinner with us means a lot to her."

Bella didn't need to say—she probably didn't know how to —but I was there to interpret it. She loved Lux. That point was undeniable. But I was stuck between two very hardheaded people: a child who didn't know how to express her emotions and an adult who might know how to express her emotions but just didn't want to.

Her eyes cast down to me, and all of a sudden, I was taken back to when she had me against the desk.

I need her again. Desire shot through me so suddenly, I had to grip the counter. Her being so close only made it worse.

Her smell. Her heat. *Her.* It was not supposed to be like this. It had never been like this with any other family.

And while no other person had ever paid a million dollars to give *me* the night of my life, there was more to it than that.

"I know," she whispered. "I just don't know how to fix it."

The vulnerability in her voice had my throat constricting. It was so hard to see someone like Lux look so... helpless. I wanted to make her feel better. I didn't know her very well, but I knew that she didn't deserve to feel this way.

Neither of them did.

Silence stretched out between us, but it wasn't uncomfortable. It was... charged.

"So, you moving in or what?" she asked after a moment.

I was finally able to look away from her and toward where Bella was playing.

The whole thing was an awful idea. It would give me and Lux far too many excuses to act on whatever this thing was between us.

But, on the other hand, it would be really good for Bella. I'd be there when she woke up, when she came back from school, and I might even get to tuck her in before she went to sleep.

I mean, if Lux wants me to. I'm getting ahead of myself. I've only been here for a few days.

"I don't think I should," I finally replied. "Even if it would be easier to take care of her. I'm afraid—"

"That you'll fall in love with me?" She met me with a smirk that had heat rising up my face and burning my ears.

"So full of yourself. You're the one pushing. I could easily argue that you're the one who's going to fall in love with me."

"I don't fall in love," she said, somehow moving closer. My back was to the counter and her thigh was now between my legs. "I fuck."

The heat intensified. *Yep. This would be disastrous.*

"That's the problem, isn't it?" I asked. "This will complicate things."

"Will it?"

There was a moment between us. Our eyes met. Our breaths stopped.

It would... right? I was Bella's nanny. I was charged with taking care of her niece. A child who was severely grieving her parents' death and who was living with a woman who didn't have the faintest clue how to deal with it.

Probably because she hasn't processed her sister's death either.

"Juliette! Come time me!"

The trance between us was broken, and I took the chance to move toward the backyard, grateful for the distraction.

But Lux's hand caught my wrist. My skin burned where she touched me, and I couldn't help the gasp that made its way out of my mouth.

I turned back to look at her. All the joking was gone, and she met me with an expression I couldn't make out.

"Think about it," she said, her voice steady and unwavering. I swallowed the knot in my throat, along with the automatic urge to say yes.

"The offer for the room or the offer for the fucking?"

A smile pulled at her lips.

"The room," she answered. "I was teasing about the... other stuff. It may be a bad idea, but I don't want Bella's nanny to be homeless. It's temporary anyway."

"Temporary," I muttered. How long was temporary? How long would I have this job? It seemed like I was about to lose it on a daily basis. But I still couldn't help but ask, "Will it come out of my paycheck?"

She shook her head.

"Think of it as a thank you for doing something I couldn't."

She was making it too hard to refuse. My parents' debts had been paid, but I wouldn't be able to afford my own apartment on this salary alone. I would still have to find some type of roommate situation so I wouldn't touch Lucas's college fund. I could always ask the girls if they wanted to find a place together, but I needed to be close to here, and that was far away from where they needed to be.

I was afraid to ask what she meant. Afraid of the answer and how it would complicate things even more. Her gaze was too hard to shake, the question too heavy to ignore.

So I asked anyway.

"Which is?"

"Making her happy."

Chapter 15
Lux

Juliette didn't work on Thursday. She had to talk to her roommates about moving into my house, and I told her she could have the day off.

I acted in her stead for the day, taking Bella to and from school for the first time. Something my niece was more excited about than I anticipated. She even asked me for help with her math homework.

I wouldn't admit it to Juliette, but I was having trouble grasping some of the concepts. So awfully, in fact, that Bella huffed and finished the rest herself, making me think that she didn't *truly* need my help. She just wanted the company.

It made me want to do better. And even with my jam-packed schedule during the day, I couldn't keep my mind from wandering back to Juliette.

For some reason, I was scared that they would try and talk her out of it. Maybe they had more sense than either of us did.

I waited all of Thursday and Thursday night for her to give me an answer, but there wasn't so much as a text. My eyes had grown tired from looking at my phone for hours in the darkness.

On Friday, I was on edge.

I didn't want to admit how fast I ran from the kitchen to the front door when I heard her car pull up or how I had waited an extra few seconds at the door, taking a deep breath before I opened it.

I watched as she unloaded a box of stuff from her trunk, multiple boxes already around her. My heart felt like it was going to explode.

She is actually moving in.

"I'll bring the rest in after work and tomorrow," she said as she attempted to haul three boxes inside the house. They were all cardboard, all looking a little worse for wear. Stains, holes, and being held together by two rolls of duct tape at least.

She'll be lucky to make it inside before one of them crashes to the ground, taking her with it.

Juliette hadn't taken more than two very wobbly steps up the stairs before I was rushing to her and grabbing the boxes from her. I don't know if my heart could take an accidental fall when just watching her like this had it pounding in my chest.

Not to mention the images my mind made up of her face-planting on the stairs.

A shiver ran up my spine.

She might be doing a hell of a good job taking care of Bella, but it seemed like she didn't care too much about herself or what happened to her.

Or maybe she's just not used to asking for help. Or having any.

I grabbed the bottom of the boxes and lifted them with ease. I was almost surprised that they caused her so much trouble since they were light. Judging by the noise they made, I was guessing there were some knickknacks in there, maybe some personal items that went on her nightstand, and a few clothes, but nothing extremely heavy.

At least not for someone who worked out regularly like me. It would be a waste of an in-home gym if I didn't. Even with Bella around, I tried to do some lifting before bed.

The look on her face as I held the boxes with ease did not get past me, and boy, did it make my ego soar. I might have flexed a little bit more.

"Hey, you don't have to—"

"And let you fall and hurt yourself and then sue me for improper workplace safety protocols? I think not."

I caught the ghost of a smile before I turned and walked into the house.

Maybe I was being a little bit too obvious about my feelings for her, no matter how many excuses I came up with for treating her differently. But today, I didn't have to worry about being seen because there was no one in the house except for the two of us.

Bella was already at school, begrudgingly and after complaining about Juliette not being here again. She had perked up when I told her she might be moving in, though—because I hoped she would, which was why I was working from home today. Both Gina and Marci got the hint that they didn't need to hang around and had gone shopping.

Which meant the two of us were completely alone.

The knowledge of that weighed on me as I walked through the house.

"It's the bedroom right across from mine," I said, trying to fill the silence of the house. "It has a queen bed, dresser, and closet; the only thing it doesn't have is an attached bath."

"That's okay." Her shoes squeaked against the hard floor as she followed me. "I don't have one now either. Actually, I never had one. Growing up, my brothers and I shared one."

I turned to look behind my shoulder at her. Well, that's something I didn't expect.

"I didn't think you had brothers," I commented, pausing at the door.

She leaned against the wall, looking up at me with a smile.

"Don't seem like a middle child, huh?"

"No," I admitted and went inside, placing the boxes on the floor. "More like an only child or the eldest."

"My older brother is much older than us. He was already in high school when I was born, and as far as I can remember, he was never around. I don't think he ever really got along with my parents, given that he was kind of the guinea pig," she said from the doorway. "We don't know him well, so for all intents and purposes, I am the eldest."

I let out a hum. I couldn't think of anyone not wanting to be around Juliette. Moving away from your parents, I could totally understand, but even as a younger sibling, I always wanted to be with my sister.

I don't know how someone could just look at her and not want anything to do with her afterwards.

"And your other brother?" I asked. "How's he? Are you close?"

I don't know why I asked. I probably shouldn't pry. It wasn't necessary for our work relationship.

But a part of me wanted to know her better. Wanted to know how she came to be such a soft, caring person. Who was she close to? When did she have her first kiss? Did she go to prom? Did she like school?

All of it. I wanted to know all of it.

Juliette was somewhat complicated for me to understand. No one had ever drawn me to them the way she had. No one ever had me this obsessed.

I could fuck. I loved it. I loved being with women. I might not have been with anyone in a long time, but no woman ever outweighed my love for working and making money.

None of them had ever been able to tear me away from my job. Yet all I could think about every day was her and Bella and how to get back to them sooner.

I would never admit it to anyone, but the time between when Juliette went home and when she came back in the morning was the longest twelve hours I've ever endured.

Even considering the possibility of her moving in had a buzz of excitement running through me. Every time I lay down in my bed, I imagined her being in the room right across from me.

I imagined what it would be like to wake up and have her in bed with me.

This was the first time I openly cared about what had made her into the person she was now. But I didn't just care, I didn't just want to know; I *needed* to know. Needed to understand how someone like her could so thoroughly change the course of my life. Change *me*.

"We're pretty close. Even closer after our parents died."

Her confession hit me like an arrow to the chest. *Shit. Of course.* It made sense why she and Bella got along so well. How she knew what Bella needed before she even knew it herself.

I suddenly saw the woman in front of me in a different light.

It made me hurt for her in a way I couldn't fully understand myself. I had never gotten along with my mother. If I were being honest, I thought she was the devil incarnate. She didn't care much about anyone except for my sister and herself. And oftentimes, even though she favored my sister, she would put herself and her image first.

I couldn't get out of the house soon enough when I turned eighteen.

But I had a feeling Juliette's case was completely different.

It felt like she had had two parents who loved her and lost them.

She was caring. She was kind, and she loved easily. I could see it in the way that she took care of Bella. And even though she had been in a traumatic situation, she never treated Bella like she was a broken doll.

With caution, yes, but never with fear that she might break.

Maybe because she knew she wouldn't.

"He's with my aunt now," she said nonchalantly, like she didn't dump the biggest bomb on me. "Not the best situation, but he's turning eighteen and going to college soon, so there's not much to say about it. He actually just got his acceptance letter."

She was beaming at that last part. Her eyes lit up, and her smile was wide on her face. It made even my cheeks ache.

She loved him like an older sister was supposed to, and I wondered if my sister ever looked like this when she talked about me.

"That must have been hard," I blurted out as I took a step forward.

My mind was telling me it wasn't a good idea to get any closer, but all I could imagine was little Juliette crying at their funeral while holding onto her younger brother, immediately turning into the caretaker.

No one deserved to lose their parents so young, but especially not Juliette. She was still smiling, and pride was still bursting out of her when she looked up at me.

"What age were you when they died?" I asked, and my question had a little bit of that light dulling.

"Sixteen," she answered with a forced smile. "I was with my aunt for a bit, but taking care of two kids was a lot, so I left my brother there and bounced around from relative to relative before I graduated and ended up living on my own."

My jaw clenched as anger clashed violently inside of me.

Her aunt just left her like that? So young and having gone through so much?

I couldn't believe anyone would do that. Even I—someone who had no experience with kids—took it upon myself to take care of Bella after her mother died. Not just because it was what my sister wanted but because I loved Bella, and I didn't want to see her suffer at the hands of my mother or anyone else who decided to take her in.

I knew she would be safe with me.

It was hard. Many times I had no idea what I was doing, but I tried. For Bella. For my sister.

I could never give her up.

Even if I was completely fucking it up and Bella hated me, I wouldn't throw out a child in need. Juliette implied that she decided to leave, but it was probably her aunt pushing her out. She would never have left her brother if she didn't have to; that much was obvious just from the look on her face when she talked about him.

"I'm sorry," she said and let out an embarrassed chuckle. "I don't know why I'm trauma-dumping on you."

"It's okay. I asked."

I hadn't realized how close we'd gotten. Or how quiet the world was when we were together, alone in this room.

I felt like she needed comfort. Needed *something*.

Needed me.

I wanted to make her forget everything that happened. I wanted to give her a life she deserved. A soft, abundant life where she didn't have to work so hard just to live.

This is more than just sex. This is about her. About us.

I am so fucked.

My fingers were itching to touch her skin. My hands had a mind of their own, slowly lifting, ready to grab her and pull her to me. Her eyes told me that she was feeling the change too.

They were wide and dilated, her mouth slightly open, giving me a preview of the pink tongue hiding there.

This was a bad idea. Both of us knew it. We needed to leave this room, but I couldn't move.

"Lux..."

Fuck, my name on her lips was sinful. I needed to hear it again. Craved it.

"Juliette..."

Just as I was about to reach out to her, she jerked back, her hand flying to her pocket. Her eyes widened when she caught sight of the caller ID.

"I knew I was forgetting something! I need to pick up my brother from school today!"

The trance was broken. The room still felt stifling, but at least my head had cleared just enough for me to take a step away.

She looked up at me in a panic. "Will you be okay if I—"

"Go," I said with a forced smile. "I'll take care of Bella's pickup today."

Even though I had multiple meetings, I would cancel them for her.

How could I tell her no? Especially after what she'd just told me. And after I saw how much love she had for her brother. There was no way.

"Is it a half day for Bella too?" she asked. "I totally forgot to check. If so, you need to leave now."

I pulled out my phone and quickly found the school calendar.

"No, it's a full day," I said. "Don't worry. You better get going. I'll show you around the house some other time."

She nodded and ran out of the room, leaving me alone to look at her things.

With a heavy heart, I put my phone in my pocket and started to open the boxes. I hoped Juliette would take it as the helping hand it was instead of an invasion of privacy. But honestly, maybe I was just a little curious about what was in the boxes.

Though the more I lingered in her room, the more I couldn't stop thinking about what she'd gone through.

How could her aunt do that to her? How could she take one look at Juliette, a child, and just throw her away like that?

Even worse, it didn't seem like Juliette was holding a grudge. It was like it was just a normal, understandable thing not to want to take care of her.

I paused when I opened the first box and found a photo album.

I shouldn't look, but that didn't stop me from pulling it out and flipping through the pages with little hesitation.

It was obviously put together by one of her parents. It had baby pictures of her when she was younger. An older boy was next to her in most of them, looking at the camera with a frown. But Juliette was oblivious to his displeasure and smiled at the camera like it was her job.

I flipped through a few. When her younger brother came into the picture, she clearly lit up. She was always holding him. Always hugging him.

She loved that little boy.

Unlike Bella, they weren't alone after their parents' death. They had each other.

But Juliette had been forced into a caretaker role. I could see it happening.

I flipped through the pages until I got to the back. During her high school years and even after, Juliette seemed to have picked up the responsibility of updating the family photo album.

The boy turned grumpier and more teenage-like in the photos, but Juliette was always smiling. Always happy.

"Damn..."

I brought out my phone, sending her a quick text.

ME

> Why don't we all have dinner tonight? You can bring him here or we can go out. Bella would love it.

I was actually not sure how Bella would feel about it. I was the one who wanted them close. Who wanted to see their dynamic in action.

I wasn't a caretaker like her. I didn't really believe I could help her, but part of me didn't want her to do this alone. That maybe if I could help even just a little bit, it would be worth it.

My phone buzzed with her reply.

JULIETTE

> Why don't I just pick up Bella and bring her back and we can all eat?

My heart dropped into my stomach. I only had a few hours to prepare. But there was something else to consider.

I raced out to the front, catching Juliette starting the car.

"Wait a minute," I said, motioning for her to step out of it.

She turned to look at me with a raised brow, but I ducked back into the house and grabbed the key to my car.

"Your car's shit—no offense—so it's safer if you take mine."

Her mouth was agape as she looked over the keys in my hand. Slowly, she came back up the steps, grabbing them from me. I didn't miss the way her hand lingered against mine.

"As much as I'd like to fight you, you're right," she said, then a small smile pulled at her lips. "That's very thoughtful of you, Lux."

Warmth spread throughout my chest. Praising Juliette was one of life's greatest pleasures, but being praised *by* her? It gave me a whole new sense of pride.

"Drive safe," I told her and watched as she made her way to my car instead. I waited until she drove off, basking in the warmth of her words. Then pulled out my phone in a panic.

I quickly canceled all my plans and dialed Gina's cell. She answered after two rings.

"Yes, Ms.—"

"You need to bring more food. We have guests tonight!"

Chapter 16
Juliette

I tapped my fingers against the steering wheel, my eyes cutting to my brother in the front seat, who kept looking at his phone.

It was supposed to be a celebration dinner where I told him that I was paying for his entire college tuition, but we'd somehow changed our plans and were now waiting in the pickup line for Bella.

"So they're, like, rich," he said, his eyes critically analyzing the car I was currently driving.

"Yeah," I answered with a sigh. "They're pretty well-off."

"Good for you," he said. "The pay must be good. Hopefully enough to get you out of that shitty living situation."

My face burned. *How will he react when he finds out I moved in with them?* I debated telling him but ultimately decided it was best not to.

I turned to him.

"How have you been lately?" I asked. "Has she been treating you well? Do you need anything? Clothes? Money? Food?"

He dropped his phone and sent me a smile.

"You can stop worrying about me. I'm almost eighteen. I can take care of myself now."

I chewed my bottom lip.

"I know you can," I said. "But I just want to be there for you. Just because you can take care of yourself doesn't mean you have to do it alone. When it's hard, you can lean on me."

The movement of kids behind him caught my eye.

"Listen, I have some good news. I was going to tell you at dinner, but since we will be with them, I think it's better I tell you here."

He lifted a brow.

"That serious, huh? Don't tell me you met someone, fell in love, and are now going to elope to Vegas."

Heat rushed to my face. His words were a bit too close to the mark, though I could never imagine whatever was happening between me and Lux going as far as marriage.

Plus, I'm pretty sure Lux would be appalled if I ever mentioned a Vegas wedding. She didn't seem like the type to accept anything other than one of those super extravagant ballroom weddings that cost hundreds of thousands.

It was honestly more embarrassing how far my mind went with fantasies of Lux than his words. Even if anything were to happen between us, it would be nothing more than fucking, and she had made that abundantly clear.

But I still couldn't stop myself from imagining us in an extravagant ballroom. Me wearing a puffed-out ball gown and veil, holding a pink bouquet while she waited for me at the end of the aisle. Her hair would be pushed back and out of her face, and she would be wearing a tight-fitting suit that showed off her—

"Oh, wait! Did you actually—"

"No!" I said hastily and turned forward, unable to look at him. "It's not like that!"

"Are you sure?" he asked in a teasing tone. "It looks like maybe you did meet someone. You can be honest with me. Come on, Julie, tell me—"

A knock on the window pulled our attention to the little girl waiting outside. Bella looked in with a questioning look.

I rolled down my window.

"This is my little brother, Bella," I explained with a smile. " He's going to join us for a meal. Lux is waiting at home for us."

This had her face lighting up.

"She's not working?" she asked and quickly climbed into the back of the car, strapping herself in.

"She took the day off," I replied, though I wasn't sure.

"My name's Lucas," my brother said, turning around and sticking his hand out for Bella, who took it immediately. "I like your bows."

Today she had two braids, both ending with bright yellow bows that matched her yellow polo and white skirt.

Wait... Had Lux done those? My heart melted at the thought of Lux paying attention enough to be able to replicate the braids so perfectly.

"Thanks!" she said, and without missing a beat, turned to me and added, "Michael and Jordan kissed behind the cafeteria today!"

I let out an exaggerated gasp. "No! Wasn't he with Danielle?"

"Yes! And when she found out, she was so upset!" Bella was already getting into it, her hands thrown up in the air, giving us an incredulous look that I could just make out through the rearview mirror.

"I'm living for this drama," Lucas said as we pulled away.

"You don't even know the half of it!" Bella gasped and went

into the whole backstory, sharing every piece of gossip that was crammed inside her little brain with him.

We barely had a chance to get a word in the entire way home.

"I feel like the teacher should know about it," Lucas told Bella as we walked in the house. "I mean, an underground candy gambling ring is a bit much."

"It's not just candy!" Bella wagged a finger. "It's the class prize as well! They're super hard to get, and Dexter always gets them, so he uses them for the gambling ring."

"Should she even know what a gambling ring is?" Lucas whispered to me.

"She's eight," I said. "You'd be surprised with what they pick up from movies and TV shows."

The smell of delicious food hit my senses. Bella ran into the house, gasping when she came across the dining table we couldn't see just yet.

"Oh my gosh! A feast!"

She said it in such a way that had both Lucas and me laughing.

We rounded the corner to see Gina prepping the plates and Lux bringing them to the table. She paused when she saw us and sent us an easy smile.

"Did you have a good day at school, Bella?"

"Who cares! Let's eat!" she replied as she climbed into her assigned seat.

Lux smiled at her before motioning for both of us to take a seat.

I put my hand on Lucas's back and guided him to the table.

"Name's Lucas," he said and reached out to shake Lux's hand. "Thanks for inviting me over."

"Not at all, we're happy to have you. And I hear congratulations are in order? Someone got into college?"

I flushed when Lucas sent me a look.

"Sure did," he said, his smile more like a grimace. "But let's not make this all about me. The food looks delicious!"

"So good," Bella piped in as she grabbed another spoonful off the plate in front of her.

Lucas sat down, and I followed suit, my mouth watering at the spread.

"Looks great, Gina!"

Gina, who was still in the kitchen, turned to me and nodded in thanks.

"Wish I could take all the credit, but Lux had very specific recipes and instructions." She gave Lux a knowing look.

Lux cleared her throat and sat down.

"Anyway, getting into college is a very big thing," Lux told him as she started filling her plate with salad. "You should be proud of yourself. Celebrate the win that it is. No need to be humble."

I placed my hand on Lucas's. I was so unbelievably proud of him that it was hard to verbalize.

"On our way back, I'll get you that boba I promised you," I said.

He shot me a smile and quickly pulled his hand from under mine so he could start to eat.

The action caused my heart to ache just a bit, but I brushed it off as him being a teenager who didn't want his overbearing older sister to get too touchy-feely.

"This feast is more than good enough." He started to dig in. "So, Bella, you were saying something about that gambling ring?"

"Gambling ring?" Lux asked, her head snapping to Bella, who nodded excitedly.

"We gamble in loads of things and get fun prizes at the end! Today we played Go Fish, and yesterday we played Uno.

Sometimes, if we get bored, we gamble on which couple will break up first. I usually win."

Lux sent me a look as if to say, *Is she being serious?* I gave her a sheepish smile.

"Show her what you won," I said.

Bella dug into her pocket and pulled out a handful of small items. A fidget toy, a fragrant pencil that smelled like berries, a single sticker, and a small, white case that I only just realized were AirPods.

"Which rich kid gave those up?" Lucas asked, jerking his head toward the latter.

"Kinsley's boyfriend gifted them to her, and she put them up in Go Fish and lost." Bella was beaming.

Lux grabbed the case and popped it open, a frown marring her face.

Just when I thought she was going to give her a lesson in ethics or something, she closed the case and gave it back.

"Not even the latest generation. And they look used," she said with a huff. "What kind of boyfriend gives her his hand-me-downs?"

"That's what I said!" Bella replied, placing them on the table so she could resume eating. "Like, he only gave them to her because he got a new pair for his birthday, and he wanted to seem all cool and stuff because Mason and Penelope give each other gifts all the time. They've been together like the whole year."

"I'm losing her with all the names," Lucas whispered, and Lux looked to me for an explanation as well.

"The popular couple," I said. "They put on a big show. Always hug and hold hands."

Lux nodded.

"I see. So Kinsley's boyfriend wanted to one-up them but failed miserably. What's his name even?"

Bella shook her head. "Not important. He's annoying anyway. He never wanted to hang out with Kinsley, and he was always running and playing soccer and getting sweaty. It's so gross."

We all let out a laugh, enjoying Bella's gossip session. Lux, Lucas, and I would chime in here or there asking questions, and she would prattle off everything she knew.

It was a cute bonding moment for Bella and Lux. Like they finally had something in common.

When dinner was over, Bella went outside to play, and we stayed seated, sipping our mint lemonade.

"So you never did say," Lux started, turning to face Lucas. "Which school did you decide on?"

Lucas visibly tensed and took a long sip before answering.

"I haven't really decided, you know? There were a few that sent me some letters, but I just haven't committed to any yet."

"What's holding you back?" Lux asked, but I already knew the answer. *Tuition.*

I didn't know what scholarships they were offering, but I was almost positive they would not cover the full cost.

Lucas looked a bit uncomfortable, like he wanted to say something but was fighting with himself on whether he should. Maybe bringing him to a stranger's house wasn't the best way to celebrate this big win.

Lucas liked to keep to himself. Ever since he was younger, he started slowly becoming more and more introverted. He probably didn't want to talk about all the schools that had sent him letters that he might decline because of financial hardships.

He knew what my situation was, but not what kind of relationship Lux and I had, so maybe it was just making him uncomfortable. I was getting ready to jump in, but then he spoke.

"I just… Okay, don't kill me, Jules."

Panic immediately rose in me. He only called me Jules when he had really bad news. I sat up straight, my nails digging into my palms.

Don't tell me…

"I just… don't think I'm a college person. I don't really wanna go."

My world crashed around me.

For other people, it might have been something really simple. They might not even have blinked at what he said. They would probably ask a few questions, but overall, they would support him, give some kind words, and move on.

But I was different. Lucas was supposed to be different.

And it totally caught me off guard. Because the boy I knew growing up wanted college. He even had a list of his favorite schools on a sheet inside his desk. One he looked at almost every day.

And now he was saying he didn't want to go?

It had to be because of money. Nothing else made sense.

I gritted my teeth, unable to believe what I was hearing. He had worked so hard to get all his grades up. I knew he didn't *love* school, but this was different. This was college. And given how we had grown up and the importance of an education, I was positive he would want to go.

"But you seemed so excited to know you got accepted," I said, my voice quiet. "You texted me…"

He looked at me with his eyebrows pushed together.

"And then I saw the cost. I did the math. I don't want to be in debt until I'm forty, Jules. Plus, I can make money in other ways."

"Lots of really successful people don't go to school," Lux supplied. "Not me. I went, but that's beside the point."

I closed my eyes, trying to center myself. Then I took a deep breath and looked straight at my brother.

"I was going to wait to tell you this when we were alone, but I'm going to pay for your school."

Lucas raised a brow at me. "You?" he asked with a scoff. "You babysit for a living. You don't have any money."

His words felt like a knife to the chest. *Does he really think so little of me?*

"Nanny," Lux corrected, her eyes narrowing at my brother.

"Right, whatever." Lucas waved her off, and Lux clearly didn't like the teenage attitude showing through. "Point stands. You're broke, Jules."

"I've been saving." I tried my best not to look at Lux as I felt her staring at me. Now she knew what I planned to do with the money she gave me and why I still needed this job.

"Not enough, Jules. These schools, they're too expens—"

"I have enough," I argued. "For all four years. I'm not kidding. Pick whatever school you want. I'm prepared."

He leaned back, his eyes looking up and down my body, scrutinizing me.

"You? The *nanny*. Saved up enough for all four years of school. Any school. Even Harvard?"

Geez, just twist the knife, why don't you?

"Yes," I hissed.

He paused, then crossed his arms over his chest.

"What did you do to get the money?"

"Nothing illegal," I shot back. I couldn't help but look at Lux. "Can you please go to Bella for a minute?"

She pursed her lips before nodding and taking her leave.

Lucas looked at her as she left, then back to me.

"Didn't know you could order your boss around." He leaned forward. "Actually, I noticed her making eyes at you all night. Don't tell me—"

"Let's stay on track, Luca—"

"This is on track," he said. I hated when he was like this. When he could see right through me. It was something only he could do. Maybe it was because we had spent so much time together growing up, but he could always read me like a book. "You're fucking her, aren't you?"

I took a sip of my drink.

"I'm *not*. Now, about your schoo—"

"I don't care if you have the money," he said and stood. "Now that I know it's not yours, I can't take it."

I stood up and grabbed his wrist.

"It *is* mine. And I want you to have it. I want you to go to school. To live a good life. To succeed. To not be like... me. Take it, *please*."

He hesitated for a moment before pulling his wrist from my grasp.

"Tell me what you did to get it then, huh?"

My entire body flushed with shame. I couldn't. There was a line I wouldn't cross, and this was it.

"Just leave it and accept the goddamn money, Lucas. Don't be difficult."

He took a step closer.

"I'm being difficult?" he asked with a scoff. "Now I *know* you opened your legs to get that money. Is that why she looks at you like that? Is there some other arrangement here? Or did you fuck some rich, old geezer just so you could get out of hard work? For the last time, I don't want to fucking go, and I don't want your fucking dirty money—"

"That's enough," Lux said, appearing by my side and wrapping her arm around my shoulder. "You're young, so you might not get it, but you should *never* talk to your sister that way."

Lucas glared at her.

"Hey, just because you think you have some weird claim on her—"

"This has nothing to do with what I feel about her," she said. "Yes, I like your sister. And that's none of your business, quite frankly. It's between me and her. But I say this because you never know what could happen. Tonight might be the last time you got to talk to her." She paused for a second. "Now, I think it's time for everyone to rest. Bella's driver will take you home."

I expected Lucas to fight, but when I stayed silent, he seemed to deflate as well. As he took a step back, tears welled in my eyes.

"I'll call you," he mumbled and walked to the door where Marci was already waiting with a scowl.

There was a long, silent moment, then the door shut and Lux turned me to look at her.

"Don't *ever* let people, even your brother, talk to you like that, do you hear? You don't deser—"

"So you really like me?"

Lux stopped mid-sentence, her face deadpan.

"That's all you got from that?" she asked, her hands gripping my shoulders. "I'm telling you, you deserve more. It doesn't matter where that money came from. You shouldn't feel ashamed. No one should make you feel that way. You're too important and too good for it."

I tried to let her words sink in, but all they did was bring back the wound my brother left.

"He's just a teenager," I said. "He's had it hard. And just because I offered him the money doesn't mean he has to take it."

She paused for a moment, her expression turning soft.

"There are many things I regret about my relationship with my sister," she said in a low voice, likely not wanting to alert Bella to our conversation. "One of them was how I treated her before her death. She was... kinder than me. Always reaching out. But I ignored her. Pushed her away when I was busy. I didn't give her the attention she deserved, didn't spend enough time with her. If I knew she would die so young... If I knew I would never see her again, I... I have so many regrets."

Her words weighed heavily on me. I couldn't see it from her perspective, as I'd always been the one worried about my sibling, always the one reaching out, always the one taking care of him.

But now I saw that Lux was more like Lucas. Someone wanting to show that they could live on their own. Succeed. Even if it came off harsh, they wanted to prove themselves.

Before I knew what I was doing, I was wrapping my arms around her waist. She froze, her breath audibly hitching. Ever so slowly, not to scare her away, I placed my head on her chest. I felt as though she could jump ship any moment, but she needed this.

Maybe just as much as Bella did.

After all, they both lost people they loved. She breathed in deeply. Her heart was racing; I could hear the rapid beating as I hugged her.

Her arms twitched, and slowly, she brought them around me, but they never touched my skin. They just hovered there, unsure. I could feel them brush against my back. The invisible weight of them.

"Juliette, are you okay?"

Before we could pull away, we heard the sound of Bella's footsteps, and her small body slammed into us. She buried her head into us and squeezed, pulling us into a three-person hug.

Lux hesitantly wrapped one arm around Bella, the other around me. I brought my hand to Bella's head, patting it.

"Lucas had to go," I finally told Bella, not breaking the hug. "He'll be back if you want another gossip session sometime."

Her lower lip jutted out, and she gave me a disbelieving expression. "He sounded angry. Did he hurt your feelings?"

"No, baby." My voice was calm. "Wait for me outside, and I'll come play with you, okay?"

She nodded and ran away. Only then did I look up at Lux.

My heart stopped in my chest before slowly breaking because Lux had tears rushing down her face. She was silent, but they never stopped, only slowed. She was looking into the distance.

I looked around to see if anyone was watching, but the chef had disappeared, and Bella was outside.

"It's okay," I whispered and leaned my head back on her chest. "Just stay like this."

I could see her fists balled at her sides as she tried to rein herself in. I let her stay there for as long as she needed.

She was so focused on Bella, she never gave herself time to grieve.

Maybe there was a bigger reason why I was here. I wasn't sure I believed in fate, but it sure seemed like this family needed some extra love and care.

And maybe I did too.

Chapter 17
Lux

The air was chilly, but it helped calm my mind.

Instead of the tears taking a weight off my chest, they only seemed to make the pressure of it all just that much worse.

Because she wasn't supposed to see that. No one was. I had always been a person that kept all my emotions carefully locked away, never showing too much, even to my family.

With the exception of my sister, no one had ever seen me cry past the age of seven. It was at that time, when my relationship with my mother was at its worst, that I vowed to never let people see me in a vulnerable state.

I took pride in my cold and unbothered demeanor. People couldn't take advantage of it like they did vulnerability.

I never intended to cry in front of Juliette, no matter how good of a person she was. But it felt like my tears had a mind of their own. One minute, I was furious because of how her brother was treating her, and then all of a sudden they were running down my face.

I was glad Bella didn't see it. The last thing she needed was to see the only person she could lean on in this world having a mental breakdown. And luckily, she was too worried about what Juliette was feeling to even notice me.

It was for the best.

I had stayed behind even when Juliette told me to leave. I hid myself beyond the sliding glass door and eavesdropped on their conversation.

I was more curious than anything else. I had a feeling that I knew what she was going to do with the money I gave her, and I was proud of her when she confirmed it.

Her needing this job made so much more sense now. She was going to use it all on her brother's education. Based on my math, nannying didn't give her much, especially after whatever cut the agency took out.

And she was going to give every single penny of it to him.

She would still work herself to the bone, live in less-than-perfect situations, never splurge on herself—or at least I assume she didn't, given the small number of boxes she'd brought so far.

It was all so he could have a chance at a good life. But he didn't want any of it.

I couldn't help but feel for her. I didn't want her to suffer like this, to work so hard for a little payout, to put others first only to be knocked down.

She seemed happy enough, but she was too sweet for this world.

She shouldn't have lost her parents so young. She shouldn't have been kicked out of her aunt's. She shouldn't have to work so hard for the bare minimum.

I should have offered more than a million for her.

She was worth far more. I looked at numbers for a living, and no number seemed enough to me.

What I didn't expect, though, was his reaction. How angry he got.

I didn't fault him for not wanting to follow the traditional path, a lot of people didn't, but to treat his sister so cruelly...

It reminded me a little bit too much of myself and my younger years, when I would talk back to my sister for no reason other than I could. I saw myself in him. And I saw my sister in Juliette, even though she was much more fiery than Juliette, especially when she got angry. But my sister, just like her, was caring. Especially when it came to her family.

"Can't sleep?"

Speak of the devil.

I trained my eyes on the pool and the hot tub, trying to distract myself even for just a moment. But it was no use. I couldn't avoid her, nor did I want to.

I turned around on the lounge chair, locking eyes with Juliette. She was in a yellow cotton pajama set. Shorts and a tank top with small little flower patterns on it.

To top it off, she wasn't wearing a bra. Because of course.

She was sin and temptation wrapped in one gorgeous, innocent-looking little package.

There was nothing inherently sexy about what she was wearing, but seeing how the shorts hugged her milky thighs and how I could see just a sliver of her stomach underneath the tank top had me feeling like this was the sexiest lingerie she could ever show up in.

Is she wearing panties under those shorts? I thought before shaking the thought away.

"No. I take it your bedroom is okay? I didn't get to show you around—"

"It's fine. Bella showed me the most important parts of the house already." She paused, probably noticing I hadn't stopped staring. "I should leave you—"

"You came at just the right time," I said, pulling my eyes from her body to meet her gaze. "Did you check your email?"

She shook her head. Her hair was pulled into a messy ponytail at the top of her head. I had the urge to pull on it and bare her neck to me.

"I left my phone back in the room. Something wrong?"

I motioned for the lounger beside me, but instead she sat on mine. Her ass was just on the edge and brushed against my legs. I moved to the side to give her more space. Her closeness was allowing me to look at details that only made my need for her worse. Like the slender expanse of her neck that I now could see had a small little freckle on the back. One that was usually hidden by her hair.

My eyes fell down her body again, stopping at her breasts. My mouth watered at the sight. The fabric was so thin that it hid absolutely nothing. Especially her hard nipples.

Her hands were placed on her thighs, her shorts riding up and practically showing me her ass. But my eyes shot up to her breasts again.

I want to pull one of those nipples into my mouth and bite.

It was incredibly hard to pull my eyes away, but I had to. This was important. I had thought long and hard about it and finally decided that I was just going to go for it.

"You're fired."

The words didn't fully sink in at first. She looked at me expectantly before letting out a shocked scoff.

"This again?" she asked, standing up and placing her hands on her hips. Anger twisted her face, and for a moment, I allowed myself to enjoy the sight of it. "Is it because I saw too much? You know what? This time I'm not begging—"

I grabbed her wrist and forced her to sit back down. Electricity zapped through us at our contact. Her eyes shot down to where we connected and then back up to mine.

"I let your boss know that while you've been the best nanny

I've ever had, I'm terminating my contract with them after one too many issues with the agency."

She gave me a confused look.

"Okay, and...?"

"And if you'd like..." I cleared my throat. *Here goes nothing.* "I want to hire you directly as our live-in nanny at double the rate you were getting before."

A frown graced her beautiful face, and I wanted nothing more than to kiss it away.

"I knew you wouldn't walk away from the agency yourself. They are shitty at best. Corrupt. They don't take care of their people, and I wouldn't be surprised if I weren't the only guardian pissed off at them. But it's less about them and more about you. I'm not offering you this—"

"Because you pity me?"

I leaned forward, making sure she could see how dead serious I was.

"There is nothing to pity about you," I said in a serious tone. "You are beyond capable. You are strong. You are caring. You are a dream of a nanny and..." I searched for a word. *Friend* didn't seem right, but she wasn't my lover either. "A person. I am offering you this because you deserve it and are being severely underpaid for what you are doing for us and your experience. I can't tell you how much it means to have you here with us. But I want to show it at least."

She looked down at her hands, which were folded on her lap.

"Why are you doing this?" she whispered.

"You deserve it."

I grabbed her hands and tugged on them until she looked at me. Her eyes were wide and slowly reddening.

"You deserve this and so much more, Juliette. Stop selling yourself short. Please."

Her lower lip trembled, and suddenly I was hit with a younger version of her who had no one to take care of her. No one who gave a damn.

My hands acted on their own, cupping her cheeks.

"Are you just so in love with me that you're trying to keep me near you?" She was trying to make a joke, but her voice was weak and vulnerable.

"Do you want the truth?" I whispered.

My eyes fell to her lips.

This is so wrong. We already crossed the line; doing it again would just guarantee it ended badly.

"Can I start tomorrow?" she asked, evading my question, and I leaned back, slightly confused.

When she got up, my heart dropped. Right. Space. We needed space between us. *It's for the best. For the best. For the—*

Her hands played with the hem of her flimsy tank top.

"Well?" she asked. "If I can start tomorrow, it means *tonight—*" She sauntered over to the inground hot tub surrounded by rocks. She sat on the edge and removed her tank top, but she was facing away from me. With her hair up, I had a full, unobstructed view of her lightly toned back, waist, and hips. I wanted to trail kisses up her spine. "We wouldn't be breaking any rules."

Jesus fucking Christ.

I got up faster than I ever had in my life and walked the short distance to her, taking off my clothes as I did. By the time I sank into the hot tub and moved in front of her, I was only in my underwear.

She opened her legs for me, and I was instantly there, kneeling on the small stone lip underwater. My arms wrapped around her, my hands cupped her ass.

Her breasts were right in my face, tempting me, but I kept my eyes on hers.

"Yes," I whispered. "The answer is yes."

"To what?" she asked breathlessly. "I think I need clarification, *sir*."

I couldn't hold back anymore. I pushed myself up and covered her mouth with mine.

She moaned against me, her lips opening to give me access.

We were in a frenzy, our tongues fighting more than dancing. The aching need for each other was obvious in the desperate way we kissed. Our bodies melded together. Our hands were everywhere. Even the smallest amount of space between us was too much.

Heat zapped from my head to my toes.

Her taste was divine. And I knew her cunt would taste even sweeter.

I tried to show her everything with that kiss.

That I was telling the truth. That I wanted her. Needed her. That she was starting to become a pivotal person in my life.

That I have fallen for her.

Since the club, I had been a goner. There was no way around it. It was a single moment that sparked my obsession. One moment that would change our lives forever, and back then, to me, it had been just another day. Just another night out looking for a fun time in the arms of a beautiful woman.

I never thought one decision would bring her into my life.

I was sure of it now. Juliette was the person I'd never thought I'd find. She was the person I was supposed to fall in love with. I knew deep in my soul that *she* was sent to me. I don't know what I did to deserve it, and a part of me was afraid that the universe would realize their mistake and snatch her away from me, so I'd make sure to hold on extra tight.

I just had to show *her* all of it.

I broke our kiss so I could leave wet, open-mouthed ones

down her throat and chest, pausing to give her perfect tits the attention they deserved.

"Fuck, Lux," she moaned and arched into me as I dragged my tongue across the rosy bud. I sucked it into my mouth, circling it with my tongue in between.

She was already becoming a writhing mess, but I was no better. I was losing control. My movements became rougher. I pulled her closer to me, my hands gripping her ass.

My teeth sunk into her nipple, and I was met with a deep groan.

"Lux, touch me. Touch me right now. Please."

"You beg so sweetly, darling, how can I resist?"

I pulled her shorts right off before I was pushing her back to lay flat on the stones.

I dove into her pussy, my mouth latching onto her clit, two fingers entering her immediately. I wasn't playing around. The first time we were together, we only had a single night, and while I made sure to make the most of it, I wasn't this desperate.

But back then I didn't know how it felt to be with her or how it felt to be without her.

All I could think about was that I only had these few hours where she could be mine, and I needed to make sure it was a night we would never forget.

I looked up to see her hands plucking her nipples. She was spread out, not hiding a thing from me. Her legs were wide open, giving me more than enough room to fuck her.

I worked her pussy hard, sucking her clit rhythmically and working my fingers in and out of her, paying close attention to the way she writhed.

When I did something she liked, she arched, and her breath got caught. When she wanted me to go harder or faster, she would spread her legs as wide as they went, her wanton begging but a whisper as she got closer and closer to her orgasm.

My name on her lips was intoxicating, a drug I wished to bottle and use whenever I felt particularly miserable.

"Don't stop," she begged. "I'm so close. Lux. Please. Please. Pleas—"

She came with a cry. Her cunt squeezed my fingers, sucking them in for more, and I made sure I fucked her hard and fast through her orgasm, my lips never leaving her clit. Even when she was done, I made sure to lick her up clean.

But once she lay limp, I got up, pulling her with me.

"Lux, what are you—"

"Quiet," I said as I carried her into the house, naked and all. "I'm not done with you yet."

Chapter 18
Juliette

I sunk down onto the large, fake cock with a whimper.

"Like this, sir?"

"Perfect, Angel," she cooed, her voice heady with pleasure.

The strap was attached to her, a low vibrating hum coming from the base. Her face was flushed, the vibrations on her clit working her to another orgasm. I didn't get the pleasure of seeing what Lux looked like when she was on the edge last time. It was breathtaking. Seeing Lux in control was one thing, but seeing her as she slowly started to lose it was something else.

I committed it to memory, knowing that in just a few hours, we would be done here. This would never happen again.

I shifted my hips, trying to take more of the fake cock. The dildo was larger than any I'd ever taken, but the need to please her was stronger than any slight discomfort. We slathered it with lube, but my pussy was so sensitive from the multiple orgasms that I couldn't help my slight whimpers.

"Tell me if it's too much," she said. I loved how breathy she got when she was getting close to her orgasm.

"No, I got it," I assured her and spread my legs further on either side of her so I could sink down.

Her fingers found my clit, rubbing quick horizontal strokes over it.

I placed my hands on her chest, leaning forward, desperately trying to keep my moans down.

It was well past three in the morning, and after an all-night fuck fest, I was starting to lose whatever control over my vocal cords I'd had up until now.

Her quick fingers on my clit sent me spiraling. My pussy was clenching hard on the dildo until suddenly it loosened, and I slipped to the hilt.

"So fucking good, Angel," she praised and moved her hands to my hips, showing me how to gyrate against her. "You're so perfect. Made for me."

I took over, finding a rhythm that had heat pooling in my belly. It got slicker and slicker between us, my wetness leaking down the toy allowing me to rock a bit harder.

It was too much. The pleasure was taking over my body and I didn't know how I could contain it all. But fuck, did I love it.

I loved how her praises felt like open-mouthed kisses across my overly sensitive skin. I loved how she seemed to know just how to push me in order to get me into one mind-blowing orgasm after the next.

"God, Lux, no one's ever made me feel this way," I confessed. It was the truth, and not some fake passionate words that someone blurted out in the throes of pleasure. When I thought back to the best fuck of my life, there was no comparison. No one ever came close to her.

She pulled herself up, holding onto me so she could push

me back down into the bed. It was her turn to take control of the pacing.

I threw my head back as she fucked me deeper than anyone had before. Her long, hard thrusts were knocking the breath out of me. I was going to feel her the next day. A sick part of me wanted it. I wanted to be lying in my bed, feeling the ache between my legs and knowing she was just a door away. I wanted to look her in the eyes while I still felt my pussy pulsating from her assault.

Because after tonight, a memory was all I'd have. So I wanted it to linger as long as possible.

Her mouth found my neck. She licked up the sensitive column, and I found myself angling my head so she could get better access. Her teeth raked against my skin and pulled a desperate moan out of me.

The pain mixed so delightfully with the pleasure.

"Tell me how good I fuck you, Angel."

"So good, sir," I forced out. "So good. Ah—*fuck.*"

I was coming again, but Lux didn't let up. She was pounding into me, our hips snapping together with a force that had me moving down the bed before her hands pushed down on my arms, steadying me.

"Tell me, Angel. Tell me how good this feels for you."

"I love it when you fuck me, sir. I love feeling you inside me. God, harder. Fuck me harder, sir. Please. *Please.*"

"Fuck, I'm coming again," she groaned. "Your begging is intoxicating."

"I want to please you, sir," I forced out as she thrust again and again at a frenzied pace. "I want you to use me. However you want. I want to be your perfect little fuck toy. Tell me what you want, and I'll do it. Lux... Sir. Again. I'm coming ag—"

I couldn't finish as another surprise orgasm had me in its claws.

Her mouth was on my nipple. I whimpered in protest, my body overstimulated.

"You *are* my perfect little fuck toy, Angel," she groaned. "So obedient. Turn around, ass up. You're not done."

When she pulled out of me, I felt strangely empty. I flipped over, pushing my ass up for her and spreading my legs.

"Fuck me harder, sir," I pleaded, pushing my head into the soft bedding. "I want more."

Her hands were on my hips, forcing me back onto the fake cock without much more pleading.

"Arch, baby, hips back. Yes, good. So good."

Her hand slipped around and played with my clit.

"Lux, I don't know if I can stop this," I confessed as she played me like her very own instrument. She was so familiar with my body, with what I needed. What was too much and what was not enough. She kept saying I had been made for her, but it's more like *she* had been made for me.

"Then we won't," she groaned. "Don't think about anything else, Juliette. What's outside doesn't matter. It's just you and me in here. You and me, Angel."

"You and me," I repeated breathlessly.

My muscles felt like jelly. I could do nothing but sink into the bed and take what she was delivering. In a way, it was the ultimate show of trust. I knew she would take care of me. I knew she'd never hurt me. Just as I knew I didn't want to leave this room.

It wasn't long until both of us were coming again.

But this time, when we were done, we slipped into the covers together, our bodies intertwined, sticky, sweaty skin and all.

"Lux..."

"Yes, Angel?"

"About your question before..."

She hummed, her eyes barely open. Long lashes brushed across her cheeks, and I couldn't help but think how unfair it was that she was gifted with long, beautiful lashes but wore no makeup to accentuate them.

"You know, if I really wanted the truth?" I pushed.

"You trying to get a post-sex love confession out of me?" she joked, her eyes popping open.

My heart stopped and my skin heated. She had just fucked me in at least ten different ways, but *this* was what had me blushing.

"And if I am?"

She pulled me closer, pushing my head to the crook of her neck.

"If you really want an answer, ask me in the morning, Angel."

I tried to stay awake, reveling in the feel of her next to me, knowing that this would truly have to be our last time.

I ran my hands down her soft skin. Pulled away to look at her unguarded sleeping face. And then, as quietly as I could, I slipped out of her room and back into my own.

Chapter 19
Lux

She didn't ask again in the morning.

But to be honest, that wasn't even what I was most upset about. Even though we both knew it was a one-night thing and that her contract started the next day, my chest still felt emptier than usual when I woke up and she wasn't next to me.

I lay there for longer than I'd like to admit, just remembering the night before, my hand caressing the spot where she was lying when I dozed off. I smelled the sheets, trying to soak up her scent for as long as I could.

It's fine, I told myself. I repeated it a few times as I got up, got dressed, and then met both her and Bella at the table.

It was better this way, of course.

But that didn't change how I felt.

Unfortunately, the one night had solidified everything I felt. And I'd come to one resounding conclusion that I had no idea how to deal with.

I'm in love with Juliette.

It wasn't just some crush. I couldn't just fuck her out of my system.

I wanted her. Needed her. I couldn't even fathom having anyone else in my bed or in my life besides her.

I just didn't know what my next steps would be.

The few days after our sex-filled night were... easy. The tension was gone, like we'd quenched our thirst, but I knew it was only a matter of time before it became unbearable again.

Hell, I started craving her the morning after, but I had to keep myself together. As much as I wanted her, I needed to make sure I did this right.

I needed to show her that she wasn't just a fuck to me. That I took her seriously. That I took this thing between us seriously, as serious as the relationship developing between her, Bella, and myself.

It was so much more complicated than just asking her to be my girlfriend.

Asking her to be my girlfriend... Who am I?

In love, that's what I am. And fucked.

I couldn't forget the ethical side. I was her boss, and I didn't want her to feel like she had to be with me to keep her job.

I would never take advantage of her like that.

So I'd have to wait for her to make the first move.

Relinquishing control, not being able to do anything about what I felt for her, made me antsy. Even as I sat through meetings, at my desk, at lunch. All I could think about was how I wanted to do it.

I thought about extravagant bouquets of flowers in her room. Roses, of course.

I thought of taking her out to an expensive dinner. Maybe something overlooking downtown.

I thought about taking her back to the club.

I had more than enough ideas, but none of them seemed right. She deserved all of it, if not more. And I couldn't wait until I could finally shed this professional cover and take her into my arms.

And then there was Bella.

I wasn't totally sure what she would think when she found out about Juliette and me.

Would she be happy? Would she be jealous? Would she be angry?

And what if we didn't work? What if she had to watch Juliette walk out of her life? She needed stability.

I won't let that happen.

I knew I could make Juliette happy if only I had the chance.

I was starting to feel like I knew her. Her likes and dislikes.

She loved to do things with her hands but didn't love getting dirty. I noticed that when she was playing with Bella, she'd immediately go wash her hands if they got dirty.

I knew what she wore when she was happy versus stressed —it was all in the shoes, really. Flats versus sneakers.

I watched as she picked at the food she didn't like but still ate some of it to be polite. She hated stem vegetables. She would eat the leafy ones, but any of the harder vegetables she avoided like the plague. She also wasn't a coffee person. I had not seen her drink any since she moved in.

Lastly, and most importantly, I knew how much she loved Bella.

Her heart was a beautiful thing. Her life might have been hard, but she didn't let that twist the beauty of it.

A ping from my laptop pulled my attention to it. There was a small notification from my secretary.

You have a lunch delivery.

A lunch delivery? I didn't order anything.

I'll send them in.

My fingers were on the keyboard, ready to tell her to turn them away, but then my door opened. Fuming, I stood, ready to rip into whoever decided they were important enough to walk into the CEO's office without prior notice.

But all of it died on my tongue when Bella's sweet face peeked around the door. Her hair was pulled back into two braids at her crown that held it back while the bottom part was curled. I could just make out the twin bows sitting at the back, matching her white-and-black plaid dress.

"Surprise!" she squeaked and pushed open the door to show me Juliette wearing a very similar outfit.

My cold-hearted mask was usually on, but it melted when I saw the two of them together. Especially when they decided to match. Bella craved the connection that I couldn't give her, and I was grateful for what Juliette was doing.

"You left so early this morning you didn't even have break-fast," Juliette said and shut the door behind her. "We thought you'd appreciate at least one home-cooked meal today." She blushed before adding, "It was Bella's idea."

My office was my space to think. To make money. To make

big decisions that could potentially cost us millions—or billions —of dollars.

It was sacred.

I never wanted anyone in my office, especially uninvited.

But that didn't apply to this moment. Especially as I watched an eager Bella holding up a lunch box, one of hers, and placing it right on my desk.

I loved everything about the situation.

That they surprised me.

How happy Bella was.

How thoughtful it was.

The matching outfits.

All of it was more than I'd ever imagined I could have.

And it was Bella's idea. She was thinking about me.

"Thank you, Bella," I said around the knot in my throat. "Where's your lunch?"

"We're going to the diner after this to get pie!" Bella said. "I wanted to take you too, but Juliette said you were probably busy."

"Unfortunately, I am today. The end of the month comes with a lot of meetings and reports that are due."

Bella nodded, a frown on her face as she backed away to stand at Juliette's side.

"That's okay, we were just popping by. We will leave you to it—"

"But since you're here," I said and stood, fixing my suit coat as I stood. "Do you want a tour?"

Juliette was going to turn me down; I saw it in the way she forced a smile to her face, but Bella was faster.

"Yeah! Let's go!"

With a laugh, I rounded my desk. "You got it, little lady. But stay close, okay?"

She nodded and did one thing I'd never expected.

She grabbed my hand, letting me pull her out of my office. My heart clenched in my chest, and my gaze cut to Juliette, who was watching us with the sweetest smile I'd ever seen.

I took my time on the tour.

Work could wait.

Chapter 20
Juliette

The days flew by.

It was hard to not get lost in Lux. Especially when it felt a bit like we were playing house. We had breakfast and dinner together every single day, with both of us spending time with Bella whenever possible. And the girl had really come out of her shell since I started as her nanny.

Sometimes school was still a bit rough, but more often than not, all it took was a good paint session, sometimes a cry, to make it better. Since that one time, she'd never had a break-down again.

It felt like she was actually healing. Even though I knew grief was not linear.

Or predictable.

So I knew something was coming. I could feel it like a breath on the back of my neck, like having someone's eyes on me and not being able to place them.

I didn't fear for my life, but there was a storm on the horizon.

And one day, when I came home with Bella after a not-so-great day, I found it as a neatly dolled-up package sitting on our couch.

She was dressed in a shimmery tweed ensemble with her black hair done in perfect curls. Her delicately plucked brows framed a face full of makeup, and she was holding a bag that I knew cost more than my life's savings—including the club money.

"Oh, you must be the nanny," she said, her chin jutting out. "Go make yourself busy while I talk to my granddaughter."

Her obvious dismissal rubbed me the wrong way. I had been in more than my fair share of situations like this, but this time something told me I had to protect Bella. There was a feeling of unease in my chest that wouldn't leave me, and it was telling me not to leave a young child with her.

She was clearly Lux's mom, but my instincts told me there was more to this person than the older lady with class and poise she was pretending to be. Bella confirmed my feelings by gripping my side.

"I'll stay here," I replied and grabbed my phone, quickly typing an SOS to Lux.

ME

Your mom was in the house waiting for us. I'm not leaving Bella alone with her. Help?

The woman let out a scoff and rolled her eyes at me.

"Who do you think you are?" she asked. "I'm not asking; I'm telling you to leave and give me time alone with her."

Sometimes being a nanny meant having to deal with people who thought they were superior just because they were paying me for a service. They didn't even stop to think that the *service* was quite literally one of the most important in the world.

No, they just saw me as someone they could walk all over.

Not today, sister.

"Juliette..." Bella whispered, stepping closer to me.

"Don't worry, sweetheart, I'm staying here." I looked squarely into her grandma's eyes. I didn't really know what their relationship was, but I ventured, "Weird that you chose a time when Lux is at work to come here. You wouldn't be planning on stealing her, would you?"

She let out a bark of a laugh. I saw nothing of Lux in her except for maybe hair and eye color.

I almost wondered how this person could even have given birth to someone as wonderful as Lux.

"You must really not know who I am." She stood, closing the space between us. "And it wouldn't be stealing." She was so close I got hit with her nauseatingly sweet perfume. "I'd be taking back custody."

It felt like a bucket of ice-cold water being thrown over me. *She won't fucking dare. I won't let her.*

Bella let out a whimper, and I could feel her silent tears dropping on my hand as she held it right up to her face.

I pulled her behind me, shielding her.

"Come on, Bella, let's go get our snack. Lux and your *grandmother* can work this out when she gets home."

Just as I was about to walk away, her clawed grip circled the wrist Bella was holding on to.

"You better fucking listen to me, you little—"

"What?" I countered, puffing up, shoulder back. I wasn't going to back down. Not when she reminded me so much of my aunt, both emotionally manipulating women who cared for nothing other than themselves.

She didn't want Bella. She didn't care for her. Her actions here only proved as much.

"I have the snacks," Gina said, appearing by our side. "Bella, honey, follow me to the kitchen."

Bella was reluctant to leave my side, but I looked down at her, breaking my staring contest with her grandmother, and nodded.

"It's okay," I whispered. "Go. Lux will be here soon."

At least I hope so.

As Bella walked away, I could feel the woman's body tensing with anger.

"Sit down, please," I said and motioned to the couch she had gotten up from. "Would you like a glass of—"

"You insolent brat!" she bellowed. "You're nothing but a nanny. You think you can talk to me like this? Tell me what to do? Keep that child away from me?"

"Lower your voice," I hissed at her. If she thought she could intimidate me, she had another thing coming. "You may not care about Bella hearing this, but I do. She doesn't need this. Not right now."

"Like you know what she needs! I'm her grandmother. You're just a lowly servant."

I looked her up and down, and it finally dawned on me just how vile this woman was.

Fuck this. I need to get to Bella.

I turned to walk away again, but this time she pulled me back with a jerk. My head whipped to look at her.

"Don't you fucking touch me—"

I saw a flash of her diamond bracelet as her hand raised, ready to strike. I didn't have enough time to protect myself, or even try to, so I braced for impact, flinching.

But the blow never came.

My eyes had closed on instinct, so I peeled them open to

see Lux's strong forearm and her hand gripping her mother's, stopping her.

Relief crashed through me. I looked up at her, finally feeling like I could breathe.

She was staring at her mother with anger clear on her face. Her eyes were wide, her jaw clenched, her breathing heavy. She looked like it was taking all her strength to stop herself from returning the blow.

I'd never seen her this angry before. And it was all for me. For *us*. She had come to protect *us*.

"Juliette!" Bella cried, running to me.

"I'm okay. I'm okay," I said and turned to hug her as she clung to me. Her small hands were shaking as they fisted my clothing. I patted her back as her breathing quickened, a sure sign that another panic attack was making its presence known. "Over here. Come on."

"Don't you walk away—"

"You don't get to order her around," Lux spat. "You don't get to be in this house."

I got Bella far enough away to have her full attention, carefully angling us so she couldn't see the showdown in the living room. Kneeling down, I placed my hands over her ears so she didn't have to hear it either and turned her so she was facing me.

Her face was already red, her eyes watery as they darted around, trying to take it all in. Ideally, I would take her to her room, but she was spiraling so fast into her panic attack I didn't want to risk it.

"Look at me, sweetheart," I said when she tried to turn her head around. "Just me."

I mimicked blowing out candles, and she shakily held up her hand before she weakly started blowing.

"Juliette," she whined, her little voice full of despair. "Don't let her take me."

My heart broke into a million pieces. I wanted to promise it. Vow that I'd never let her get taken.

But it wasn't in my power, and promising her that would only exacerbate matters if her grandmother was ever granted custody.

"I told you to never show up here uninvited again," I heard Lux growl.

"I'm allowed to see my granddaughter," her mother huffed. "I'm the one who's supposed to have her anyway. I don't know what you did to make your sister change her mind, but I know for a fact I was the one supposed to be her guardian."

"Have? *Have?* Do you hear yourself? Bella is not a *thing* to have. She's a beautiful, resilient young girl who doesn't need this. Doesn't need you. Now leave on your own before I make you."

Bella tried to turn around again, but Gina was there now too, blocking her view. She crouched down at her side and held out three fingers.

"Blow them out."

Bella took a deep inhale and blew one out, her breath shaky. Slowly, Gina lowered it and gave her an encouraging smile. Bella hesitated, then did one more.

"You see what you're doing?" Lux asked on a whisper. My gaze shot to them to find them staring at us, both scowling but for entirely different reasons. "Leave if you really care about her."

"We're not done," she warned and sent me a glare before storming out of the house.

When the door slammed behind her, there was a collective exhale from all the adults in the room. I waited a few moments, making sure she was completely gone, and only then did I take my hands from Bella's ears.

"You did so good," I said with a small smile. I ran my hand down her hair, fixing the bits that had gotten messed up. "I know it can be hard, and blowing out the candles can seem a bit silly, but you did so good."

Lux was suddenly on her other side, kneeling down like us, and as soon as Bella saw her, she wrapped her arms around her shoulders.

"Don't let her take me, Auntie Lux," she pleaded, her eyes wide and her lip quivering.

Lux rubbed her back. "I don't know what she told you back then, but I won't be letting you go without a fight."

She pulled away and looked at Lux with tears in her eyes. "Promise?"

"I promise," Lux said, wiping away the remnants of her tears.

I didn't know it was possible, but in that moment, I fell for Lux even more. Not just because she had protected us, something no one had ever done for me before, but because of how gentle and caring she was afterwards.

Lux had admitted that she didn't think she was made for this, but I knew she was. She just needed a little help to bring it out. She had changed in the short time that I had been here.

Maybe I have too.

"What did she say to you last time, Bella?" I asked once she was calm enough.

Bella looked down at the floor, her hands gripping the side of her dress.

"She said I wouldn't be here long and that she'd come get me soon. I thought that's why she was here."

Poor girl.

I only wished I could do something for her. No child should have to deal with this.

Lux's gaze on me had me freezing.

"Did she hurt you?" she asked, her hand reaching out for me. My heart skipped a beat in my chest, and I quickly stood up, unable to bear her touch.

My face was already flushing, my skin hot, butterflies unleashing in my belly.

It's like I'm a goddamn virgin with a crush, even though she railed me within an inch of my life not long ago.

"No," I said quickly. "You got here just in time. Thanks."

She stood up too and reached for me again, like she couldn't stop herself. "I was already on the way, but when I saw your message, I—"

Gina cleared her throat.

"Lemonade?"

"Yes, please," I said with a sigh, taking the exit. "Bella, do you want some quiet time? Maybe some food? We could play games or...?"

She pressed her lips into a thin line before shyly looking up at us.

"I think I want some playtime outside, if that's okay."

I looked at Lux, who nodded.

"Go on."

Bella ran off without another word, still not her usual self but steadier than a few moments prior. When she was far enough away, Lux appeared by my side.

"A word in my office?"

I looked at Gina, who was already locking eyes with me.

"I got it," she said. "You two go."

Nodding, I followed Lux, but she walked right past her office and into... *her room.*

I paused as she silently opened the door and waited for me to make the decision to walk inside.

I'm her direct employee now. It would be highly inappropriate for me to enter her bedroom.

But my feet were already moving. She slipped in behind me, closing the door with a soft click.

My back was to her front as she inched closer. Her hands never touched me, but they hovered by my sides, her fingertips close enough that I could feel the electric current working between us. Her hot breath fanned against my neck, and I cursed myself for wearing my hair up.

"I've never been so angry in my life," she muttered.

I took a deep breath in, inhaling her scent.

I was starting to get lightheaded just remembering the last time we were in a bed together.

My mind screamed danger, but I couldn't move.

"She's awful," I admitted. "Poor Bella. She was really affected."

"I mean about you," she said. "I've never wanted to protect someone so badly."

The unspoken *besides Bella* was there, but I couldn't bring myself to be snarky enough to add it. Or to joke about how much she loved me.

Because I was starting to get the distinct feeling that she truly did have feelings for me. And I knew for a fact, especially after what just happened, that I did too.

But I couldn't let it happen. I couldn't jeopardize this. I needed to be smart.

And fucking my boss was definitely *not* smart.

"You shouldn't say those things," I murmured and slowly turned to face her. My eyes traveled up from her chest to her eyes, and my breath caught.

I don't think anyone ever looked at me with such longing.

Her eyebrows were pushed together, her lips in a slight frown, the need for *me* clear in her eyes.

She was begging me. Silently pleading for me to close the space between us.

But it wasn't entirely sexual. She looked like she needed a hug again. But this time I was afraid of what it would open us up to.

"I can't help it," she said. "You've been running rampant in my head. Every night I lie down and close my eyes, I see you. I see you in everything I do. In the blue flowers on my way to work that almost perfectly match your eyes. Every time I catch just a glimpse of a color you wear, I'm immediately checking if it's you. Even your laugh seems to haunt me, always playing in my mind. I can't sleep without you haunting my dreams. I can still smell you on my sheets, and I can't bring myself to wash them because of just how much I need to feel like you're close to me. I can't get you out of my mind, Juliette."

The last came out as more of a complaint than a compliment.

"Sorry to inconvenience you." I tried to look away, but her fingers found my chin and forced me to look up at her. The need in her eyes was only intensifying.

"That's the thing, I don't *want* to get you out of my mind. I want to hear you laugh all the time. Twenty-four-seven. I want to wake up to you and Bella chatting together in the kitchen. I *love* leaving work to come home to both of you. Do you under-stand I haven't looked forward to something in years? I don't even remember the last time I was actually excited about some-thing, but you've changed that. I'm ecstatic to get home. I can't wait. Because you're here waiting for me."

I swallowed the knot in my throat.

"I want you in my life, Juliette. In my arms. In my bed. I

need you in every way you're willing to give yourself to me. I can't pretend anymore."

There was no lie. No joking. Her face was telling me everything I needed to know. Everything I'd ever wanted to hear, she was serving it to me on a silver platter.

"And if I don't want to give myself to you? Just keep it professional?"

Her jaw tightened, and her hand dropped.

"If you can look me in the eyes and tell me that's what you want, then I'll leave you alone. But you can't lie to me, Juliette."

Looking into her eyes now, I wasn't sure I'd be able to get the words out.

"I need this job," I whispered, hoping she could see everything else I wanted to say but couldn't.

"And you'll have it," she said. "No matter how long you need it for. Whatever happens between us won't change that."

I tried to look down, but she forced my head back up, this time using both hands to cup my face gently as if I were going to break.

"Look at me. Tell me, Angel. Tell me I'm the only one feeling this way. Tell me you don't look forward to seeing me every morning. That you don't wish you were in bed with me every night. Tell me you've never thought about how good we'd be together."

It's so wrong. And so dangerous.

But she was right.

Every night when I went to bed, I thought about sneaking into her room. Every time I saw her in the morning, I longed to walk right into her arms.

"I *can't*," I whispered. "I can't say any of those things, Lux."

Her eyes flashed.

"Your move, Angel. Tell me what you want to do about it."

"I—"

A knock at the door had us freezing.

"Juliette, you left your phone in the kitchen. Your brother called you like three times. I think it's urgent." Gina's voice sounded worried.

I paused, my eyes locking with Lux's. My brother never called me, and given what happened last time, it was even more unlikely that he was reaching out just to chat.

"A rain check, then," she said and sidestepped so I could force my unstable legs to carry me to the door and open it, quickly taking my phone from Gina.

My heart dropped when I saw the message.

LUCAS

Aunt Kath had a heart attack. In the hospital now.

Chapter 21
Juliette

I looked down at my aunt, who was staring up at me with a look of disgust.

"Only decides to show up when I'm on my deathbed," she snapped. Her blonde hair was pulled into a messy bun on the top of her head, and even though she had tried to paint her face with heavy makeup, the tiredness was seeping through.

Aunt Kathy.

She had obviously been through a lot, but I wouldn't let it sway me. I wasn't the teenager she'd pushed out of her house. I might have let her live in peace for the sake of my brother, but Jesus, did I hate the woman in front of me.

Just like Lux's mom, she was rotten inside and out.

I turned to look at Lucas, who had his eyes trained on the floor.

"If you don't want me here, I can leave." I readied to do just that, but Lucas grabbed my wrist.

"I called you for a reason," he said, still not looking at me. Then, so softly, "Insurance doesn't cover everything."

I stood there, understanding slowly washing over me. Then hurt. Then disbelief.

"You won't take my money for college, but you'll call me to save *her*."

He saw what she did to me, and no doubt she hadn't been a saint to him either. Why was he taking her side on this?

"As I understand, you've come into a large sum of money," she blurted out, her eyes narrowing at me. "*Questionable* money."

My head snapped back to Lucas.

"What did you tell her?"

He opened his mouth, but she was faster. "That you spread your legs for it."

My body deflated. I couldn't believe Lucas had really said that. I regretted a lot of things, but meeting Lux, even in a situation where I was selling my body for money, wasn't something I'd allow myself to feel shame for anymore.

I turned without a word, ready to walk out, when her voice followed me.

"I took care of you and that brat of a brother of yours for years! It's the least I deserve."

Lux's words rang in my head.

I'm telling you, you deserve more. It doesn't matter where that money came from. You shouldn't feel ashamed. No one should make you feel that way. You're too important and too good for it.

She was right. No one had the right to make me feel bad about myself. Least of all, my aunt.

I had taken this shit from her my whole life. Not anymore. Maybe it was watching Lux stand up to her own mother that gave me the boost of confidence. Or maybe it was Bella's panic attack, a visible representation of what I often felt on the inside.

But it didn't have to continue. That much I was starting to figure out.

I turned around, glaring at my aunt.

"*Deserve?* You don't deserve anything from me or from my brother. You were a shit aunt to me. I lost my parents, I needed you, and you pushed me out!"

"You little whore! You're an embarrassment to this family! Your parents would be ashamed of you. And don't act like I never gave you anything—"

"You didn't! And you don't get to judge me, especially when you're the one begging me for my *questionable* money."

"I'm not begging!" she said with a huff. "I'm asking for what I'm owed!"

I scoffed. "You ever just sit and wonder why you're alone, Kathy?"

"Why you little—"

"It's because you're fucking rotten," I hissed. "All the way down to your soul. And you know what? I'm glad you pushed me out because I *never* could have dealt with this bullshit." I took a deep breath and centered myself. "I'm done here."

Lucas looked at me, his face hardening. He would have to deal with the fallout. I didn't want to leave him here like this. I felt bad.

But I also couldn't just take this lying down, especially after what he'd said. Even if I loved him.

"My offer still stands for you, Lucas," I said, my voice softer. "If you don't want it, that's fine. But I'll only give you one more week to decide."

He didn't answer me as I turned on my heel and walked back out into the hallway. Lux and Bella were there, waiting for me, looking at me with pitying expressions.

They probably heard the fight.

I opened my mouth, ready to greet them, but the words

wouldn't come out. The weight of what had just happened was heavy.

My eyes stung, and I looked to the side, trying to hide my tears from Bella.

She didn't need to see this. She already had so much she had to deal with. She didn't need her nanny having a mental breakdown on her.

What I didn't expect was for them to clock it right away and for Bella to come rushing to me, her arms wrapping around me.

I gritted my teeth, but it did nothing to stop the tears from filling my eyes. I was usually so good at hiding my emotions, but seeing her beautiful wide eyes looking at me with such concern had my guard crashing down.

"I want ice cream," she said, taking my hand and tugging me along with her toward the entrance. "Lux, we're going to Thirty-One!"

I couldn't bring myself to laugh at what she was calling Baskin-Robbins or her obvious attempt at cheering me up. Instead, I let Lux take my other hand and quietly followed them to let myself be taken care of.

"Can you help me braid my hair?"

I turned to the small voice that carried across the living room, putting down the craft supplies I was cleaning up.

Bella was peeking behind the wall of the hallway, already in her matching pink princess pajamas. Her hair was wet, indicating that she had just showered.

By herself.

Even after knowing Bella for some time now, I was shocked at how independent she was.

I stood up, sending her a smile. "You got it, but let's dry your hair a bit more first, hm?"

When I reached her, I held out my hand, and she took it right away, leading me to her room. It was mostly dark, save for the light by her bedside table and the one leaking from her bathroom.

We went into the bathroom, where the brush and hair ties were already waiting. She stood in front of the mirror, her eyes on me.

I picked up the brush and immediately got to work, brushing out any knots before attempting to dry it.

"You're very independent for your age," I commented. "Have you always liked doing your bedtime routine alone?"

When she looked down at the counter, I took it as my sign not to pry and reached into one of the cabinets, looking for the dryer.

"My mommy would wait in my bed for me with a bedtime story," she whispered. "She was proud of me when I did things by myself, so I—"

Her voice cut off. I leaned down and gave her a small one-sided hug, placing my cheek on the top of her head.

"I'm proud of you too," I said in a low voice. "But if you want any help, you let me know, okay? There are many things you *can* do alone, but it doesn't mean you *have* to."

She didn't respond, her gaze still locked in on the counter. Through the mirror, I could tell how close she was to breaking down.

I gave her a few moments before I pulled away and started setting up the dryer.

"I'm going to dry your hair now, okay?"

She nodded but said nothing else.

I started on the lowest setting and ran my fingers through her hair as I dried it. I worked in silence, letting her mind wander. I wondered if she was imagining her mother in my place. Remembering her fingers running against her scalp. Her mother's warmth behind her. Her scent.

It hurt because I'd been there. I knew what she was probably thinking.

Many times, I would find myself hoarding my mother's old perfume in my bathroom, spraying it when I missed her the most.

"My mom was the one who taught me how to braid," I said when I was done drying her hair. "She was *really* good at it."

"Do you miss her?"

I paused before running my fingers through her hair to start one of the two braids.

"Every day," I whispered, my throat clogging. "Even more in moments like this when I remember us doing the same thing."

"I can't dry my hair," she said after a pause. "I don't... do it good."

I finished one braid and started on the next. *No wonder she wakes up with hair sticking up everywhere sometimes.*

"I can help with that if you want me to." I sent her a smile in the mirror when I realized she was looking at me. I placed the finished braids over her shoulders and squeezed them. "Bedtime?"

She nodded and left the bathroom. I followed closely behind, turning off the light. She crawled into her bed and under her covers, her eyes flicking to me.

"Is it okay if I help you turn off the light?"

She nodded. I crossed the room, stopping at her bedside table.

"Sweet dreams, Bella. I'll see you in the morning, and I'll be right outside if you need anything."

As I reached to flick off the light, her little voice reached my ears.

"It's a bit silly, but... I like *Goodnight Moon*."

The book in question was on the table, just under the light. It looked well loved, with its cracked spine and the binding peeking through it.

"So do I," I said and grabbed it. "Shall we read it together?"

She nodded and scooted over in her bed, making space for me. I crawled in but stayed over the covers and opened up the book.

Bella's hand found my waist, and her face buried into my arm. I started reading as slowly and rhythmically as possible. I wanted this to last. But the book was short.

When I reached the end, I felt droplets sink into my clothes. Bella was still holding on to me.

"I think we can go one more time," I murmured and flipped the book over to start again.

She relaxed into me and, slowly, after our third read-through, fell into a deep sleep.

"No skinny dipping tonight?" Lux asked as she joined me in the backyard.

The fire was roaring, warming the space, but as soon as she showed up, the air turned scalding.

Bella was fast asleep, had been for almost two hours. Story time had knocked her right out, and I even stayed for ten minutes afterwards so as not to wake her when I left. She was out for the night, leaving me and Lux all alone together.

She sat down across from me, her long legs crossing. She had a silk pajama set on that shone in the light of the fire. It looked like it cost some serious money, but I was used to that about Lux by now. Everything she owned, down to her socks, was by some expensive brand.

But she never made a big deal out of it, and she never made me feel less than.

I showed her the glass of red wine I poured myself. The rest of the cheap bottle was in front of me. I had gotten it one hour before at the nearest liquor store.

"Heard hot-tubbing and drinking don't mix well," I said.

She leaned forward, turning the bottle so she could take a look at the label.

"Why didn't you get something from the wine cellar?"

I didn't know you had one.

Plus, even if I did, it just felt wrong to raid your alcohol like that.

But I chose to keep that to myself and instead went with, "There was a sale."

She grimaced and stood up without another word. When she returned, she was holding two glasses of red and offered me one.

I hesitated before placing mine on the table and grabbing hers.

When I took a swig, I immediately tasted the difference. Dry. Fruity. And extremely smooth.

"Okay, this is much better."

"There's a few things I live by in this world. One of them is not wasting time drinking shitty alcohol."

"And the other?" I asked, bringing the glass to my lips.

A smirk pulled at her lips.

"If I want something—I mean, *truly* want something—I won't give up until I get it."

Her eyes were trained on me, the meaning obvious.

Even with everything else going on, it was impossible to forget what happened between us earlier.

"Can I ask you something?"

I was immediately on alert, so I sat straighter before giving her a short nod.

"Mint chocolate chip, really?"

There was a pause before I snorted.

"Is that why you were looking at me like that in the ice cream shop?" I asked, unable to hold back my laughter.

The ice cream shop was cute, and our time there was mostly spent with Bella and me talking and sharing bits of each other's ice cream. Lux didn't get anything; she just stared at us with an expression I couldn't make out.

"It's an abomination," she said casually and took a sip of her wine. "Just like that sorry excuse for wine you brought back. If you want to get drunk, let me know and I'll get you the good stuff. Don't waste your palate on that shit."

I gave her a forced smile.

"I don't like drinking," I admitted. "Nor do I ever get drunk. I just wanted to... relax."

She gave me a long look.

"Maybe you haven't had the good stuff, so you don't know you've been missing out. Some stuff is worth getting drunk on."

Was there a double meaning there? I couldn't tell. My head was buzzing, and not entirely because of the alcohol. Her presence had me on edge, and all I wanted to do was fall into her arms again. Forget everything other than us.

But that's a bad idea and unethical, I reminded myself. *She's your boss.*

"Actually... I told you my parents died. It was an accident. They were hit by a drunk driver," I said. "I couldn't ever really bring myself to drink much after that."

Lux's eyes fell to her wine.

"My sister died in an accident too. No one was drunk, though. Just a shitty driver who ran a red light. Luckily Bella was at school."

I took another sip of my wine, hoping it would give me the courage to say what I needed to. But it didn't. I was floundering on how to bring up the inevitable.

Lux beat me to it.

"They asked you to pay for her bills, didn't they?"

I nodded, my eyes falling to the wine.

"Did you hear?"

"Only the volume," she said. "Not the words."

"She wanted my dirty money. My brother basically spilled everything he told me that night to my aunt. Neither is very proud of me."

"Juliette."

I looked up to meet her darkened gaze. She was looking at me that way again. The mix of seriousness and longing had me wanting to close the space between us and curl up against her.

"You are worth every penny I spent on you. More, even. If you asked me for another million—a fucking billion—I'd give it to you. And no one has the right to call *you* dirty."

I swallowed thickly, the tears coming back. *Why does she have to say all the right things?*

"Do you understand me, Juliette?" she asked, her tone demanding my answer. "Don't let anyone ever make you believe otherwise."

"I understand, Lux."

I had been confident inside that room, the anger pushing me to fight back. But now, after the fallout and feeling all the shitty emotions it brought up... My confidence was slowly being eaten away at.

I told her I understood, but the more time I had to think,

the more I didn't. The shame I felt when they attacked me was too much to bear, and suddenly I regretted ever going to that club.

In my heart, I know there was nothing wrong with it. I had a good time. Everything was consensual. What Lux wanted to spend her money on was her decision and hers alone.

But... Did I embarrass him? The look on my brother's face when he put two and two together still felt like a punch to the gut.

I jumped when Lux's hand brushed against my cheek.

I hadn't heard her come over to my couch or felt her sit down until she was holding my face and forcing me to look at her.

"Try again, Angel," she whispered. "I can see what's going down in your mind."

My grip tightened on the glass, and my stomach dropped when I realized I was displeasing her. All I wanted to do since I met her was to be a woman worthy of her praise.

"I just never thought he'd react like that," I admitted in a whisper. "I thought that this was his way out. Like a miracle. You may not get it since you're loaded, but this type of money was supposed to be life-changing. But somehow... I messed it all up."

This time I didn't bother to stop my tears.

Lux grabbed the glass and placed it on the table before wrapping her arms around me, enveloping me in her warmth and scent. My body relaxed into her, and my tears sped up. Every time she touched me, it was like a wrecking ball to all the carefully erected boundaries I'd raised throughout the years. The ones that were supposed to protect me and keep people away.

Her hand found my hair, stroking it softly and just staying there while I cried out all the hurt.

Everything I'd done to give him a good life. Everything I'd done to live away from my aunt. Everything I'd done to survive. All of it had been weighing on me and came crashing down in that moment.

"You didn't mess anything up, Juliette," she whispered. "If he can't see what you're doing for him, that's his problem. You've done enough."

You've done enough.

Had I, though? Had I done everything I could to make sure he lived a good life? I felt like I hadn't. Like I could have worked harder. Faster.

"You've done enough, Juliette," she repeated. "You've done good. It's time to rest."

My crying slowed until I was just lying there, letting her hold me while I worked through it all.

She didn't rush me. Didn't try to push me away. We just sat there in silence.

"Okay," I whispered and pulled away.

"Okay?" she asked, her eyes searching my face. "Repeat it back to me then."

"No one has the right to call me dirty or make me feel like it."

Her smile had my heart skipping in my chest.

"Perfect, Angel," she praised. "Well, except for me, but in very different—very pleasurable—circumstances."

Before I knew what I was doing, I was placing my lips on hers, my hands tangling in her hair. She let me push her back onto the couch. Her hands were on my hips, holding me steady as I straddled her, her fingers slipping through the loose fabric of my shorts.

She responded to my kiss with gentleness. I tried to attack her much like she did when she took charge, but she slowed us down, her hand moving to my neck, keeping me in place as she explored my mouth.

Her tongue flicked against mine, pulling a moan from me. Her gentleness was unlike anything I'd experienced before. And it was far more intoxicating than when we were going at each other.

This kiss felt like she was savoring me. Like she was trying to pour everything she said into it, forcing me to pause and take it in.

Lux was *worshipping* me with her mouth.

She pulled away, breathless.

"Take a seat on your throne, Angel. I want to taste you."

My breath caught. *We shouldn't.*

But I couldn't stop myself even if I wanted to.

I wanted my boss. From the moment she bought me at the auction until now, my desire for her never wavered.

"Fuck it," I whispered and did exactly as she told me to.

I climbed on top of her, placing my knees on either side of her head. She did the work of pushing my flimsy shorts to the side, and slowly, I took my seat.

Her lips attacked me. From my clit to my entrance, there wasn't a single inch she neglected. Within minutes, she had me shaking.

My hands on the armrest kept me steady. As I felt heat coil inside me, I threw my head back, looking at the countless number of stars above us. When looking at just how massive the sky was, I felt so small, but the feelings I had for her felt too big to squash down.

This was more than just sex. Just like always, she was treating me like a queen. Like someone worthy of her full and undivided attention. Like someone whose pleasure was just as, if not more, important as her own.

She made me feel like the center of her world, and I drank

it in greedily. I jerked my hips against her, riding her tongue like I was owed the pleasure. This time, I took, and she generously gave me everything she had.

"Lux," I moaned, my hands coming to my nipples.

She hummed against my folds, her tongue running back up to my clit before she was spearing me again.

"I'm coming," I gasped as I felt my core clench. She didn't let up. She kept going, letting me jerk against her as I rode out my orgasm. But I couldn't get enough, and apparently neither could she.

As soon as I came down from my high, she was pushing me back against the couch, climbing on top of me, her lips coming to my neck.

"Say you'll be mine, Juliette," she breathed. "I can't take another day without knowing if I have you or not. It's killing me."

Her tongue ran up the length of my neck, and she pulled back to look me in the eyes. I placed my hand on her cheek.

"It's an awful idea," I whispered.

"I've never been very smart," she joked, but we both knew it was a lie. I couldn't help but smile at her in response.

"I'm already yours, Lux. Have been since you first bid on me."

She let out a breath, and I caught sight of the twinkle in her eyes before she was kissing me.

"Mine. *Mine.*"

I gasped as her fingers found my cunt.

"*Yours,*" I vowed and fell into the ocean of pleasure she promised me.

Chapter 22
Lux

Keeping things professional in front of everyone was harder than I thought.

After Juliette finally admitted she was mine, I wanted nothing more than to spoil her.

It was the least she deserved.

The more I learned about her—about how she grew up and the people who abandoned her—the more I wanted to make up for all the lost time.

She was so perfect. I knew from the start that she had to be mine. I tried to fight it for so long, but it was hopeless.

It was like everything I'd been looking for my entire life finally showed up on my doorstep in a nice pretty package just waiting for me to open it.

The days passed in a blissful blur. Each day I spent with her seemed more perfect than the last. During the day, we would keep up the facade. We would meet in the kitchen with Bella, have breakfast, and separate for the day so I could go to work and she could take Bella to school.

She would give me updates on what they were doing, I

would sometimes reply with a not-entirely-professional thing or two, and then I would come home and have dinner with everyone. Sometimes we all had lunch together.

Then we would spend the rest of our time together before Bella went to sleep. It wasn't long before Bella started asking Juliette to accompany her during her bedtime routine, which I later learned meant braiding her hair and reading her the bedtime story my sister did.

Bella had come a long way from insisting she did it herself and locking everyone out to padding out in her pajamas when she was ready for Juliette.

I wish one day she'll trust me that much.

But I was content with this for now. Because at least she was opening up to someone.

And that someone being Juliette had my obsession with the nanny only deepening. She was an integral part of our life. Both Bella and I desperately needed her, and I was unable to hide it any longer.

Once Bella was asleep and everyone had gone home for the day, Juliette would sneak into my bed.

It was starting to feel a little bit unbelievable. Like at a moment's notice, the powers that be would realize just how well things were going for me and would snatch it all away. I had held onto her extra tight at night over the last few days as the feeling started to weigh on me.

I hated that as soon as things started to feel good in my life there was this overwhelming sense of panic and fear that everything would go wrong.

Even if it would, I tried to push everything to the back of my mind. I tried to enjoy what I had.

"I can't believe she's actually playing with someone," I murmured as Juliette and I sat next to each other on the grass.

My fingers were just barely grazing her hand. I was being extra careful so we wouldn't get caught. We were at a large park filled with trees, and the sweet smell of blooming flowers permeated the air. There was a large playground with a handful of kids, and Bella had found a playmate to play frisbee with.

She was laughing and looking happier than I'd ever seen her. She had been hesitant at first, but after a few minutes, she really got into it, and she was barely looking back at us anymore.

"I know," Juliette murmured. She shifted so she could brush her fingers across my own. "I'm so proud of her."

"Me too."

My heart swelled every time I looked at Bella. Just a measly almost eight months now, she had been a shell of a child. Her eyes were hollow, she would barely eat, she wouldn't get enough sleep. She had no interest in doing anything, and her grades were slipping.

This was a completely different child. A child reminiscent of the Bella she used to be before her parents died.

That's not to say that there weren't bad days. She had them for sure. But they were few and far between when compared to before.

"It's all because of you, you know?" I said and stole a glance at Juliet.

She was wearing a yellow dress and a large sun hat, looking perfectly in place at the park. Her blonde hair was pulled back into a little ponytail, and she had accessorized with cute flower jewelry that I hadn't seen before.

She took my breath away. Every single day I saw her. It didn't matter if she was dolled up or in her sweats or in that skimpy pajama set I loved.

She turned to me, smiling, and opened her mouth to say

something, but then we both heard, "Why don't you go ask your mom? And I'll go ask mine."

"Okay!"

Bella ran over to us, grinning, her feet taking her as fast as her small legs would let her. When she reached us, she was breathless. She was wearing a cute yellow shorts-and-tank set that had small embroidered flowers on it.

Bella didn't have her ears pierced, but Juliette had taken the time to braid her hair and place small flower pins to make up for it. She also wore a matching necklace with a single pink flower in the middle that matched Juliette's.

"Gloria wants to know if I can go get a frozen yogurt with her!"

She was addressing... me. My mind went back to the first day Juliette came to our house, and she mistakenly called me "Mom" in front of Bella. It ruined Bella's day, but now she didn't even bother to correct the other girl.

It made my heart soar.

I never wanted to replace my sister, but seeing that Bella hadn't broken down because of the mistake was a huge step forward.

"Yeah," I said with a smile. "We don't have anywhere to be after this, so that sounds perfectly fine to me. Why don't we meet her there?"

"She said we could walk. Is that okay?"

"I'd like to walk," Juliette replied and got up, brushing off the remaining grass that stuck to her dress. "Where is her mom?"

"I'll go find her!" And Bella was off in a flash.

I looked away for a second to send Juliette a wink. One goddamn second.

But that was enough for me to lose sight of Bella.

I was on my feet in seconds, my heart pounding in my

chest. I took a moment to find her, just in case I was freaking out for no reason, but after coming up empty, I really started to panic.

"Where'd she go?" I asked frantically. Juliette was by my side, her hand gripping mine as she scanned the park with me.

"I don't see her," she whispered, fear lacing her voice.

How the fuck did this happen?

My eyes scanned everything. The playground. The place where I saw the little girl she was playing with run off to. All the trees. Various people sitting on the ground having their own small dates. Everyone was happy and smiling, and there was no sign of Bella.

No. No no no no.

This can't be happening.

We started moving further into the park, getting more anxious by the second, and then I saw her with someone who was all too familiar.

Before relief could even show its head, rage hit me.

I rounded on them, walking as fast as I could, anger boiling in my veins. And then Juliette saw it too, and I watched the fear on her face, even if she wasn't fully aware of what my mother was capable of.

"Oh no."

Bella was looking down while my mother's hands were on her shoulders. All the happiness had drained from Bella's face, and now she was standing there with a frown, looking like she wanted to be anywhere but there.

"Bella!"

Bella's panicked face cracked my heart as she saw me and ran to me. Juliette grabbed her, hid her behind me, and hugged her, making sure my mom couldn't get anywhere near her.

"What a coincidence," she said, though her voice and the

look on her face told me it was anything but. And I knew this woman would do anything to try and get Bella.

Even if it meant stalking us.

There was no such thing as coincidence with her. Because of how important her image was to her, she made sure she had everything planned. Nothing surprised her. Nothing rattled her.

And the only thing we had in common was that she would not let something go until she had her way.

"I told you I didn't want to see you again," I hissed and kept Juliette and Bella behind me. Bella grabbed my hand and held it close to her face. I could feel Juliette shift so she could hold onto Bella tighter.

My mom looked at me with hatred in her eyes.

The thing about my mother was that she had always loved my sister. She had been her first child—the first everything. She was perfect. And while it annoyed me, I loved her. She took care of me when my own mother cast me aside for not being perfect enough.

My mother volunteered at schools. In her community, people knew her as the friendly lady across the street.

But they didn't know that she hated her mistake of a second daughter.

My sister and I did not have the same father. But both of those men decided to leave my mother. I figured that they saw the true her and couldn't bear to be with her regardless of their children.

Nothing I ever did had been enough for her.

I did everything right. I got straight A's. I never skipped school. I graduated at the top of my class. I went to an Ivy League college. And I owned my own fucking company.

But none of it was good enough because she never wanted me.

Maybe I was a constant reminder of a man she had loved and lost. One who had wanted nothing to do with her. And every single day she saw me, it reminded her that she'd lost him. She'd let him slip out of her grasp.

When my sister died, she was devastated, but she knew that if she could have Bella, she could still keep a little bit of my sister with her.

Her reaction when she found out that I was named the guardian had been nothing short of explosive. I never heard her cuss so loudly.

At first, I had tried to keep their relationship strong. I thought Bella would need her grandmother. But after she'd shown up back home, looking broken-hearted and asking never to see her again, I changed my mind. Bella's mental health and feelings were more important than any blood ties. I vowed to never have her near Bella ever again.

But she keeps fucking showing up.

"If you keep interfering like this, I'm going to call the cops," I warned, the threat clear in my voice.

"You wouldn't dar—"

"I will," I promised. "I'm not playing around anymore, Mom. You want to keep crossing these boundaries? Then I'm going to enforce them. And you don't want me to get a fucking restraining order. Leave Bella alone."

"I was just walking around the park and I happened to see her," she huffed. "What are you saying? If I see her outside, I can't even say hi to my own granddaughter?"

"No," I said simply.

She clicked her tongue and crossed her arms over her chest, looking around as if to see if anyone was watching. A few moms were, and they were holding their children far away, clearly looking like they were not going to take her side, a mix of pity and morbid curiosity in their gazes.

If there was one thing my mom hated, it was looking bad in front of a crowd, so I leaned into this, speaking a little louder than necessary.

"I'm serious. This is your last warning. I have custody, I don't need to remind you of that. And if you keep trying to take her, you'll be charged with kidnapping."

She still had her arms crossed, and she had an exasperated look on her face, but I should've known that she was up to something because instead of stomping away, she stood her ground, and her eyes went straight to Juliette.

"You know, I heard something really funny recently," she started, ignoring what I said about the kidnapping entirely. "Did you know that your Aunt Kathy and I go to the same floristry class?"

When Juliette's hand grasped the back of my shirt, my heart sank into my stomach.

I knew exactly where she was fucking going with this. Again, my mother never showed up unprepared. It has been quiet recently—a little bit too quiet—and now I realized it was because she was scheming in the background instead of licking her wounds.

Not only did I not want to have Juliette go through this again with my own mother, but I also could not bear to have Bella hear the words that were going to come out of her mouth.

She will ruin us if she has the chance.

"You better watch what you say," I warned. "Not only is Bella here, but Juliette is important to me, and I will not have you disrespecting her again. I don't care what you heard. I don't care what her aunt said. You *will not* repeat it here."

"Come on, Bella," Juliette whispered, starting to pull her away. But my mom, being the bitch that she was, decided she needed to speak up.

"So it's OK for you to hire your *whore* as your nanny?" she asked loudly, drawing attention. Onlookers' faces started to shift. They started to look at Juliette and her flower dress and hat. Criticizing her. I could feel it in their gaze. I grabbed her hand, squeezing it. "Should we talk about how your *nanny* recently came into some money?"

"Juliette... My chest feels tight."

I looked down to see Bella gripping Juliette's dress, her face buried in it. We had to stop this. I wanted nothing more than to make my mother pay, but doing it in a park full of children was not the way. And neither was exposing Bella to all of it.

"You're going to be hearing from my lawyer," I said to my mom before quickly scooping up Bella, grabbing Juliette's hand, and rushing to our car.

"Don't you listen to her," I said to both Juliette and Bella. "I promise she's not going to do that again. I'll fix this, okay?"

Bella had her nose buried in my shirt and was inhaling deeply.

"Okay," she mumbled, and then I heard her whispering, counting down from fifty. Something else Juliette had taught her to do.

"That's good, Bella," Juliette cooed, her hand coming up to rub Bella's back as we walked. "You're doing so good. You've gotten so good at calming yourself down."

But Bella said nothing. When I set her down, she actually pulled away and buckled herself in the car. We followed suit, wanting to get out of there as soon as possible. None of us spoke. I knew both Juliette and I were thinking the same thing.

If my mother decides to open her mouth, we will be in a lot of fucking trouble. Trouble Bella doesn't need.

As usual, just when I thought my life was perfect, it was all threatening to crash down.

I leaned back in my chair with a sigh. "Great, Laura. Again, sorry to bother you so late..."

"Don't worry about it, Lux. I'll finish this tonight and follow up tomorrow."

We hung up, and I was left with an impossible heaviness on my shoulders.

This is it. We're actually doing this.

Some part of me always knew it would come to this, I just didn't want to admit it to myself. I wanted to believe that even if my mother was a manipulative bitch to me, *maybe* she could redeem herself for Bella.

But that was wishful thinking.

I stood up from my chair, stretching out the ache in my muscles. Walking out of my office and down the hallway, I paused when I reached Bella's room. The small, muffled sound of Juliette reading to her reached my ears.

The exhaustion was starting to overtake me then. I leaned my head against the door so I could hear her more clearly. Her smooth, rhythmic voice filtered through, and I found myself relaxing because of it.

When she finished, I found it hard to pull myself away. I wanted to slip in and crawl into bed with them, fall asleep to the sweet sound of Juliette reading.

"Again?" Juliette asked in a voice barely discernible through the door.

"Maybe... more... if that's okay," Bella said in an even smaller voice. I couldn't make out everything, but I was grateful she was asking her to read again. It allowed me a selfish moment with them.

Even if we were separated by a wall, both emotionally and

physically, this was the closest I'd felt to them. I enjoyed watching them together. Loved seeing the comfort they found in each other.

It was okay if I was still on the other side of this wall, watching over them like a guardian angel. But I couldn't help but think Juliette was the real angel here.

I didn't have Juliette's ability to get Bella to open up. To get her to forget about everything. Yet she came in and did it effortlessly.

I'll fix this. For them.

I promised to keep Bella safe. Make her happy. Even if that meant spilling blood. My mother was unpredictable, and after the years of abuse at her hands, I knew she'd be capable of anything.

Whatever came our way, I would protect both of them. *Our new little family.* It was us against the world.

Chapter 23
Juliette

"The restraining order will be in place tomorrow," Lux told me as I got settled against her, my head on her chest.

Bella needed me to read *Goodnight Moon* five times before falling asleep tonight, and even then her little hands were gripping me so tightly I couldn't slip out until she was sound asleep.

I hated seeing her like this and knowing there was nothing I could do about it. But Lux was already ahead of me. And for that, I was grateful.

I knew it was coming. She was nothing if not efficient, and I knew her lawyer would work quickly—still, this was a hell of a lot faster than I expected.

"That's for the best," I murmured, then went quiet. Finally, after a day of trying to make sure Bella was okay, I had time to let my mind wander.

The thing that had been bugging me all day was how did she find my aunt? Or was it my aunt who found her? Either way, it felt icky. It felt like an invasion of privacy, and I definitely didn't want those two talking. Who knew what kind of havoc they could wreak if they were together?

"What are you thinking about so hard over there, Angel?"

"I don't think it's a coincidence that she found my aunt," I said after a moment.

Lux exhaled. "There's no such thing as a coincidence with my mother." Annoyance filled her tone. She reached up to brush her hand over my back, soothing me. There were still tingles every time we touched, but this time I could actually revel in the comfort it provided. "I have someone working on it, don't worry. She's gone too far, and I am not going to sit still this time."

I nodded and let out a long breath. I could trust Lux. She was a good person, and even if she didn't like to show it, she cared a lot.

"Who is this *someone?*" I asked, unable to help myself. "Sounds mysterious."

I could feel her laughing. "I may or may not have a *very* reliable information broker who can look into things like this for me."

I paused for a second. Maybe I shouldn't ask, but I needed to know. If we were to fight whatever this was together, I had to know all the facts.

"Lux, I don't mean to pry or make you tell me things if you're not ready to, but what happened? Why is your mother being such a—"

"Gigantic bitch?"

A smile tugged at my lips.

"Exactly."

She hugged me closer with a sigh.

"She should never have had children," she said after a short pause. "She hated me for some reason and made it known as I was growing up. Part of me worked so hard in high school and college to spite her. I was thinking that if I was successful afterwards, she'd finally have no choice but to respect me."

"People like her don't change," I murmured, thinking of my own aunt.

"No," she agreed. "They don't. But I was young and naive, thinking that if I could just *prove* how useful I was to her, maybe she'd rethink everything. But she's still the same mother who chose my sister over me. The one who obviously loved only one of her children. It's why she wants Bella so badly. She doesn't care about her. She's just the last part of my sister left in this world."

My hand found hers and squeezed.

"I'm sorry," I whispered. "You deserved better than that."

Poor Lux. I hated imagining how she was neglected like that as a child. She didn't deserve it.

"Bella deserves better."

There was another pause.

"But you do too. You know that, right?" My thumb ran circles over her wrist. "Past Lux, a child unable to fight for herself, and present Lux, an adult forced to protect her niece against her own mom... Both of them are worthy of love."

I could feel her swallow and her chest catch, but I didn't move. I let the words simmer between us.

"Thank you, Angel... for always knowing what to say."

"Just being honest," I whispered and placed a small kiss on her skin. I ran my hand over her heart, feeling it beat in her chest. "I wish I could help somehow."

"You help more than you'll ever know." Her hand came to grab mine again. "Since I met you, my life has only changed for the better."

Maybe it was the darkness that gave us the ability to talk like this. To spill our deepest worries and secrets. But it also made me worry. Worry about our future. Worry about what would become of us.

All of us.

"I don't want Bella to know how we met," I said quietly. "I don't regret it at all, but that's not for a little girl to know. On top of that, I don't even know how we'll explain our relationship to her."

Lux's other hand went to my chin, making me look at her even though I could barely see her in the dark.

"I know. It's my fault. I went after you, but I didn't think hard enough about what we would tell Bella. I should've prepared for this. I'm sorry."

The vulnerability in her words caused my chest to tighten.

"It's not your fault," I told her, grabbing her hand. "We'll think of something together, okay? But if we're serious about this..."

"I've never not been serious about you, Juliette." My heart soared at that. "Even though I knew we shouldn't, I couldn't help myself. There is no one better for me in this world than you. We just happen to have met under not-so-great circum-stances."

I couldn't help but smile.

"I actually think the *circumstances* were pretty great," I joked.

"I'll show you circumstances."

And even after it all, Lux made me forget everything else in the world.

We were both sitting in the kitchen when Bella came out, dressed in a sparkly pink dress. This time, she had a small bandanna on her head, but it was slightly tilted, so I took the chance to fix it for her.

"Very cute," I commented with a smile. "Where did you come up with this one?"

"I saw a couple of girls wearing one at school," she replied with a big smile.

I had seen a couple of girls wearing them in the pickup line, so I had actually added a few of those to my shopping list.

Lux cleared her throat, causing us both to look at her.

"If you want to go to school, I'll definitely take you, but I wanted to offer... a mental health day?" she asked, sounding almost unsure. "We can do whatever you want. Go get ice cream, go to the park, go to Adventureland... Just me and you. Juliette gets the day off today."

I looked at her suspiciously.

What is this about? And why is it the first time I'm hearing about it?

Bella let out a noise of excitement and jumped up and down quickly. "Let's go to the mall!"

Lux smirked. "Deal. Then maybe, since it's Juliette's day off and all, she'd like to join us. We can split ways and then meet again in, like, an hour or two?"

I still didn't understand what she was up to, but I agreed, so we packed up to go to the mall.

Lux called in for Bella, citing that she wasn't feeling well and that she would be back tomorrow. I had to sit in the backseat with Bella and try to stop her from giggling and blowing her cover.

It was cute—even a little wholesome—and I was glad to see both of them enjoying themselves.

It wasn't until we got there, parked, and entered that Lux pulled me aside and explained in a little voice, "I decided how to tell her. We'll have a fun day, and then before we meet again,

I'll let her know that I've liked you for some time and I want you to be more than our nanny."

Ah, I see. The talk.

My heart warmed. She might have made these plans on a whim, but they were both gentle and attentive.

"I think it's perfect," I said, giving her a smile.

Only then did I realize how nervous she was. Pulling at her clothes. Her eyes moving back and forth, shooting between me and Bella. Even her hands were a bit shaky.

I wanted to kiss her, but I quickly brushed her arm and mimicked taking a deep breath instead.

"It'll be fine," I reassured her. "It's really thoughtful of you to do it this way."

"Do you... want to do it with me?" she asked, her voice unsure. "I feel bad about making you go off on your own."

How cute.

"You're not *making* me do anything," I said. "It's best this way. She should hear it from you. I don't want to pressure her into accepting it just because she doesn't want to hurt my feelings. Plus... this is a bonding moment for the two of you."

She took a deep breath and nodded.

"You have my card. Use it. Do whatever you want. Maybe even get your hair and nails done. Pamper yourself."

My smile widened.

"I have my own money to spend, Lux. You pay me, remember? I really don't think this is a proper use of a black card."

She gave me a look. "Do I really have to remind you?"

I raised my brow at her, confusion washing over me.

"I told you you're worth every penny. I don't care whether it's five dollars or five million. You spend that money and treat yourself. And you bet your fine ass that if you don't spend enough, I'm going to come back here with you and show you how to really spend money."

God. Why does she make butterflies go off in my stomach so easily?

Lux could just look in my direction and they'd be off. But there was something oddly comforting about someone wanting to spend money on me. No matter how random it was.

"Okay," I replied and motioned for her to go back to Bella's side. "We'll meet in two hours. Text me where you are."

She nodded, quickly squeezing my hand before turning to take Bella farther into the mall, but not before the little girl turned back and waved at me. I waved back with a smile.

I waited a moment before moving away, making sure that they were fully out of sight.

To be honest, I hadn't ever thought about pampering myself. It was a foreign concept. I never had the money for it. *Pampering* for me was a nice meal that I couldn't usually afford or an article of clothing that I had my eyes on for a while.

With the whole mall at my disposal, I had no idea where to start.

And honestly, after living with Lux and Bella, I didn't really need much anymore. My housing was taken care of, I ate delicious food every day, and I didn't really need any new clothes or shoes or anything like that.

I turned around, taking in the expansive mall around me.

I can always get some snacks or get my hair and nails done like she suggested.

But the more I sat with myself, the more I realized it had been a while since I'd been able to just be alone like this. Not just alone—alone without having anything to do.

I wasn't worried about money or paying rent. I wasn't wondering where my next meal would be coming from. I wasn't so exhausted from work that I'd just crash on my bed as soon as I got there.

So I let myself sink into the feeling of not knowing what to do with myself. I let it sit heavy in my chest, allowing the anxiety to creep in.

Then I shut that shit down, puffed my chest out, and went for it.

I was going to do exactly what Lux recommended. Hair and nails.

Maybe I could dye my hair red.

I almost texted Lux to tease her about it but decided not to. And then I decided to get some nice lingerie she could peel off me later. Definitely something we'd both enjoy.

I stopped by a coffee kiosk and got a small iced tea before walking into the salon, which—thankfully—had spots open.

I zoned out more than once when the tech was working on my nails. I knew I was supposed to be enjoying it, but all I could think about was how Bella and Lux were doing.

How *the talk* was going.

It hoped it wouldn't be a shock to her for the one person in her life to come out of nowhere and tell her she and her nanny were together.

I hope she doesn't hate us for it.

That was the worst thing I could imagine as I sat down in the hairdresser's chair. I breathed in and kept busy sipping on my tea and listening to the gossip around me.

Until my phone buzzed.

Excitement and panic swirled in my chest, thinking Lux and Bella had finished early.

But it wasn't them.

It was my brother.

LUCAS

Do you have time to talk?

. . .

I was hurt, but I wouldn't say no to him. We were the only real family we had.

So I texted Lux.

ME

Hey! How are you guys doing? All done?

She replied almost instantly.

LUX STERLING

Still need some time. I haven't gotten to it yet.
Maybe get yourself a snack?

ME

Okay. Lucas is coming over for a chat so I'll
go meet him.

Text me when you're ready.

And don't worry. I'll be fine. We'll be fine.

The hairstylist started cutting my hair while I typed Lucas back.

ME

Meet me in the first-floor coffee shop at the
mall. I'll be there in thirty.

And now I was spiraling. She trimmed my hair and gave me a
deep conditioning treatment, making small talk along the way,
and I nodded through it, but my mind wasn't there at all.

I was running through exactly what I was going to say,
word for word, in my head as my hair was getting blow-dried.

*I'm sorry I put you in a hard spot, but what you said to me
was not okay.*

I don't want it to be like this between us.

*If you don't want to go, that's fine, but at least let me help
with other things.*

The anxious rumblings in my head only got worse when I
got there. And once I was sitting there, pretty and pampered
with matcha between my newly manicured nails, I started
thinking that maybe it wasn't such a good idea to meet him in
person.

I didn't know what he wanted to talk to me about. I didn't
know if he was going to berate me again, even though I was sure
I wasn't going to just take it. But he was my brother, so I would
take the chance because I loved him. And it broke my heart that
we weren't talking.

When he walked in, my breath caught. He looked awful.
Deep bags under his eyes, rumpled clothes, hair a mess.

*What the fuck happened? Is this because of what happened
with Aunt Kathy?*

His eyes met mine, and a small, easy smile spread across his
face. His entire body sagged as if he was letting out a sigh of
relief.

He maneuvered through the small shop and took a seat across from me. I pushed a hot latte toward him. He looked like he needed it.

"Thanks," he muttered, his eyes falling to the table. "And thanks for meeting me."

"You're my brother." I reached over to hold his hand. "Regardless of what happened, I will always be here for you."

"About that," he said and cleared his throat. He sat up straight, his eyes finally meeting mine. "Ever since you left the hospital, I just felt so bad. The guilt is eating me alive, Juliette. I'm so sorry. I let her get inside my head with her comments and thoughts and I shouldn't have."

My heart broke at his words. He sounded so... broken. Regardless of how rude he'd been to me, I didn't want my brother to feel this way. *Ever.* I'd rather take whatever they gave me tenfold than see him hurt like this.

"Hey, *hey,*" I said, dropping my voice. "It's okay. I get it. How is Aunt Kathy doing, by the way?"

To be honest, I didn't really care, but seeing that it caused my brother stress also messed with me.

"Better now that everything is paid for. She doesn't know I'm here. After you walked away, she wanted nothing to do with you. The whole thing rubbed me the wrong way. The way she spoke to you... The way she talked about us..."

"Lucas, she's a horrible person. And I can't wait for you to get out of there." His words dawned on me. "Wait. Everything is paid for?" I asked, an eerie feeling creeping up now.

"Yeah..." he trailed off, giving me a look. "By you. That's why I'm here. To say thank you. I know she never would."

I didn't like my aunt. I didn't like her when I was younger, and I surely didn't like her after the way she spoke about my brother.

I would never pay for her hospital bills. Especially when it was her own fault that she didn't have insurance.

I also knew that she had money stashed away. I didn't know exactly how much, but I knew it had to be a comfortable amount.

"Why would you think I paid for it?" I asked, lowering my voice to a whisper. "Especially when you implied I was selling myself for money and she literally called me a *whore*."

His fingers gripped the cup tighter.

"That was wrong of me. I didn't mean it and I hope you know I'm sorry. I just... I don't wanna go to college. *There*. I said it."

He looked up at me, his face completely serious.

"I'm done with school, Juliette. I know I planned to go, I know we talked about it, but people change. I'm not the same kid who used to love TV shows with college roommates and think that was the awesomest thing ever." He paused for a second. "I know you always wanted the best for me, and you want me to succeed, but I would much rather do something else with my life."

I ground my teeth together. He was right. He had the right to change and choose his own path in life.

"Lucas... I get it. But you still need a plan," I said, urging him to look me in the eyes. "You don't have to take my money if it offends you so much. But I just want you to be able to provide for yourself."

Regret was clear on his face.

"It doesn't offend me, Juliette. I was just taken off guard when I put two and two together. You and your boss—"

"I'm going to stop you there. To be honest, whatever you think is your problem, not mine. What Lux and I have is our business, and *only* our business. Hopefully one day you'll understand it."

He paused again at my tone. Lux was right. I wasn't just going to take it anymore. I didn't deserve it.

"I'm... I'm sorry. That came out wrong. I don't have an issue with Lux and you together or with the money. I just don't want it for college."

Hope sparked in my chest and a smile threatened to pull at my lips.

"Then what do you want it for?" I asked, leaning forward.

"Trade school," he said, looking up at me hesitantly. "I wanna be a lineman. You know, those people who fix the power lines? That's what I want to do."

I was taken aback both by his honesty and by what he had decided on as a career.

"Okay," I said after a moment, my voice trailing off. "You don't *have* to go to college. I won't force you to do anything you don't want to. If this is what you want and you're serious about it... I'm more than willing to pay for everything."

For the first time in a while, his face lit up with a smile, and suddenly everything else faded into the background.

This is what I really wanted when I offered to pay for his college tuition. For him to be happy.

It was never really about college at all. Yes, I thought it would give him an advantage in life and make it so he could get a high-paying job and never worry about money.

But at the end of the day, all I wanted was to see him happy.

I squeezed his hand.

"I don't want to fight with you." My tone was soft. "You're my brother, and I love you."

"I love you too," he said, holding my smile, but then just as quickly as it came, it disappeared. "So you're positive it wasn't you? The money, I mean. It was in your name."

"No," I said, and took a sip from my matcha.

But what I didn't tell him was that I knew exactly who it had come from, and I was not going to let it slide.

Chapter 24
Lux

I looked at Bella as she took heavy gulps of her sugary drink.

The drink was on the table in front of her, and her hands were filled with bags. She refused to let them go even as we sat down. I had a few by my feet as well.

All of them contained clothes, accessories, jewelry, and honestly anything that caught her eye. I wasn't going to tell her no today.

Or any day, if I was being honest.

It was the first time I'd actually seen her enjoy shopping. When she came under my care, I'd brought her here because I didn't have anything in my house that was suitable for her. But she didn't seem very interested, which left me having to pick a lot of the things myself, and I had no idea what to buy for a little girl her age.

But now she happily looked through all the clothing and trinkets, carefully picking out everything she wanted. She would even stop and tell me which she saw people wearing at school. How they wore it. Who wore it better.

She was a completely different girl, and I kicked myself for not doing this sooner with her. Though I'm not sure if any time before this would've been right.

Back then, her mother and father had just died, and I wasn't any better to be around since I was deep in my grief as well. Neither of us knew how to be around each other.

While I had spent time with her now and then every time I visited my sister or we met up somewhere, those had been short amounts of time. Nothing like being forced together for hours or living together.

Nothing like becoming her new person.

But now, and because of Juliette, I could see us slowly healing. She was opening up. Enjoying school and life more. She smiled more than she frowned now. She didn't have any of those explosive tantrums anymore.

The pain would never go away, I knew that. Losing my sister was a trauma that would be forever scarred onto our psyche.

But we could take our lives back. We could be happy. All three of us.

And that brought me back to the conversation I needed to have. All the worry came back with a vengeance.

I was obsessed with Juliette. I loved her, and there was no denying it now. And it wasn't fair to her to hide our relationship or what I felt for her. She deserved someone who would love her out in the open and freely, not to be hidden away like some dirty little secret.

I wanted to do the right thing for both my girls. I wanted to give them the life they deserved in every way. And that meant not hiding Juliette but not keeping secrets from Bella either.

But I didn't want Bella to feel like she was being left behind in any way. She never would be. So I had to get this right.

"Where is Juliette?" she asked, looking around the food

court of the mall, no doubt hoping she'd be coming around the corner any minute now.

"She's meeting her brother," I said.

Bella's face twisted, and she took another sip of her drink before whispering, "Uh-oh, should we... go save her or something?"

If it were any other time, I would have laughed, but I was just as concerned as she was. Just because I loved Juliette didn't mean I felt the same about her family, no matter how much she cared about him. He had been awful to her last time, and I didn't want her to have to go through it again. Especially alone.

But I knew that he was probably there because *I* had done something I shouldn't have.

Something I would definitely be hearing about later.

But right now, it was about me and Bella. About coming clean to her that I was in love with her nanny, and I wanted to be in a relationship with her.

I took a deep breath, nerves racing through me. My heart was pounding in my chest. My palms were sweaty.

Facing the eight-year-old was more nerve-racking than most of the things I did on the daily as a CEO.

What if she likes her fine as a nanny but can't accept her as my girlfriend? What if she gets mad at Juliette for taking her aunt away from her?

Bella didn't have many stable people in her life, which was why I wanted to keep the lines between me and Juliette clean. So she could have me, her aunt, and Juliette, her nanny and confidante.

I wanted her to be able to tell Juliette anything she couldn't tell me. For her to lean on Juliette without worrying that she would instantly come running to me afterwards to spill her secrets.

At least until she feels comfortable coming to me herself

with anything she needs, I instantly thought. Because I wanted to be that for my niece too.

"Bella, I have someone to talk to you about."

Her eyes went wide. *Shit.* "Did something bad happen?"

"No, no," I said quickly. "It's actually a very good thing."

She perked up at this and leaned forward as if to say, *What is it? I'm all ears.*

I swallowed thickly, nerves acting up again. *It's now or never, Lux. You're a grown woman. You got this.*

"I really, really like Juliette, and I want her to be my girl-friend." The words tumbled out in one breath. Too fast. Kind of low. Bella looked at me for a long moment, and I realized she probably hadn't heard me.

Shifting in my chair and taking another deep breath, I tried again.

"I said that I really, really like Juliette, and I—"

"I thought she already was your girlfriend," she said with a confused look.

I sat up straight, palms on the table in front of me.

"Why would you think that?"

"Because you guys look at each other like my friend looks at her boyfriend." The grimace on her face was kind of cute. "All googly-eyed and gross."

I opened my mouth to say something, but nothing came out. I didn't really know how to respond to that.

Okay? You're right? I guess the cat's out of the bag?

I guess Juliette and I weren't as secretive as we thought.

"Wow. I didn't see that coming." She giggled, and her smile radiated happiness, which had a weight lifting off my shoulders.

"I also saw you kissing one morning when you thought I wasn't around," she said, taking a sip of her drink.

Yeah, that would do it.

"And are you... okay with it?"

She shrugged. "As long as you don't take my time with her away, I'm fine."

Their time together? What about our time? I felt a little bit insulted.

"You're worried about *me* taking *your* time together away but not her stealing me? Your aunt?"

She coughed and waved me off, taking a nonchalant sip of her drink and looking very grown-up. I wasn't sure I liked it.

"You don't paint with me, or tie my laces, or pick me up from school, or braid my hair, or help me with my math home-work, or get me out of school to go have a secret piece of pie... Oops. I wasn't supposed to say that."

I laughed and ruffled her hair. "I get it, you really like Juliette."

She got serious for a moment, her eyes falling down to the table.

"I do," she said quietly. "And I hope she stays around for a long time."

"Bella, even though I don't do a lot of those things with you, I hope you know—"

"I really like you too, Auntie Lux. And I like it when you come get me out of school too for lunch and when you try to braid my hair, even though it doesn't look as cool."

The emotions were clogging my throat again, and I was at a loss for words.

"So don't mess it up, okay?" she finally added.

And all the heavy feelings were gone with a snap of her little fingers.

"I won't," I promised. "Now let's go find our girl, hm?"

She nodded and bounced off her chair, taking my hand as we walked back through the mall to the coffee shop where I knew she was waiting.

"You're gonna ruin it before you even start," Bella said as we piled out of the car and back to our house.

Juliette had been noticeably quiet and angry at me since we met her in the café. Her brother was gone, but she was there with a matcha in her hand and a frown on her face, shooting daggers at me. Bella obviously didn't miss that.

The worst part? Juliette would barely even talk to me. It was my first experience with her being actually mad at me.

"Oh, stop," I whispered. "Go play in your room for a little bit, okay? Maybe try on your clothes and you can give us a fashion show later?"

She sent me a glance, but the promise of her very own fashion show was too enticing, and she happily skipped toward her room, her tiny arms carrying as many shopping bags as she could. I would take the rest in.

Once we were in the kitchen, I turned around and faced Juliette, who was staring at me with her arms crossed over her chest.

She's cute when she's angry.

And that is the wrong thing to be thinking right now.

"Well, Bella took it really—"

"You know I hate my aunt, right?"

I rocked on the balls of my feet and shoved my hands in my pockets. "I don't think you hate anyone."

Juliette frowned. "Fine, but you know I don't like her, right?"

"Yes," I said, my lips pursed.

She closed the space between us, looking up at me with fire in her eyes. This was a new side of Juliette that I'd never seen before, but I definitely wanted to bring it out again when we were alone and in the bedroom.

I knew my mind shouldn't be in the gutter, but I couldn't help it.

"Then why did you pay for her hospital bill?"

Of course he told her. Up until then, I tried to tell myself that maybe she was mad about something else. That maybe something her brother said pissed her off, but reality was sinking in. And I really wished Lucas would've stayed silent, but it seemed that was not his strong suit.

"Because she's your family, and I knew it was stressing Lucas out since he is the one who lives with her."

She opened her mouth to speak, but I held my hand up.

"And I know that as soon as Lucas is unhappy, you're unhappy. You didn't need to spend your heart and money on her. She doesn't deserve it. But I have more than enough money to go around, and if it makes your life easier and someone you care about happy? I am willing to spend it."

She frowned, her eyebrows pulling together.

"She really doesn't deserve your money."

"No, she doesn't. I know." My hand went up to cup her cheek. "But *you* do. Remember what I said? I'll keep saying it until you get it. Every cent I spend on you, whether directly to you, your family, or whatever else, is a cent I'm glad to spend. That especially includes the new lingerie I know you bought. Yes, I saw the bag." I was hoping for a smile at that, and I got one. "The point is, I want to help, Juliette, wherever I can. I don't want you to worry about anything. Not anymore."

She let out a sigh and then quickly buried her head in my chest, her arms wrapping around my waist. I hugged her back.

"Thank you," she whispered. "You know me better than I thought."

"No need to thank me, Angel. Your heart is too kind. Your

mind may tell you to cut ties with your aunt, but I know you'd feel guilty as soon as you saw how it would affect your brother."

She looked up at me. "Even so, it's too much money. I'm really not used to spending this much on myself. Or for a partner to spend it on me."

"Does it make you uncomfortable?" I asked, and she gave me a nod. I leaned down to kiss her lips. Just a quick peck before I was pulling away. "Well, you better get used to it, Angel, because I have *years* to make up for. All those years you were struggling, alone, and hurting. All those years you had no one to take care of you. All those years you worried about where your next meal was going to come from or if you could keep your place. All those years you wished you had someone—*anyone*—to turn to, but your side was empty." I kissed her lips again and held her face in my hands. "I'm going to make up for all of it. I'm going to show you, and not just with money, how important you are. You deserve to be *cherished*. You deserve to be taken care of. You are important to me, and as each and every day goes by, it gets harder to imagine a world without you in it."

"Lux..."

Her eyes watered. Her lower lip trembled. She looked so vulnerable in that moment.

"You don't have to say anything," I said as I ran my thumb across her cheek. "Just know that I will remind you every day until, finally, you get it in your head just how important you are to me... and Bella."

She was silent for a moment. "So she took it well?" I didn't mention how shaky or thick with emotion her voice was.

"She already thought we were together," I answered with a laugh. "I think she realized before we did. Apparently, we make googly eyes at each other."

She let out a laugh of her own. I left out the part where she'd seen us kiss. It would probably mortify her.

"Are we that obvious?"

"Yes." A voice came from behind us that caused us both to look. Both Gina and Marci were standing there. Marci's hands were on her hips, giving us a wicked grin. Gina was holding a fresh batch of groceries, her expression flustered.

Marci leaned toward Gina. "You owe me twenty."

Gina sighed and handed her a crumpled twenty-dollar bill from her pocket.

"What was the bet?" I asked.

"I voted you'd get together in less than three months."

Gina shrugged. "I knew Juliette had really high professional standards, so I thought it would take longer to break her down."

Juliette's face turned a beautiful pink at the jab.

This is how it was meant to be.

It was everything I wanted. Fun, easy, seamless. My girl, my niece, everything was slowly fitting into place and giving me a life that I never could've imagined just a few months ago.

I thought losing my sister was the end of the world. I loved her, and I had no idea how to give her child the life she deserved. But Bella and Juliette were teaching me how to live a better life for them—how to enjoy what I have.

Before this, more often than not, I would go to the office seven days a week, even if just for an hour. Nothing else mattered.

But I wasn't that person anymore.

She truly is my angel.

No one could convince me that she wasn't sent to make my life better, and I wouldn't stop until she knew how much she meant to me. How obsessed I was with her. How much I loved her.

I didn't care if it took weeks, months, or years.
Because she was mine.

Chapter 25
Juliette

"You're not giving up on me now, are you, Angel? Remember the safe word."

Bubblegum. And there was no way I was going to use it.

I braced myself on the bed as Lux dragged the vibrator from my clit to my entrance and back again. I was barely hanging on. My entire body was shaking. My breathing was labored.

This time, she had my feet planted on the ground with my body lying on the bed and my ass up in the air. I had to push my face into the sheets to stop the moans from tumbling out of my mouth.

I was completely naked, and she was still in her work clothes—an entire suit—but she had unbuttoned the jacket and the first few buttons of her shirt. It gave me a mouthwatering view of her chest and the tattoo on it.

I was itching to get a taste of her. I didn't have many chances to. She was in total control in the bedroom, and more often than not, all she wanted was to pleasure me. Just like tonight. She was on me like a hound. As soon as Bella went to sleep, I was ushered into her room, ordered to strip, and forced to lie on the bed as she worshipped me with her mouth.

That was hours ago, and she wasn't ready to stop anytime soon. There were no breaks this time. She was far too ravenous for that.

My legs shook harder as she brought the vibrator to my clit and pushed.

I let out a muffled cry as the orgasm started building up again. It swirled in my belly, and my core got tighter and tighter and tighter until—

She pulled away with a chuckle.

"Be quiet or I'll have to gag you," she warned. My pussy squeezed at the thought of it.

Her hand came to rub the back of my thigh, my ass, and then my back before it tangled in my hair and she yanked my head back. I couldn't hold a gasp as her lips kissed my ass cheek before she lightly bit it.

"What's gotten into you?"

"Are you saying you don't like it?" she asked.

As if to tease me, she pushed the vibrator against my entrance, pushing it inside me slowly before pulling out and doing it all over again. I moved my hips to try and meet her shallow thrusts, but every time I did, she would just pull away.

"I fucking love it," I panted. "Make me work for it, sir. I'm not worthy of it yet."

"Oh, you're worthy, Angel," she replied, laying her entire body over me as her lips brushed against my ear. "But that doesn't mean I don't love to see you beg for it."

"Please," I gasped and was rewarded with the lightest pressure against my clit. "Please let me come."

"Again, Angel."

But I did one better. I turned around and pushed her away

from the bed so I could sink to my knees in front of her. My hands were gripping her pants, and I looked up at her with my best puppy dog eyes.

She met me with a smirk and turned off the vibrator.

"You look good on your knees. Why don't you give me a show?" As she said it, Lux pushed her shiny shoe forward just barely. "*Ride it.*"

My breath caught. I had never done anything as dirty as that. Before her, I was quite vanilla, which was why going to a sex club was so out of character for me.

I'd always had fantasies. Dreamed about meeting someone like her. Someone I could finally submit to. Someone I could trust enough to give into my every desire without fear of being judged.

"Will it please you, sir?" I asked and climbed onto her foot, placing my wet cunt right on top of it. The material was cold, and combined with the wetness leaking out of me, slippery. But it was just hard enough to put that very much needed pressure on my clit.

I love the way she's looking down at me.

Her dark hair had been pushed back and out of her way. Her eyes were hooded, her mouth slightly open, my cum still on her lips.

She looked down at me like she was starving. Like she hadn't been fucking me for the last few hours. Like she had only gotten a taste and it had turned her into a ravenous animal.

She was insatiable. *For me.*

And goddamn, did I want to try this with her.

As a test, I jerked my hips back and forth, grabbing onto her leg, grinding down harder on her shoe. A moan spilled from my lips as heat shot through me, and her hand ran through my hair, a small gesture that let me know she liked what I was doing.

"Just like that," she murmured. The clear desire interwoven

with her praise had my breath catching. "You're such a good girl, aren't you? Willing to do anything for me. Can you come like this for me?"

"Yes," I breathed and moved faster against the hard material.

I'd make myself come if that's what it took to have those sweet, warm praises fall from her lips again.

I was already so sensitive and worked up from before that my orgasm would hit me in a matter of moments. A curling heat twisted in my belly, my pussy already pulsing.

It was all so overwhelming. The whole situation. How dirty it felt. How ready I was. And most of all, her sultry eyes taking me in. All of me.

She was my undoing.

I shattered completely, unable to hold my orgasm back as it tore through me.

And as it hit me, I whispered, "Please let me taste you."

I didn't mean for that to come out. I meant to do this at her pace, no demands. After all, it was her I wanted to please.

But pleasing her included giving *her* pleasure. Making her come at my hands.

I stayed there, my cum leaking down onto her shoe as she stood looking at me, her hand still in my hair.

Her nostrils flared, and a fire lit in her eyes.

"Only if you think you're up to it," she finally said. "I'm warning you, it can be difficult to make me come, especially with oral."

I smiled. "Challenge accepted."

"You're so perfect," she praised as I lapped up the wetness spilling out of her.

I finally had her lying against her pillows, me between her legs, naked and completely bare to me.

My mouth was everywhere. Her entrance. Her clit. Biting into her thigh. Even if it wasn't easy, I wasn't a quitter, and nothing would feel better than making her fall apart.

I didn't care how long it took. I didn't care how tired my jaw was after. The words falling from her mouth along with moans of pleasure were all the fuel I needed to keep going.

I speared her with my tongue, my thumb coming to her clit and rubbing furious circles over it.

Because I wasn't in a rush, I took my time to study her.

Lux required a bit more pressure and intensity than I did. Something that would have me shaking in seconds wasn't much for her at all.

So I went harder, faster, and I knew I got it right when she let out a gasp, her back arching, her hand fisting my hair like she needed something to hold on to.

Her head fell back, the muscles in her throat quivering as she sank into the pleasure I was pulling from her.

There was a light sheen of sweat falling down her forehead, and I watched as it made the journey down her face and neck to her breasts. It followed the lines of her tattoo before dispersing into her skin.

"Just like that. *Oh fuck*, just like that."

I brought my other hand, reaching out to pinch her nipple, the rosy bud just begging me to give it some attention.

"Yes, yes, *yes*."

There was nothing more beautiful than Lux as she came. She was wild, almost crazed as it ran through her. Her orgasm was like a tidal wave, threatening to destroy every-thing in its path, and she was just a casualty. Like it had a will of its own and only showed itself when it was coaxed into being.

She thrashed against me. Her moans cut out, and she was stuck there, frozen as her cunt pulsated.

I did this. I fucking did this.

Just like I thought, there was nothing more rewarding than seeing her unravel because of me.

"You're so beautiful," I cooed as she came down. Her eyes were wide, her breath heavy. She stared up at the ceiling like she was trying to catch her breath after a marathon.

I climbed up her body but kept her legs spread open with my thighs and my fingers between her legs, teasing her sensitive cunt.

I didn't want to stop. I wanted to see it again and again. I lazily circled her clit, making sure to keep the pressure before letting my fingers travel down and entering into her slippery cunt.

"So you want to top me now?" she joked and ran her hand through my hair and pushed it to the side so she could get a look at my face.

I didn't bother replying. Actions spoke louder than words anyway.

I slipped my fingers in and out of her. She was so obscenely wet that we could hear it through the silence of the room. I picked up my pace, pumping into her and slamming the heel of my palm against her clit. I almost thought it was too much, but then her body jerked against me, and I felt her cunt squeeze my fingers.

"Oh *God*," she said with a laugh. "No one's ever made me come twice in a row."

A burst of pride flared through my chest. It was so potent it had me lightheaded.

"It's just that no one ever knew how to treat her right," I

said, panting as I moved down her body. She spread her legs further for me, her head falling back into the pillows and her mouth opening again in that silent scream as she came, my fingers never stopping. "Isn't that right?" I asked her pretty pussy. "You just needed someone to show you the littlest bit of attention."

I expected Luz to shoot something snarky back or make fun of me for that, but instead I was thrown on the bed, her lips at my throat.

Before I knew it, we were starting all over again with her hand between my legs this time.

It was perfect between us. Maybe even more so because we had nothing to hide.

I almost couldn't believe she was mine. Couldn't believe that I was so lucky.

Having Lux was something I couldn't have dreamed possible. I could say she was the woman of my dreams, but she was far more than that.

She was everything I never knew I needed.

And I wanted to hold on to her.

Because I knew that as soon as I let my guard down, something bad would happen.

That was just the way life worked.

Chapter 26
Lux

It was a normal morning. We had gotten up, and Juliette had just finished braiding Bella's hair and added a special pink sparkly bow that she had gotten for her at a boutique we randomly walked by one day.

She had kept it a secret until she finally found a chance to give it to her as a present. Juliette had been happy to give it to her, but there was also that small bit of anxiety thrumming underneath. She had been worried Bella would hate it.

But Bella would never.

It warmed my heart to see Bella immediately lighting up when Juliette hesitantly gave her the package. She let out a squeal of happiness right then and there, and an even louder one when she actually opened it.

It just reinforced how perfect they were together. How perfect *we* were. And how lucky I had been to find someone like Juliette.

Less than half a year ago, it felt like my heart had been torn out and ripped to shreds. I had been overwhelmed, unsure. Everything seemed like it was going to shit.

Now, I just couldn't believe this was my life.

I was sipping my coffee and looking at the two of them as they interacted.

Juliette had her hair up in a messy bun, her face bare but glowing. She wore her lounge clothes, an oversized light blue shirt and sweats. When she looked at me, she sent me a warm smile.

She's so perfect.

Bella was in front of her, chomping on some waffles.

"No, you should try it, really. No one in my class could do it."

"I am positive I cannot lick my elbow," Juliette said with a light laugh.

My smile widened then as Bella shot me a glance.

"Try it, Auntie Lux! If anyone can do it, it's you!"

I shook my head and took a sip of my coffee. "I was young once too, believe me. I've tried."

Bella pouted, and just as she was about to push us to try again, the doorbell rang.

"I'll get it," Gina said, placing the dishes back in the sink. I thought nothing of it. Even though we didn't usually get visitors, my mind was only on my girls.

But when she answered the door and her voice cut out, I knew immediately that there was an issue. "Hey! You're not supposed—"

Before I knew it, my mom was rounding the corner. As always, she was dressed as if she was going to some type of city council meeting. Perfectly coiffed curly black hair, flawless makeup, not a single wrinkle on her outfit.

She wielded a large white stack of papers in her hands as her eyes sat on me. She had this look on her face. One I had seen many times growing up. *She thinks she's won.* That whatever was in her hands was the key to getting one up on me.

Even when I was a young teenager, she had wanted to be better than me. Always had to knock me down. Whether that was through ignoring me, paying more attention to my sister, or pointing out—or feeding—my insecurities.

She's thinking she's better than me. She wants this to hurt.

Juliette moved in front of Bella immediately. My niece held onto the back of Juliette's shirt and glared at my mother. If it weren't such a dire situation, I would've applauded her for her courage.

I was up immediately, but she simply shoved the papers into my chest and made a beeline for Bella. My hand reached out and gripped her arm.

"I told you you're not allowed—"

"I'm taking you to court for custody of the child," she said, and yanked her arm out of my grasp. She sent me a glare, looking me up and down, a disgusting smirk spreading across her painted lips. "If you make this easy, I won't ruin your image, but if you plan on fighting me, it's only going to go one way. *My way.*"

Anger boiled inside me, working its way up my entire body. It was so potent I felt the need to pull at my skin to find some sort of relief. It was either that or punching my own mother in the face.

"You can't take—"

"I *can* if you want to keep your livelihood," she said, looking Juliette straight in the eyes. She was goading her.

But instead of taking the bait, Juliette paused, looking at my mother. Then something seemed to dawn on her.

"You know something."

My mother let out a huff. "I'm resourceful."

"I don't think that's the right word for it," Juliette replied, her arms crossing in front of her.

Bella was still holding onto her for dear life, but her glare had not let up yet. I moved to them, a united front.

"It's all in the files, but let me tell you, it sure is damning. If this goes out, you'll never be able to work with children ever again."

Stillness washed over Juliette, a sense of calm I wasn't feeling.

"We know you talked to my aunt," she said, and then corrected herself. "No, you probably *stalked* my aunt and then waited until you could get a chance to speak to her. What did she tell you exactly?"

"Oh, I didn't *stalk* anyone," my mother said with a huff. "I just met her at my normal floristry class, and as we were talking, I realized who she was. She told me some *very* interesting things about you, including that you'd recently come into some money. Given in exchange for sexual favors to my daughter."

Rage coursed through me as I took a peek at the papers in front of me and saw what she was alleging as a reason to change Bella's custody order.

I couldn't tell which was worse. Her aunt giving up this information or my mother using it as blackmail.

My reasoning stands when it comes to Juliette, but I fucking regret paying for that bitch's medical expenses.

"This is low even for you," I spat and threw the papers on the counter. They scattered all over the island and down to the floor. "If you take this to court, and this becomes public, we're not the only ones whose reputation will be damaged."

She turned to look at me with a villainous smile that took her evilness to a whole other level. *She's enjoying this.*

"Oh no, I already have my press tour ready," she said and batted her eyelashes. "You're no child of mine. All of *that* came from your father."

Juliette leaned forward and grabbed the papers without

leaving Bella's side. Her eyes scanned them, and she let out a light gasp.

Meeting my eyes, I gave her a nod. It was even worse than either of us could've imagined.

Somehow—maybe by following me, possibly by bribing a few people, including someone there—my mother had found out that we met at a BDSM club. And while that wouldn't usually be an issue, she was using it as proof that I was an unfit guardian to Bella. Furthermore, she intended to use Juliette's presence here and the money I paid her as even more proof that Bella was not in a stable household.

I didn't even want to get into the rest of the defamatory document. It was ridiculous. But I knew it could work. Ridiculous lies and the prospect of "keeping children safe" took well-meaning, normal individuals and turned them into angry, mindless beings that wanted nothing more than to destroy anything they didn't understand.

And she knew that as well. She would harness their ignorance and unwillingness to learn and make an impossible case against us.

She's turning what Juliette and I have into something disgusting. Something dirty.

All she needed to do was convince a judge that I was twisted and had brought someone like-minded around Bella. That Bella's safety was at risk.

My fists clenched, and I had to take deep breaths through my nose and out through my mouth.

How dare she—

No.

I quieted my mind immediately. This was no time to let anger get the better of me.

I needed to get my lawyer, and fast. But if my mother actually did go to the courts with this... I was afraid I might lose Bella forever.

I looked at Bella and leaned down, grabbing both her arms. I made sure that she was looking me in the eye and not the vile woman behind me.

Her eyes were already watering, and I could tell that she knew what I was about to say was truly bad news.

"You're going to have to stay with her for a little bit," I said. Each word felt like I was trying to pluck out barbed wire from my heart. The pain on her face made it all so much worse. "It's temporary. I'm going to find a way out of this, and I'm going to bring you *home*."

"No, she's not," my mother said as she walked around me, her hand grabbing Bella by the shoulder. "You're going to come and stay with me like you should have from the very beginning. *Permanently*."

Juliette was there, pushing her hand off Bella.

"Give us one day to prepare," she asked, her voice softer than mine ever could be at the moment. "It's the least you can do. *For Bella.* She has things to pack. Let's not make this worse for her."

For the first time, my mother seemed to consider her words. She took a step back, her eyes running down Juliette's frame with a scowl.

"One day. But then I want her at my doorstep. If you don't comply, this will look even worse for the two of you."

Juliette nodded, but I said nothing as my mother left.

When the door slammed behind her, there was silence.

What the fuck am I going to do?

Gina came over, offering us all water. I had forgotten she was there at all. Juliette took a bottle, but Bella and I didn't. She was looking at the ground, and I was too busy looking at her.

I can't lose her. But I need to tread carefully, or else I truly may have no other option.

Then Bella finally spoke up.

"You promised," she said, her voice hollow. Even if my heart hadn't been on the verge of breaking, that would have done it.

"I did. I did, and I'm sorry," I told her, trying to keep my voice from cracking. "I don't want this. And you deserve so much better than this. I'm going to fix it."

I looked at Juliette.

"Just in case, prepare her room and her stuff. I need to call the lawyer."

She nodded and gently took Bella from me. With one last glance at her, I hurried to my office to dial the only person I thought could help me.

"So... You have custody, which means she can't just take her from you," my lawyer, Laura, explained as she looked over my mother's documentation.

She looked every bit like the professional she was, and that helped calm me. Her long, brown hair was straight, and today she was wearing a finger-hugging emerald suit that showed the tiniest bit of cleavage. Her fingers, neck, and wrist were all splashed with gold jewelry.

She had on an extravagant pair of gold frames that I assumed were mostly for examining documents like the one in front of her.

I didn't fully remember who had introduced me to Laura. Likely Sloan, the same person who had recommended I go to Club Pétale. Sloan was an associate I had done business with on more than one occasion. She had owned quite a few companies at one point, and I used to contract some of her services and materials, but that was *before* she got arrested.

I refused to do business with her after that, and she didn't seem too upset about it. I mean, she still offered for me to come to the club where she worked.

Laura was as good as they came, and if she truly could help us with this, I might have to give her a large bonus. I haven't needed her for much and was sure I wasn't nearly as big as some of her other clients, but I appreciated how fast she got to me nonetheless.

"I know," I said, and took a swig of whiskey. The stronger stuff that I saved for exactly a moment like this.

I could hear Bella crying softly as Juliette tried to pack up her stuff. I hated all of it. I couldn't face seeing her like this, so I tried to push it out of my mind and focus on what was in front of me.

"I'm a criminal defense lawyer, but as my first time seeing the case like this... it's bad." She gave me a look. "While no crime has been committed, you're right to be worried about this getting in front of a judge. They don't typically see people in the BDSM world as innocent and... *well-meaning*. Especially if it's an older judge."

It looked all sorts of wrong, I knew that. Juliette and I met under circumstances that some people would not understand, and then instead of firing her when she came to my house, I let her stay on as the nanny. To top it off, I was now in a relationship with her.

My mother was planning to go in front of a judge and tell them how worried she was about Bella and what my *lifestyle* might mean for her safety and upbringing.

And while I knew that was bullshit and that no one would

love Bella as much as Juliette and I did, I also knew how it would be perceived.

"What can I do?" I asked, lowering my voice. Even though the door was closed, I was afraid Bella might still hear me.

Laura set the papers down with a sigh and slowly took off her glasses and folded them. I knew that sigh. It was one I used too, especially when things were not about to go my way.

"Honestly? You need to get her to drop it. We could take this to court, but listen, your best shot is to handle it outside it if you want a chance at keeping her."

I took a big swig of alcohol and placed the glass on the table a little harder than I meant to. Laura gave me a pitiful look.

"I know," she said as she got up. Her phone had been buzzing for the last five minutes in her purse. "None of this is ideal. But... Off the record?"

I nodded.

"Dig up some shit on her and blackmail her back. I know people who can get you the things you need. Obviously, this is not my advice as a *lawyer*, but there is not one person in this world that is squeaky clean. And once you have that? It's in the bag."

"You're willing to help me if I get it?"

"Willing?" She laughed. "I will be happy to. Let's call it my specialty."

A burst of confidence sprouted in me. "Perfect. But I don't need anyone. I have an information broker, and she's dangerous enough as it is. I don't need more of them hanging around."

Laura's lips twitched as if she wanted to smile, but instead, she just nodded and headed to the door, her heels clicking against the floor as she went.

Once the door was shut behind her, I let myself unravel. Groaning, I placed my head in my hands.

I didn't want things to go this far, but I would not allow

Bella to spend time in my mother's house if I could help it. Not only did Bella obviously hate and fear her, but I knew what my mom would do to her behind closed doors.

She was never physical, but damn, was she able to inflict some emotional wounds.

I allowed myself a few minutes to breathe. To take in everything and make sure that what I wanted to do was get that crazy bitch involved.

There was only one possible answer.

I picked up my phone, clicking on her contact, and she picked up on the second ring.

"I need you to get me all the blackmail you can on my mother," I said, not even wasting time on a hello. "The worse, the better, and I need it all within a day or two. As fast as you can get it. Hell, if you can get it today, I'll pay you triple."

There was a little chuckle on the other end.

"What makes you think I haven't been preparing for this very moment since I met you?"

Her response struck me, and I sat up straight.

"Do you collect blackmail on all your clients' families?"

"No." Her voice sounded amused. "Only the crazy ones. But I'm busy today. I'll be over tomorrow morning."

Before I could say anything else, she hung up, and I was stuck there trying to figure out if the can of worms I just opened would be worth it.

Chapter 27
Juliette

"There's no way this is real," Lux said, staring down at the petite woman who sat on the other end of the table. Bella was due to be at her mother's house in less than an hour, and somehow the girl in front of us was going to save her.

Her pitch-black hair was cut in a bob with bangs. She wore an oversized hoodie that was at least three sizes too big on her as well as baggy jeans that hid her figure. On her neck was a pair of headphones, and on her back a large backpack, which I quickly came to learn had multiple laptops and documents inside, along with blown-up pictures that now lay in front of us on the counter.

Her name was Mia, and she was apparently our saving grace.

"Yep," she said, popping the *p*. "Your mother cheated on both her partners with each other and was surprised when they both left her because of it. Your father is still alive and tried to fight her for custody, but she did some shady shit just like she's trying to do with Bella. All details are in the file. And that's not even half of it. If you want to dive deeper on the "donations" she's been giving to some of these charity and school events, I could dig up some more stuff. Let's just say that it's more about paying off a few particular friends that have sway in her little community than actually wanting to do good."

Lux sat there stunned, and if I was being honest, I was just as stunned as her.

To be hit with the information so nonchalantly—that Lux's father had not abandoned her and that he had fought for custody of her—could not be easy.

Even worse, I knew that the small woman in front of me knew way more than she was letting on too.

I probably should've been scared of her, but I was mostly impressed. It wasn't easy to dig up this kind of information. And while her methods might have seemed a bit crazy and cluttered, she seemed to have a system and she knew all the whens and wheres of Lux's mother's timeline.

Bella was at my side, gripping my hand. Neither of us had the courage to leave her out of this meeting. She hadn't stopped crying since the showdown the day before. She even crawled into bed with us, seeking comfort.

And while Bella probably didn't fully understand what was going on, there was a renewed sense of hope between us.

It may be awful, but it's our only way out.

Mia looked at us expectantly.

"So, do you need more than that or...?"

"No, I think that will do it," Lux replied, though she sounded a little unsure, no doubt trying to digest what she'd just heard. Something was nagging at the back of my brain. I tried to push it away and leave this to Lux, but I couldn't help myself.

"Is there anything a little bit more illegal?" I asked. "Besides the shady donations?"

Lux gave me a look, but I couldn't tell if she was appreciative or skeptical.

Mia leaned forward, her eyebrows wagging. "Oh, you know, I have something. But this one's more of a rumor, so we're gonna need to get a little more proof if we want it to pack a punch."

"Tell us," Lux ordered.

"Nine years ago, she was driving under the influence, or at least that's what the records insinuate. She was never taken into custody, but she was in a car accident and later taken to the hospital. My guess is she either knew the policeman on the scene or sweet-talked him into taking her name out of the papers. Maybe both."

The world stood still.

There's no such thing as coincidence with my mother.

Lux had said those words to me before. My body caught up before my mind did, and I started to shake. I didn't want to believe it.

Nine years ago. Something had happened in my life nine years ago. Something that changed its whole trajectory. Something that still to this day affected every part of it.

"What else do you know about it?" I asked, trying to keep the horror out of my voice, my nails digging into my pants.

"Just that it was in New York and her car was totaled. In fact, the car seems to have disappeared altogether."

No.

There was absolutely no way Lux and I were connected by something so horrible.

But they died nine years ago.

The supposedly drunk driver was never found. It was in New York. It was labeled as a hit and run. I had grieved my parents, having to come to terms with the fact that their murderer might never be caught.

The universe had to be playing a fucking joke on me.

There's no way. I don't want to believe it. I can't.

"Get me those files," I said, looking at Mia. "I need them now. *Yesterday.*"

"For that, I need a lawyer," she replied with a grimace. "I can only go so far so fast. Now, if I had someone with credentials on my side..."

"I have one," Lux said. She reached her hand out to mine, squeezing it. The look she gave me told me our minds had gone to the same place. "She can help with whatever you need. She specializes in this apparently."

"Great!" Mia hopped off her seat. "Now, if you excuse me, I am going to get started on that for you. If you need to buy some time, you can always throw your father's situation—or the *donations*—in her face."

"I'll keep that in mind. Thank you," Lux said, gaze cast down to the blown-up photos Mia left behind.

The sound of the front door shutting echoed through the silent house. It felt heavy, like a hit to my chest.

"You don't think—"

"Come on, Bella," I told the child, maneuvering her off the chair. I regretted her even being a part of this conversation even more now. "We're not going to school today, but that doesn't mean you can slack on your homework."

"But it's still so early!" she exclaimed with a pout.

"And the earlier you finish, the earlier you can play," I reasoned, and this time she didn't fight me.

Lux was still looking at me, her gaze heavy. But I didn't want to meet her eyes for fear that I would give everything away. I needed time to digest this, to talk myself out of spiraling.

There's no way. There is no fucking way, and I refuse to believe it. Not just because of what it meant for my family, but what it would mean for Lux and me going forward. For Bella and me.

I could already feel it souring things between us. *And that somehow felt like my fault.*

But as I sat with Bella at the table and felt Lux watching from afar, I couldn't help but think of my parents. Of what their last minutes had been like. Of how terrifying it must have been. And how, if it were true, her mother had gotten away with it for years.

I thought about how she found my aunt. And how she was so hostile to me from the beginning.

Has she known who I am all along?

Maybe she already knew I was their daughter. Maybe her going to my aunt wasn't just to get dirt on me and Lux and just her way of doing damage control because it shocked her that her daughter and I had found each other and might be one step closer to figuring out who the fuck she really was.

Another voice in my head whispered something even worse.

Maybe it is truly just the world's most awful coincidence.

Maybe there wasn't a bigger scheme. Maybe there wasn't some villain trying to ruin my life and instead just a woman who wanted to cover up her crimes.

And all the while my mind kept going to one thing. *Can we make it through this?*

I tried to put on a brave face for Bella, but I could barely focus, and Lux saw right through me.

"Juliette, can I talk to you?"

Fuck. I looked up at Lux, trying not to show her just how afraid I was of this conversation.

"Does that mean I can go play outside?"

"Go ahead," Lux replied before calling, "Gina!" When she appeared around the corner with refreshments and a small snack for Bella, Lux added, "Can you watch her outside for a moment, please?"

"Of course! Let's go, girl." Bella took her hand and skipped off, happy not to have to deal with her homework, and Gina gave me one lingering glance before following her out.

I was silent as Lux took me to her office, but then as soon as the door closed, I couldn't help but spill everything that had been crowding my mind since the information broker showed up.

It was a nonstop tumble of every single thought in my head. Everything from her mom and her dad, how sorry I felt for her, how worried I was for Bella, and then finally, when I got to the car accident, I paused.

"What else, Angel? Tell me."

"I can't... It can't be, right? Nine years ago. New York. My parents." Lux nodded, moving closer. "Did your mother..."

I couldn't bring myself to finish that sentence as I grabbed her shirt. Tears were already filling my eyes.

Lux's expression had never wavered, only showing me the calm, collected version of her. But when she finally spoke, my heart sank down to my feet, creating a chasm where it once was. A blackened, dark hole void of hope.

"I think it would be fucking crazy if it's true. But... Angel, she's a horrible person. I wouldn't put it past her to have taken a few lives. So let's wait to see what Laura and Mia can dig up, okay? We can't get carried away. Right now, we need to focus on keeping Bella here. We can figure out the accident later." She held my chin, making me look at her. "And if it's true, we'll deal with it together."

I nodded and leaned against her chest, inhaling deeply. *In and out. In and out.* Just like I taught Bella. I let her warmth and sureness envelop me, finding comfort in her. I pushed away everything else.

It was just me and her. And all we wanted to do was keep the little girl we loved safe. That was it. That was our reason, and I just needed to focus on it.

Though I had a feeling that I would need something much stronger than breathing exercises to get me through the next twenty-four hours.

Chapter 28
Lux

There was one thing I knew about my mother, and it's that she would always try to find a way to surprise me.

Not this time, though. I knew it was coming when we failed to drop Bella off at her house the day before. The only thing that surprised me was that she hadn't come sooner.

I had taken Bella out of school for the week while we sorted this out. The last thing I wanted was for her to show up there and actually kidnap the little girl. After I saw her at the park attempting to do just that, I just didn't trust Bella out of my sight.

My mother had been blowing up my phone since the day before. Calling, texting, leaving threatening voice messages I forwarded to my lawyer, until finally I just went ahead and blocked her completely. She then got a hold of Juliette's number—I didn't have to wonder from whom—and started doing the same until she blocked her as well.

Luckily, she didn't know how to use social media for the most part, so she hadn't found any of our profiles, but honestly, it was only a matter of time. She was nothing if not persistent.

I got up from my place on the couch while Juliette and Bella shot me worried glances. They were huddled together under a blanket and had controllers in their hands, but they'd paused the game they'd started playing after getting up at the crack of dawn.

We knew this was coming. We could handle it.

We had opted to stay inside for the day for fear that she might get to Bella somehow—or find someone to do it for her. Paranoid behavior maybe, but... who knew?

"If you keep this up, I'm calling the cops," I threatened, and the pounding stopped immediately.

"If you do, I'll tell them the dirty secrets you're hiding!" she yelled, her voice raising an octave. "Do you think they'll let you keep Bella then?"

I opened the door and crossed my arms, blocking her way in case she meant to walk in.

"I have rightful custody," I explained. "You taking her would *literally* be kidnapping."

"I'm saving her!"

I exhaled and pinched the bridge of my nose with my fingers.

"I suggest you stop this," I said, trying to keep my voice calm. I had to buy Mia and Laura time to find out the rest. "Unless you want me to bring up your fake donations to the children's center to the police. Or maybe the influence those *donations* buy you? Orange isn't really your color. And, oh my, what would your friends think? I can't imagine."

"What are you talking about?" she asked, but there was a hint of alarm to her voice that told me Mia's information was spot on.

"You heard me. And that's just the tip of the iceberg. Want

to threaten me with my relationship with Juliette and how we met? That's fine, I can dig up your skeletons too. So go ahead, yell louder."

She stood there, fuming.

"I'm taking you to court," she finally said, and then paused as if she was waiting for me to beg and plead her to stop.

Not going to happen.

"If you do, I'll spill *everything* I know."

She let out a huff before turning away, stomping. The next sound we heard was the slam of her car door.

Juliette came up behind me, her hand running up my back. My shoulders sagged immediately. Even just the smallest of her touches could stop the whirlwind my mind was going through.

"We have a meeting with Laura and Mia soon. Let's get everyone ready, hm?"

I nodded and let her bring me back into the living room, where Bella was back to playing her game as if she hadn't heard anything that had just gone down with her grandmother.

She's so strong. If I were in her position, I wouldn't know what to do. Nor would I be able to emotionally handle it.

"It's okay, Aunt Lux," she said, just barely looking up from her game. "I'm not going to freak out anymore. I trust you and Juliette and that weird lady you invited to the house."

I didn't trust Mia. Not one bit, but I knew she'd deliver.

"You can trust me and Juliette, forget about the other girl." I patted the top of her head gently. "But she will be useful, so let's get ready to go meet them."

"Okay!" she chirped and turned back to the game, hastily slamming her fingers on the buttons.

I gave her a weak smile, but I couldn't bring myself to be positive yet. I had won this battle, but the threat was still there, looming over us.

I have to beat her. I have to keep us safe.

Suddenly, Juliette was there by my side, her hand gripping mine. It was the strength I needed to keep going.

"I love some good ol' blackmail," Laura singsonged as she looked at the iPad Mia handed her with all the juicy details on my mother's drunk-driving experience.

"Drunk driving, indeed," Mia said as she looked at us.

I held onto Juliette's hand, feeling the nerves through our touch. As much as I wanted shit on my mother, I didn't want it to turn to this. Juliette didn't deserve this. If what we thought was true, there was no making light of this situation.

The lack of sleep was weighing on me, the stress and pressure of it all making it even worse.

We had decided to visit Laura's office to make this more official. Mia was sitting on a chair next to her, handing her anything relevant, while Juliette and I sat in front of them. Bella was originally behind us, supposed to be doing extra homework, but she got bored and went into the waiting room to play with Laura's assistant.

I didn't want to let her out of my sight, but as long as I could hear them, it made me feel much more at ease.

"There's not much here that proves it was her, though," Laura said. "Do you have anything from the cop that got her off?"

Mia leaned over and started scrolling on the iPad before coming to a pause. Laura's eyes widened.

"It would seem like this cop was investigated multiple times for misconduct, especially related to letting women go for a little bit of action," Laura explained, annoyance clear in her voice.

Disgust filled me. I really didn't want to hear what my mother would do to get out of jail, but if it meant I could keep Bella, I would.

I knew my mom was awful, but I never knew she would stoop so low.

She likely killed people, for God's sake. And she just walked around every single day of her life, not giving a fuck.

"Can you just be straight with me?" Juliette asked, leaning forward. "My parents died in a drunk-driving accident that same year, and I need to know if this is just a weird coincidence."

Laura let out a hum, her eyes looking over Juliette. Mia was the one who scrolled back on the iPad and started reading all the information.

"It was at night, on 124th Street. Two victims, a couple. They were taken to the hospital, but they didn't make it. Their names have been blacked out of this report... Which is a bit weird," she added with a frown.

"She could have paid someone or traded another favor to get this blacked out." Laura said it and shrugged like it was no big deal as she kept scrolling. "You'd be surprised with what some people are willing to do for so little."

"I'll get you the names," Mia vowed, her brows furrowed as she grabbed her phone. "I have a contact I'll reach out to."

Juliette nodded and leaned back in her chair. She was barely breathing.

This is my fault.

Realistically, I knew my mother's actions had nothing to do with me, but I couldn't help but think that if I hadn't bought her at the auction that very first night, she would never have had to go through this.

But then I wouldn't have her.

All it took was that thought to stop me from blaming myself.

"I know it's not much, but does that information match?" Laura asked, her eyes never leaving Juliette. Lawyers were usually perceptive, but I had a feeling Laura was looking straight into Juliette's soul.

"The more I think about it, the less sure I am," she replied, her voice shaking. "I was young, and it was a long time ago. I don't remember where they said it happened. I mostly remember my reaction to the police showing up at our door."

I let my hand trail up her arm and rubbed her shoulders, a soothing gesture I hoped provided her with some sort of comfort.

"It's okay," I said in a soft voice. She nodded, but I could feel that she was just putting on a brave face for everyone else. Inside, she was barely hanging on.

Seeing her this way gutted me. Regardless of whether it had been my mother, the emotional torment she was putting us through made me hate her even more.

There was nothing I could do to help remedy this situation. We needed to know the truth, and while I couldn't bring her parents back, I damn well was going to try to get my mother to pay for it.

Mia's phone started vibrating, and she stood up, hastily leaving the room.

"It's not what I usually do," Laura started. "But if you need help with a civil suit, or maybe we could even go as far as bringing charges against her, I'll try everything in my power."

Juliette nodded and gave her a weak smile.

"If it's true... I'm not sure what I want at this point. I need to talk to my brother but also... Knowing that she tried to get close to my aunt—my family—just makes it all feel even more sickening."

Her eyes shifted to me, and I wished I could do something. *Anything*. Knowing I would do anything for her but having my hands tied like this was killing me. I felt so useless.

Mia walked back into the room, her face sullen. All of us turned to look at her. Juliette let out a pained noise as if she could read the answer on her face.

"Hayes. Trish and James Hayes."

Chapter 29
Juliette

"**G**oing for the good stuff this time, huh?"

I looked up at Lux with a forced smile. There was a bottle of red wine in my hand and I was drinking straight from it. I had taken her advice on raiding the wine cellar, and while I didn't know what I got, from the silky taste of it on my tongue, I knew it must've been expensive.

I handed it to her as she sat by me.

The air was warming, but I still opted for a light sweater and sweat shorts. Lux was dressed in her normal silk pajamas.

I wanted nothing more than to climb onto her lap, straddle her, and bring her lips to mine to forget everything that had happened over the last few days.

There was so much buzzing around my mind that it felt like I could only rely on the red wine in my hand and the feel of her lips against mine. The only two constants in this world. The only two things that had the ability to make me forget the outside world.

Her hand found my bare thigh and she squeezed.

"We'll get her," she vowed, her voice taking a serious tone.

"Even if she's your mother? Even if it means putting her away?"

I took another swig and boldly looked up at her. She was already staring at me. I expected her to frown at my obvious attempt to fight, but she just smiled.

"I love you, Juliette."

All the air was sucked right out of my lungs. My skin heated unbearably, and I sputtered for a response, but my mind was at a complete standstill.

"Wait, that's how you're choosing to confess your undying love to me? Now?" I asked, my voice raising.

Her smile only widened, and she shifted so she could put an arm around my shoulders.

"I love you, Juliette," she repeated, leaning closer to me to grab the bottle and place it on the table, not far from us. I was rendered speechless.

Her hand cupped my face, her thumb grazing my cheek.

"I. Love. *You.*"

There was emphasis on each word, all of them packing their own separate punch.

My eyes stung. *Why am I going to cry right now?*

"I love *you.*"

"Can you stop saying that?" I muttered weakly. Her eyes traveled my face like she could read every emotion I was feeling.

"I'm going to keep saying it until you realize that it doesn't matter what happens to her. Doesn't matter if she goes to jail or has to pay millions of dollars in fines or if she disappears off the face of the fucking planet because of it. I love you, and I would do anything to bring your parents' murderer to justice."

I couldn't stop it then. The tears were already falling.

Lux easily pulled me to her, maneuvering me so I was

straddling her and forced to look her in the eyes. Her hands gripped my hips, holding me steady.

"Are you sure?" I asked, my voice hollow.

There was one thing I didn't expect to come out of this—the guilt. I expected the anger, the sadness, and even the shock, but nothing could prepare me for the amount of guilt I felt.

The accident had nothing to do with me. I had been a seventeen-year-old at home with her little brother. But somehow, as it all went down, I felt responsible for what was going to happen to Lux's mother and Bella's grandmother.

I felt like I had the power to make this as easy as possible for them. That maybe if I could just turn the other way and pretend it didn't happen, they'd be able to live a normal life where their grandmother didn't kill people.

Because I loved Lux too. I loved Bella. We had created a little family I didn't know I needed. A little family that seventeen-year-old me would've died for.

My entire life, I'd had to beg people to pay attention. To love me. To even look my way.

To be loved and seen had been my greatest desire and biggest fear in this world. And Lux was here, giving me all of it. I didn't even have to ask her.

And that was why I felt unbearably guilty.

Because I didn't deserve it. I didn't deserve this level of love. I did nothing for her, but here she was, trying to help me. Trying to change my life at the expense of her own.

"Tell me what you're thinking, Angel." She said it in a low tone that made me want to spill everything.

"Is that a command, *sir*?"

Her eyes snapped up to mine at that question.

"No, Juliette. But I would really like to know. Would you indulge me?" When I didn't speak right away, she tacked on, "Please?"

I swallowed thickly.

"I want to take her to court," I admitted in a whisper. Fear crept up my back, and I couldn't look at her, so she brought her finger to my chin, forcing me to.

"I'm not going to get mad at you," she said. "I truly don't care what happens to her. I care about what happens to you. To *us*."

"Are you just saying that to make me feel better?"

Her jaw tensed.

"Is that what you really think?" she asked. "Would I lie to you?"

"I can't tell what you're thinking." I shrugged, and we both knew I was the liar in this equation. Even if she wasn't telling me how much she loved me in words, it was written all over her face. It might be hard for me to read her at times, but not this time. This time it was clear.

I was the one holding us back. There was this invisible wall between us. I could feel Lux trying to break it down, but it was a two-person job, and for some reason, I couldn't help her.

Yet.

That single word brought me comfort.

"I'm thinking you don't want to believe anyone can love you this much." Her words were an arrow straight to my heart. "That you can't believe what I'm saying. That I would give up my family for you. That I would burn it all to the fucking ground for you."

"I can't," I admitted. "Believe it, I mean."

"I'm not giving up anything, Juliette. I don't want her in my or Bella's life. In *our* life."

"But she's your moth—"

She pulled me closer. "And you're the love of my life. Even if it came down to a choice between you two, there's no doubt in my mind who I would pick every time."

I placed my forehead against her, closing my eyes and inhaling her scent deeply.

"Why are you pulling away from me?" she asked.

"I'm right here," I whispered.

"You know what I mean," she said. "I thought out of the two of us, I was the one who had trouble sharing my emotions."

She was right, of course. But how could I have seen any of this coming, let alone know how to deal with it?

I didn't want to say any of that, so instead I moved forward and captured her lips with mine. She didn't move at first but then slowly started kissing me back.

I used it as a sign to take things further, and I tangled my hands in her hair. She groaned against my mouth as she let me in. The world fell away around us as I explored her mouth and her hands traveled my body just like I knew they would. We couldn't stay away from each other for long.

But then she pulled away.

"Juliette, if you don't want to have this conversation, I understand. But I don't want to use what we have as a way to just stop talking about it."

"I want you," I said and touched my lips back to hers, my hands already pulling up my sweater, but she pulled back again, her hands on my face.

"Check-in. What are you feeling right now? Red, yellow, green."

It was the first time she was using the stop system with me, but I know it was common in other BDSM relationships.

"Green, of course," I replied and dove back in, but she evaded my kiss.

Frustrated, I tried again, barely catching her lips before she murmured against mine, "Bubblegum."

I jerked back, rejection and betrayal flooding my system. She met me with a slight frown.

"I'm sorry," I said as I tried to crawl off her, but her hands were holding me steady again.

"Angel, it's been a long day. A long, *traumatic* day." Her voice was soft. "I think we both need some rest and tomorrow we can try again."

This time she let me climb off her, but she followed, standing up. She took my hand, leading me into the house, and stopped by my bedroom door. The one I hadn't slept in since we got together.

I paused, not knowing what to say, as she retreated to her door and opened it, giving me one last glance.

"Get some rest, Juliette. Remember what I said."

And then she went in, leaving her door just a smidge open. Letting me know I was welcome to come in.

Remember what I said?

A lot of things had been said that night, but I knew she meant those three words. *I love you.* Something I hadn't said back or I felt like I deserved.

My hand gripped my doorknob, the cool metal burning its way up my arm and dousing my heated skin.

What am I doing?

I forced myself into my room, closing the door behind me, but I didn't even make it to the bed before I was falling to the ground, the tears finally spilling from my eyes.

How am I going to do this? How are we going to do this?

I didn't know if I could handle it. Sitting there in the dark, tears streaming down my face and silent sobs racking my body, I knew for a fact that I couldn't. That maybe I wasn't strong enough for this.

And both Bella and Lux deserved someone stronger than me.

Chapter 30
Lux

"I quit."

I knew we needed to have a conversation in the morning, but I didn't expect this.

It had been hard rejecting her last night, but I knew it wasn't right. If not for her, then definitely for me. I didn't want to turn sex between us into something dirty. Into something used to escape.

And now...

Fuck.

I looked up from my phone and into Juliette's eyes. Her hair was up in a bun today and she wore a simple crewneck and sweats. Her puffy eyes told me she'd spent most of the night crying. It hurt my heart to see it. I left my door open in case she needed to talk—hoping she did—but when she didn't come in, I took it as a sign that she didn't want me around.

In her hands, she had a single white paper that she placed in front of me. It was the first time a nanny was giving me notice instead of me firing them. I took the paper, reading it

quickly. There wasn't much on it, but the first sentence caught me off guard.

Instead of a two-week notice, it was a *two-day* notice, letting me know she was quitting her job and moving out.

Everything came crashing down. All my hopes, wishes, dreams, and I was left to feel the destruction of it all.

It hurt like a bitch. I put myself out there, and all it got me was pain.

But I didn't blame her. She didn't need to be around the daughter of the woman who murdered her parents and made her life a living hell. I might have made it my mission to make her mine, but I would never force her to stay in a situation where she was uncomfortable.

No one could've expected the tragedy that tied us together. Maybe it was why we were pulled together from the beginning. Maybe it was the universe simply trying to repair its mistakes instead of giving me something unbelievable like I originally thought.

The only things running through my mind were selfish thoughts.

I want to tell her that I loved her and that no matter how far she went, she couldn't change what we had. That she would realize it and find her way back.

I wanted to remind her how good we were together. How it felt like we were made for each other.

Then my mind went somewhere else. It panicked. Selfish thoughts turned into desperation.

I wanted to beg her to stay. I wanted to tell her that I needed her more than I had ever needed anyone in my life. That she was the most perfect person for me, and I could not even imagine a life with anyone else. That I would be lonely for the rest of my life if I couldn't be with her.

I wanted to tell her that Bella needed her just as much as I did. That she'd never been happier. That she looked forward to waking up every day just so she could get her hair done by her. That she loved it when she took her to school and they could have their alone time together.

That Bella told me not to mess this up. And even if I tried my best, it still felt like I did.

But I couldn't bring myself to say any of it because it felt disgusting of me to try and keep her when she needed to go.

So I stared at the paper. Bella wasn't up yet, thankfully, but I didn't know how I would explain this. Especially when I already felt the emotions clogging my throat.

"I can have Gina or someone help you pack your stuff," I finally offered, looking back up to her.

Her eyebrows were pulled together, and her eyes showed me the pain her words never would. I felt like there was a wall erected between us, and it was so thick I couldn't possibly reach over and take her hands like I wanted to. My fingers flexed, my body trying to fight back, trying to fix this somehow.

"No need," she replied. "I actually packed all of it last night, and today, while Bella is at school, I'll move everything out to an apartment I got for me and my brother."

I nodded, though I was shocked to hear that she and her brother had reconciled enough that they could move in together.

"We can still continue with Laura," I said, hoping she'd take me up on the offer just so I could be near her again.

It was her turn to nod. "Please see it through. I'll show up at the trial if it gets to that."

I deflated immediately.

"Are you sure this is what you want?" I asked, my voice a whisper. I reached out to grab her hand but stopped myself at the last second.

This is your last chance, my heart told my brain. But my brain knew that she had already been through too much.

She paused. "No," she admitted in a soft voice. "But I don't... I think I need some time. Is that... okay?"

"It's more than okay."

The careful mask she had been wearing started to crumble, and I was up, pulling her into my arms.

"I'm so sorry, Juliette," I said. "I never wanted anything like this to happen and I'm so sorry for my involvement in it."

She sniffled, the sound breaking my heart even further.

"You did nothing but be born to an awful woman." She buried her face against my chest. "I don't want this to end."

"It doesn't have to," I said, desperation leaking into my voice. "You take all the time you need, and I'll be here, waiting for you."

She pulled away and looked up at me, using her hand to wipe away a few stray tears.

"Looks like you're going to have to find a new nanny." She tried to smile, but it was weak. As was the half-hearted smile I gave her.

"No one could ever live up to you," I admitted.

She had changed everything.

From the moment she came into my life, work, money, the company—it all started to take a backseat.

Over the last few months, I had been intentionally delegating more and more stuff to my team and, of course, to Dominic. He complained a little bit, but I know he liked the power that came with it.

Just as I liked the freedom. It meant that I could spend more time with them—my family. Weekends. Trips. Having lunch with them whenever I wanted.

It meant I didn't have to worry about choosing between

them and work because after the last half year, they would always come first.

"What are you going to do?" she asked.

"Don't worry about us," I said, and reached out to grab a lock of her hair, twirling it around my finger. "You focus on yourself."

She brought her bottom lip between her teeth.

"Lux, what you said last night... I want to tell you that I—"

I covered her mouth with mine, stopping her words. It was a quick kiss before I was pulling back.

"Tell me when you come back."

It was a selfish request. One that would save me from likely breaking down in front of her and Bella.

I didn't know what would be worse. Her leaving without telling me she loved me or telling me she loved me but still choosing to leave anyway.

She hesitated and nodded just as Bella bounced into the kitchen.

"Juliette, can I have twin fishtails today?"

Juliette looked down at her as she came in, forcing a smile.

"Of course you can't, sweetheart."

I sat down, folding Juliette's resignation and hiding it in my pocket. And then I watched them, knowing this might be the last breakfast we had together.

"Why are you here?" Bella asked from the backseat.

She glared at me slightly through the rearview mirror, already coming to a conclusion that was probably not too far from the truth.

"Can't I pick you up after school and take you to your favorite diner?" I asked.

But she still looked at me suspiciously.

"Where is Juliette?"

I took a deep breath as I pulled away from the school. I really didn't want to have this conversation.

"Did you fire her or something?"

"I did not." I looked back in the rearview mirror and she was pouting. "But she's going to be taking a break for a while."

"How long?"

I paused. I didn't want to lie to her, but I also didn't want to tell her, or admit to myself, that there was a possibility that she might never come back.

"However long she needs," I replied. "Until then, I will be working from home again."

There was a silence before she demanded, "Take me home. I want to see her."

"Are you sure you don't want to get some pie—"

"No," she growled. "I don't want any *stupid* pie."

I stayed silent the rest of the way, unable to tell her that when she opened the door, Juliette would not be there waiting for her.

As soon as I parked, she unbuckled herself, jumped out of the car, and stormed into the house.

I followed her, quickly catching sight of her as she went to the kitchen and then looked at the backyard before disappearing into the hallway that connected our rooms.

She was there for quite some time before I heard the shuffle of her feet.

When she reappeared, her eyes were on the floor and her shoulders sagged. The fight and anger had disappeared.

She didn't move, just stood there, staring at the floor, so I walked up to her and knelt. My hands came to her arms, and I rubbed them up and down in an attempt to be comforting.

"It's because of Grandma, isn't it?"

I couldn't lie to her, so I said, "That's right."

"What's drunk driving?" she asked. I was a bit surprised that she hadn't asked before, but I was also kicking myself for letting her hear any of our conversations.

"When people drink alcohol, they can get drunk. It makes your head woozy, like you can't think clearly. It's not easy to stand or do much, let alone drive. So drunk driving is very dangerous."

"But couldn't she just stay?" she asked. "Does she hate drunk driving so much that she's willing to leave us for something Grandma did? She didn't even say goodbye."

I pursed my lips.

"Did Juliette ever tell you she lost her parents too?" She nodded, her eyes shifting to mine. "It was an accident with a drunk driver," I explained. "So it brings up a lot of not-great feelings."

"What if we tell her that Grandma's not coming back?" she asked. "Do you think she'd come back?"

The truth was that we needed to end this. Even with the blackmail, we needed to gather evidence on her and take her to trial. There was no telling how Juliette would feel afterwards, and I was not about to tell my eight-year-old niece that her grandma had killed Juliette's parents.

"Sometimes people just need time," I said.

"Did you ask her to stay?"

I swallowed the knot in my throat.

"I did."

Finally, the tears started welling in her eyes. She threw her arms around my neck and held onto me for dear life as she sobbed into my shoulder.

"I know," I whispered, finally letting the tears that had been lingering since last night fill my eyes. "I'll miss her too."

Chapter 31
Juliette

I lied to her. I wasn't going to live with my brother. He was actually still living with my aunt.

I was going back to the place where I'd felt most comfortable.

Well, not the same *place*, but the same *people*.

"Jules is back!" Harmony screamed as I entered, holding champagne in both hands.

I'd actually been here for a few days already, but this was the first time everyone was back together again. Moving back in with them wasn't ideal since they had only rented a three-bedroom house, so I was stuck on the couch. But honestly, as long as I was with them, I felt a little better.

I didn't know if I could handle being alone at the moment.

Erin and April were already sitting at the small circular table they had stolen from the landlady's house. They had a glass of champagne and small pastries sitting in front of them.

I couldn't help but smile as I took the champagne from Harmony.

281

"So you got fired from the nanny job," Erin said as she picked apart a croissant.

"I quit." I raised my glass in a small toast before taking a sip of my champagne.

"Wasn't it like some rich family though?" Harmony asked and motioned for me to sit down at the empty seat at the table. She stood with her back against the small kitchen counter.

"She was pretty rich. She was taking care of her niece, unfortunately. Her parents passed away in a tragic accident."

Damn it. My voice cracked toward the end. I hoped it went unnoticed, but as soon as I looked up at my ex-now-current roommates, they all had the same look on their faces.

"Why'd you quit?" Erin asked, never one to ignore the elephant in the room.

"I... uh... thought it would just be better to move on," I said, chewing on a piece of the overly sweet donut.

Silence.

"Oh my God! You fucked your boss!"

"Harmony! I did not!" I sputtered, heat automatically rushing to my face.

April let out a small squeak, and Erin let out a mock scandalized gasp.

"Oh, you *totally* did." Erin's grin made her look like a feral cat. "Did it get too real? Did your employer find out? No, let me guess—she turned out to be awful?"

I couldn't find the words, so I slammed my mouth shut. I didn't want to think about Lux. Especially in that way. If I was being honest, I wanted to try and forget her as much as possible.

It had only been a few days, but I missed her more than I cared to admit to myself. And every night I lay on that couch, I looked up at the ceiling and thought of how much of a mistake I'd made to leave her and Bella.

I wondered if Bella was being well taken care of. If Lux was overwhelmed again. If both of them were getting their emotional needs met.

And mostly, I just wanted to be with them.

My eyes stung with unshed tears.

"Guys," April whispered.

"Was she a hot MILF?" Harmony asked in a conspiratorial tone.

"I don't think she's technically a MILF," Erin muttered.

"I mean, she has a kid now, so it counts—"

"Guys, stop! Look at her!"

All eyes were on me, and they watched as I quickly broke down in front of them.

I couldn't hold in my sobs anymore.

"Oh shit. Oh no. Juliette, I'm so sorry."

Harmony was by my side in a second, wrapping her arms around me. I took her hug, but it wasn't the hug that I wanted. I wanted to be back in Lux's arms. No other arms would do.

April came up to my other side and wrapped her arms around me while Erin grabbed my hand, squeezing it.

I let everything out. All the pain from reliving my parents' murder. The hurt from leaving Lux and Bella. The regret for not being able to tell Lux that I loved her too.

They might have just been roommates once upon a time, but they were the closest thing to friends I had.

"I'm sorry," I said through my sobs. When I tried to pull away, Harmony and April just held me tighter.

"Nothing to be sorry about." Harmony placed a chaste kiss on top of my head. "I shouldn't have said that stuff. You know sometimes I don't really think before I speak."

"Obviously," Erin muttered.

"You're not any better," April spat, though her voice didn't hold much weight.

When they finally let me pull back, I took a deep breath.

"I may or may not have fallen in love with her," I whispered. "And it got complicated, so I... I just need some time, I guess."

All eyes were on me, and after a moment, I felt uncomfortable with all the stares.

"I think I know what we need," Harmony said, her eyes narrowing on me.

"More booze?" Erin asked.

"A night on the town!"

I couldn't protest as I was dragged out of my seat and forced into Harmony's room.

It seemed like a bad idea, but maybe it would be the perfect way to forget.

I was wrong.

I took a sip of my margarita as I looked at the girls, all of them mingling with their preferred partner of the night. Harmony was dancing with hers while Erin and April were sitting at a booth, drinking with two suitors on each side.

I was the only one still lingering by the bar.

The club was classier than the ones I'd been to before. Dimly lit, music not too loud, small jade-colored lamps on every table. It was also the most expensive I'd been to in a minute.

I had thought it'd be good for me to forget, but every time I looked at how happy and inebriated people were, I kept thinking of Lux's mother.

I motioned for the bartender and paid all our tabs.

As I was signing the receipt, she looked over at my barely touched margarita.

"Can I get you something else instead?" she asked. "Hate for you to pay for something you hated."

I gave her a smile. "It was delicious, actually. I'm just..."

"Ready to go home?"

I nodded. "Something like that."

I handed the receipt back to her. As I turned back to let the girls know I was going to leave, a figure was there, blocking my sight.

Lux's mother. How the fuck did she find me here?

"Let's talk, shall we?"

She left without waiting to see if I was going to follow her. Because she knew I would.

I should text Lux and tell her, but something held me back.

Maybe I can get a confession.

I still hadn't heard from Lux or Laura, so maybe this was my chance to get something out of her. I could guess what she wanted from me. So I'd let her think she could get it.

On one condition.

I followed her out without a look back at my roommates.

She led me out of the bar and to a small bridge just across from it that overlooked the river. It was used mostly for pedestrians with a two-way lane for cars. Not many people were crowding it, so it gave us enough privacy to talk.

She leaned against the railing, looking down at the river. The sound of it lapping against the bridge and rocks below hit my ears.

"I'm glad you got out of there," she said. "My daughter ruins everything she touches."

Unable to help myself, I snapped back, "Must get that from you."

"Such confidence for a nanny."

"Not one anymore. What do you want?"

She turned to me.

"I want you to go and convince Lux to let me see my grand-daughter."

I let out a laugh. "Are you serious? What finally made you realize your scheming wouldn't work?"

"It's not *scheming* if I'm trying to save my grandchild from *her*," she spat.

The small bit of alcohol that had been dormant in my system until then decided to show itself. Feeling a burst of confidence, I leaned closer, dropping my voice to a whisper.

"Bella is better off with Lux than a murderer," I hissed.

She stared at me for a second, her face giving nothing away.

"Lux is spinning tales again, isn't she?"

Anger flared through me.

"You can lie to the police, you can lie to your kids, but you *cannot* lie to me," I said, my voice raising of its own accord.

Her nostrils flared then, the only sign I got that she was angry.

"Who do you think you are?"

"The daughter of the people you murdered while you were driving drunk."

Her eyes widened for just a fraction, and then she was back to looking out at the river, her hand gripping the railing so tight her knuckles turned white.

"And here I thought you knew all along," I said, taking a step back. She refused to look at me again, confirming what I said. "Lux is coming after you. If you know what's good for you, drop any attempt at a custody battle. It won't look good for you."

I turned away, grabbing my phone from my pocket to call Lux.

Seeing her mother in person and giving her a piece of my

mind had given me a strength I didn't know I had. I was going to get that bitch, and nothing she could do would stop me from being with the love of my lif—

Pain erupted from the back of my head. My phone clattered to the sidewalk. Ringing exploded in my head. Black spots flashed across my vision.

What?

I stumbled against the railing, the only flimsy thing keeping me from falling into the cold depths below.

I forced myself to take deep breaths through the pain, but it was too much. I tried to scream, but my entire body was uncooperative. Useless. My eyes shot to the ground. There was a rock lying there. Blood on it. I could just barely make it out with my fucked-up vision.

There was no one else around besides her mother. No one to help me. No one to save me.

My body felt like it was getting weaker by the second. My stomach lurched.

Move. Move NOW.

I tried to put one foot in front of the other, but my ankles buckled.

Hands gripped me, forcing me up. Hands with cool rings that stung against my heated skin.

No. I hung onto the railing for dear life, but she was stronger than me. I was forced over, my eyes meeting the black water below.

Stop, please. Someone save me—

And then I was falling. I had no control over it. The last of my strength had been used to hold onto the railing, and she had pried my hands from it.

I'm going to die.

Even in my stupor, I knew there was no way I would survive a swim in the river.

I'm going to drown.

No. Not here. Not now. Not when I still haven't told her.

My arms flayed. I grabbed onto something rough. My nails dug into it, searing pain stemming from it. But I didn't let go.

I looked up to see her mother in the light. She looked crazed, wide-eyed and breathing heavily. For the first time I saw her perfect mask crack.

Her hair was a mess, her shirt rumpled by the effort it took to push me off the bridge.

"Just fucking die, you useless—"

I let out a cry as her heel crushed my fingers. I swung my other arm up, gripping the lip just as my other hand dropped.

She moved quickly to stomp on the other one.

"I'm not going to jail for this!"

No, she won't.

I realized in that moment she would probably continue to get away with whatever she wanted, regardless of how bad the crime was. People like her always did.

She killed my parents, and now I was next.

I wish I had told Lux I love her.

My hand slipped from the ledge, and time slowed. I was falling again. And this time, there would be no stopping it.

She looked down at me with a vindictive gaze. She knew she had won. I closed my eyes, ready for the impact of hitting the water, but it never came.

Warm fingers grabbed my wrist and yanked, pulling me against the hard rock of the bridge. I gasped and looked up to see that someone's arm had slipped through the bottom railing just in time to grab my wrist.

The person was lying on the ground, their shoulder hanging off the bridge as they held onto me. When their other hand came to grab me, I saw the beautiful brown eyes that changed my life.

The ones I fell in love with all those nights ago. The ones I saw when I went to sleep at night.

"Hang on, Juliette!"

"Lux!" I cried, my voice hoarse.

She came.

She gritted her teeth and began to pull me up. But she wasn't alone. People had seen or heard me, and they were there too. Bystanders were helping pull me up.

Saving me.

A silly thought passed my mind as I was pulled back onto the bridge.

I never had a large group of people care for me before.

They swarmed me, Lux at the forefront. I made out my ex-roommates toward the back of the crowd rushing to get to me.

"An ambulance is on the way!"

"Yes, we're right on the pedestrian bridge—"

"I saw her get pushed over!"

Lux's hands were on my face, holding me close. They were shaking. Tears filled her eyes.

"Oh, thank God," she said. "I got here in time. I made it, Juliette."

I gave her a weak smile. My head was pounding so hard it felt like it was going to rip my skull in two.

"You saved me," I forced out and fell into her chest. Her hands left my face, and I caught sight of how bloodied they were as they retreated. But I couldn't care. Not when she was here.

"Juliette?"

My vision blackened. I looked up at Lux, her face barely visible.

"I need to tell you something."

"Later," she said, her voice hitched. She looked around at

what I assumed was the crowd, but I couldn't see them anymore. "When's the ambulance coming?"

"Lux," I forced out, calling her attention back to me. "I love you too. I'm sorry I couldn't say it earlier."

"Stop saying that," she said. "I don't want to hear you say sorry ever again."

"But I need to say it." My eyelids fluttered closed. "I love you."

"Juliette? Stay with me!"

I could vaguely feel her hands on me. But everything was getting colder.

"I love *you*," I forced out, just as her muffled voice sounded again.

"I... love... *you*."

Chapter 32
Juliette

Beep. Beep. Beep.

I peeled my eyes open, bright light entering my vision and forcing me to close them right away.

My head was still pounding, though much less than after—

My eyes popped open again. I looked around, noting that I was in a hospital room.

I'm alive.

My eyes settled on the lump of a person with her head in her arms on the edge of my bed.

Lux. Her shiny black hair was a mess around her head. Her clothes rumpled and stained. Maybe blood.

My blood?

I took a moment to look at her. To *truly* look at her.

I could just make out her face. The bags under her eyes. The paleness of her skin. She must have been by my side for a while.

How long have I been here?

She came for me.

I lay there for a moment, thinking through everything that had happened.

I never thought her mother would come after me like that. That she would try to kill me. That she would almost succeed, or how scared I'd been.

Suddenly, everything I had been worried about felt like nothing at all. It all fell away.

In that moment, all I could think about was how much I loved Lux and how I should've told her from the beginning instead of running away.

It didn't matter that she was my boss—to be honest, did it ever? Didn't matter how complicated things were with her mother and the death of my parents. Didn't matter if people found out about the BDSM club. That brought me Lux. Let people think whatever the hell they wanted.

What mattered with us and Bella.

And in the moment when I was hanging off that bridge and my life was passing right before my eyes, all I could think about was them.

Being with them, living a life with them.

I will never leave them again.

I don't know how long I lay there just staring at Lux, but it must've been a while because a doctor peeked her head in the room. I motioned for her to be quiet as I reached out to touch Lux's hand, noticing for the first time my hand with all the IVs in it.

The doctor slowly shut the door behind her and walked to my side.

"Ms. Hayes, I'm happy to see you're awake," she whispered.

Lux didn't even twitch.

"How long have I been out?" My throat ached as I spoke.

"Just a little over twenty-four hours."

My eyes traveled to the covered windows. There was no

telling what time it was. The hospital's fluorescent light made it look like permanent daytime, and my body just felt exhausted, even after the long sleep.

"The police have been waiting for you," she said, her eyes shifting to Lux. "They wanted me to let them know as soon as you woke up."

I grimaced.

"Can I convince you to give us thirty minutes alone?"

She smiled and looked at her watch.

"Would you look at that? It's time for my lunch break," she said, and without another word, turned and left the room.

Hesitantly, I turned back to Lux and ran my fingers through her hair.

Her eyes fluttered open and shot to me. It took her a moment to realize what was happening, but then she jerked up, eyes wide, tears already filling them.

"Thank God, Juliette. Do you feel okay? Does anything hurt? Let me go get the docto—"

"She was just in," I said with a smile before grabbing her hand. "Thank you for saving me. I feel fine now."

Her expression changed.

"Juliette, I am so, so sor—"

"I love you," I said, cutting her off. "I'm the one who's sorry for not saying it sooner. I loved you then, and I love you now. I was just too afraid to say it. I can't believe it took me almost dying... Lux, I regret not saying it sooner—"

She was up and pulling me into her arms in seconds.

I sank into her, a feeling of calm washing over me.

This is it. This is all that matters. It's as simple as this.

"I love you too," she said and hugged me tight before suddenly pulling away. "Shit, does that hurt? Am I hurting you—"

"You're not, but even if you were, I'd be fine with that."

We stayed like that for a couple of minutes before she let go and sat back down, but she still reached for my hand.

"How did you find me?" I asked.

She flinched, the memory probably hitting her hard.

"I was following my mother," she said, and I frowned. "It's not like that. Ever since we found out what she did, Laura advised me to get someone to do that, but my thoughts were plaguing me, so I asked Gina to keep an eye on Bella and went myself too. I wasn't going inside the bar—in fact, I was about to leave when she came out with... *you*."

"So you saw everything... That must've been hard."

"Juliette... You were the one who was hit over the head and thrown off a bridge. How are you worried about *me*?" she replied, her eyes going watery again. "I'm so—"

I cupped her face.

"Yeah, it hurt like a bitch," I said with a smile. "But listen to me. None of it is your fault. *You* saved me. I wouldn't be here if it weren't for you."

She moved to kiss my lips, just lightly, touching my cheek like she couldn't believe I was there.

"Can you promise me something, though?" I asked.

"Anything."

"Can you please change your clothes? I really don't want to continue looking at my blood."

She looked down at herself before a smile pulled her lips.

"Anything for you, Angel. But can I do that when I'm sure you're not just going to disappear on me somehow?"

"You can. But I'm not going anywhere."

We sat there in silence for a moment, hands touching, just enjoying each other's company, but it wasn't long before there was a knock at the door.

"Come in," I said, and as soon as I did, the door burst open, and a little blur was running to me.

Bella climbed up on the bed before Lux had the chance to warn her about it, her panic and tear-stained face filling my vision. I opened my arms for her and let her climb into them. She buried her face in my chest, still sniffling.

"It's okay, sweetheart. I'm okay."

I brushed her hair with my fingers as she cried. It hurt a little bit with the IVs pulling on my arm, but I didn't care. She came first. I nodded at Lux so she knew it was okay.

A breathless Gina leaned against the doorframe.

"I'm so sorry," she said, panting. "I tried to stop her, but she heard some of the nurses saying you were awake."

I looked at Lux, who gave me a small smile.

"She's been here for a few hours," she said. "I tried to keep her at home, but she wasn't having it."

"I wanted to see you!" Bella said as she pulled away. "When Auntie Lux said you were in an accident, I was so scared."

I frowned and wiped the tears off her face.

"I know how scary that must've been." She was no doubt comparing it to the day when she'd lost her parents. "But I know you were brave for me, weren't you?"

"Not even a little bit. I cried the entire time," she answered with a pout.

I couldn't help but laugh and pull her back in for a hug.

"I'm okay, Bella. Don't worry. I'll be out of here soon."

"Will you come back home with us?" she asked, her voice muffled.

Lux was staring at me as if she wanted to hear the answer to that question too. I reached out and grabbed her hand.

"Just try and stop me. Yeah, I'm coming home."

The smile Lux gave me was blinding, and she stood up, pulling us both into a hug.

"Juliette, my God!"

With a sigh, we looked to the door, which now held Harmony, Erin, and April. All of them looking like I quite literally ruined their day.

They rushed to me, not caring that Bella was still in my arms.

"Are you okay? When I saw you bleeding out, I had no idea what to do! I thought you were going to di—"

"Let's not talk about that when there's a child present," Erin said, shoving Harmony out of the way.

April's hand made its way to my shoulder, and she squeezed.

"I'm okay, guys. Thanks for coming."

Harmony jumped into her recount of the night while Bella cuddled into me, not ready to let go yet. I didn't mind; I enjoyed the cuddles.

Lux stayed by my side, listening to my ex-roommates, even smiling every now and then.

But just when I thought it couldn't get any more crowded in the hospital room, Lucas popped his head in.

"How... Was this you?" I asked Lux.

"I sent him a text. Sorry, I took your phone. I didn't have Lucas's number."

Everyone made way for Lucas.

"Who's that?" Harmony asked in a hardly concealed whisper.

"The brother, I think," April whispered back.

Bella turned to glare at Lucas.

"Juliette, are you okay? Does anything hurt?" He then paused to look at Lux. "Who sends a goddamn message saying my sister is in the hospital without—"

Lucas stopped when he noticed us holding hands. When he looked at me, I just nodded. He nodded back and gave me a small smile, and I knew he got it.

Lux, Bella, and I were together, and he needed to get with the program.

A burst of warmth spread throughout my chest as I looked at the scene in front of me.

Bella still had her head on my chest and was hugging me as hard as I could possibly allow her. My roommates were talking off to the side about what types of food they were going to sneak into the hospital room for me.

My brother was in front of me, concern on his face, no doubt wanting to know what had happened. And I would tell him all about it. I wouldn't leave anything out.

They were all here for me. *Me.* I couldn't believe it. All these people were here because they cared about me and worried about me. Something seventeen-year-old me would've never imagined.

But that wasn't the end of it.

Marci poked her head in through the door and smiled when she saw me, a tray of drinks in her hands.

"How many people did you text?" I asked, looking at Lux.

The cutest blush ran up her neck and spread across her face.

"I think that's all," she replied, but then both Mia and Laura walked through the door.

"Oh my God," I said with a laugh.

"Is this some type of party or something?" Mia asked just as Laura crossed her arms over her chest.

"Have the police come yet?" Laura asked more seriously, and just as she did, two uniformed officers showed up behind them.

"Ms. Hayes?"

Laura turned around immediately, handing one of them her card. "She won't be answering questions at this time. You can come back later."

"And who are you—"

The other cop let out a heavy sigh once he read Laura's card.

"You're not gonna win this one," he told his colleague, pulling him back by his vest.

"We need to—"

"This is not a hill you want to die on, trust me. I know her."

With that, they were gone faster than they arrived, and Laura looked at me with a large smile. Marci walked to her, handing her a hot coffee.

"One latte, nonfat milk, with one sugar."

Laura thanked her, but my attention was pulled back to Lux when she lifted my hand and placed it to her lips.

"If you want them to leave, let me know."

I shook my head and sent her a smile before looking out at all the people who showed up because they cared about me.

"This is good. Thank you."

I leaned down and placed a kiss on top of Bella's head. Only then did I realize that she was asleep against me.

Tears pricked my eyes. It might have taken me a while to get here, but finally, I got a taste of what having a family felt like.

It was warm. It was fun. And I couldn't ask for anything more.

"I love you," I whispered to Lux.

"I love *you*, Angel."

Lucas made a gagging noise. "God, I'm gonna be sick." There was no venom in his voice, though. In fact, he looked... pleased.

I laughed and took the matcha Marci handed me. And for the first time in my life, I let myself be cared for and pampered by the people who loved me, knowing they were here to stay.

Juliette

I'd never been in a courtroom before.

Not even when my parents had the accident because there was no culprit. I mean, there was, but they could never find *her*. Until now.

Even if she ran away from the scene at the bridge, I was glad so many people had witnessed what Lux's mom did to me, most of whom had volunteered to testify against her.

Not only that, but I was finally getting justice for my parents.

Lux and I stood in the courtroom side by side. A united front. We hadn't let Bella come with us this time even though she wanted to. The now nine-year-old didn't seem to fully understand what was going on, and that was for the best. She didn't need to know her grandmother was a killer. We'd get to that when she was old enough to grasp it.

We watched as Lux's mother tried desperately to reason with the judge. Her lawyer's head was down as his client decided to take matters into her own hands.

She was frantic. Crying, pleading, begging. Crying so hard her makeup was running, ruining the picture-perfect image she never let slip.

She was no longer the rich, put-together woman involved in charity who had raised two kids and gained everyone's sympathy when one of them had been taken too soon.

Here, she was... unhinged.

"She's a fucking liar! I have never hurt a fly. You heard my character witnesses. They all say I'm a great and loving person! She's lying!"

"Mr. Fritz, if you cannot get your client under control—" the judge started.

"So maybe I did, but I didn't kill anyone! She talks about some random car accident and blames it on me even though I've never driven drunk in my life and I've never killed anyone!"

The judge leaned forward, clearly out of patience. "Ms. Sterling, were you paying attention to anything that was said in court?"

That shut her up. I wouldn't be surprised if she truly wasn't listening. Every time she saw Lux and me, she still acted like we were the ones to blame for this.

Turns out the policeman she had slept with to cover up her crime liked to keep note of the *favors* he did. And Mia and Laura were a force to be reckoned with. I would not want to be on their shit list. No lawyer, no matter how expensive, would be able to get her off the hook now.

My hand found Lux's, and I took a deep breath. Laura looked calm and collected as ever, but I could see just the barest hint of a smile pulling at her lips, and I knew she was proud of what she had done in this courtroom.

"You are without remorse and still trying to save yourself. I fear there is no hope for you. On top of the already issued life sentence, I am ordering you to pay two million dollars to the Hayes family for the wrongful death of their parents. One million for each parent. One million for each life you took."

His words had tears filling my eyes.

When the judge brought down his gavel, I looked back into the audience and met Lucas's eyes. I was taken back to the small boy who wouldn't let me go when he heard the news of our parents.

He was much older now and stronger too. His eyes were red, but his shoulders were back and his chest was puffed, showing the entire world just how proud he was that our parents had been vindicated.

And I was beyond proud of him. He had come right from his training, still wearing his lineman vest. He had moved out and left our aunt behind when he realized the part she'd played in helping Lux's mother. But more than that, he was pursuing his own goals in life, and I couldn't wait for him to have everything he wanted.

I turned back to the judge and watched as they dragged Lux's mother away, kicking and screaming.

"Court is adjourned!"

We all filed out, but Laura stopped us at the door.

"I'm glad I could see this to its end." She gave both Lux and me meaningful looks. "It's not every day we get a happy ending like this."

"Thank you for everything," I said, and wrapped my arm around Lux.

I looked up at her to catch her smiling at me already.

"We really appreciate it," she told Laura. "I'll be in touch."

Lauren nodded, ever the professional, and took her leave.

"Since this ended early, how about I take you out to lunch?" Lux asked.

"Only if it's at the diner," I said, knowing Bella was probably waiting for us at home.

"Deal." She was about to pull me away but paused when she caught sight of Lucas. He was standing not too far away from us. "Yes, you can come too. Family lunch."

A blinding smile spread across his face.

"Let's go get our girl, hm?" Lucas asked. "I need to hear the newest school gossip. It's like a soap opera I can't get enough of."

Lux laughed. "She's already waiting outside for us."

Over the last year, Lucas had become closer with all of us. It was awkward at first—and a bit painful if I was being honest

—but slowly he began to warm up to us. To the idea of me and Lux.

And, of course, to Bella. No one could resist her for long, but especially Lucas. She became the little sister he never had, and she helped him explore his inner child. The one that had been forced to grow up too fast after our parents' death.

Playdates. Arts and crafts. He did it all, any chance he got. He even bought matching aprons for when they took baking lessons from Gina.

It was everything I could have asked for and more.

Sure enough, Marci was waiting with a very impatient Bella. Lux met her first, trying to coax her back into the car, as Lucas came to my side, nudging my arm with his.

I looked up at him with a raised brow.

"This looks good on you," he said, side-eyeing me.

"What?" I asked and looked down on my bland court clothes, which consisted of a cardigan and a white blouse.

"Don't be stupid," he said with a huff. "Happiness. It looks good on you."

The air rushed out of my lungs, and I looked back at Lux and Bella, who were bickering playfully.

Warmth blossomed in my chest.

"So cheesy," I teased, leaning against him. "I didn't know you had it in you."

He cleared his throat and pushed me away.

"I am human, you know? I'm allowed to care about my sister." There was a small smile on his face. "Just make sure I'm the best man at the wedding."

Heat sprouted all over my body, and I struggled for a reply, but he was already gone and dipping into the car before I could stop him. Bella went in with him, and Lux was just... there.

She was always there. Wanting me. Loving me. And now waiting for me with a smile so wide it had to hurt her cheeks.

She held out a hand for me.
"Coming, Angel?"
Butterflies unleashed in my stomach.
This is what love is supposed to feel like.
I giggled as I placed my hands in hers.
"Yes, sir."

Chapter 33
Lux

My hand ran slowly up and down Bella's back as we stared down at my sister's grave.

It was only the second time we'd come back here since the accident, and I wasn't sure how she would react, but I had been ecstatic when she'd agreed to come on the anniversary of their death.

"You can say a few words if you want," Juliette said, the bouquet of flowers she brought coming into view as she handed them to Bella.

"I... don't know what to say." I could sense a bit of embarrassment in her words. I turned to Juliette for encouragement. She was already looking at me, the message clear on her face.

But even still, I couldn't bring myself to say anything.

"I miss you guys," Bella whispered. "I think about you every day." She looked at Juliette for confirmation, and she nodded. Her hand came to squeeze her shoulder.

"It's okay."

Bella took a deep, shaky breath.

"I'm doing fine," she said. "I shower by myself. I got an A on my last math test, even though Juliette helped—"

"Hey, I did too," I complained. When they both looked at me, I sent them a sheepish look. "Once or twice."

Bella shook her head and let out a light laugh.

"Juliette reads to me, Mom, and Lux got way better at braiding hair."

My chest puffed at her compliment.

"So I'm okay. I'm okay," she repeated. "I love being with Auntie Lux and Juliette, but I—"

Her words stopped just as the tears started falling. I pulled her into a side hug, bringing Juliette along.

"I know," I whispered. "I miss her too. I wish she could see how great you've been doing. She'd be so proud."

"They both know," Juliette said. "They see."

Bella let her tears fall, her silent sobs filling the space between us.

"I miss you so much," she said through her tears. "But don't worry about me, okay?"

My heart broke in two. Even though she thought her mom was up there—wherever that was—worrying about her baby girl, Bella was worried about her mom.

"We have her," Juliette said, addressing the headstone with my sister's name carved into it. "Always."

We stayed there a few more minutes in silence, my heart getting heavier the longer I stayed. Maybe this had been a mistake.

But as soon as the thought crossed my mind, Bella straightened.

"I'll visit you again soon, okay?" she said. "And next time I'll remember to buy the flowers."

Juliette let out a small laugh. "Ready to go?"

Bella nodded and stood, but I found myself unable to leave my spot.

"Auntie Lux?"

I hadn't realized tears had started to fall until Bella's small hand was there wiping them away.

"I miss them too," I explained and looked at my niece. "I'm sorry, Bella."

Bella looked at Juliette before sitting back down on the ground in front of my sister's headstone.

"Let's stay for a bit longer."

I nodded and leaned into her. Juliette joined us shortly, her arm wrapping around both of us.

"Thank you," I whispered. "For giving me a family. For changing my life in ways I could never have imagined. I promised to take care of Bella so you could rest. I intend to keep that promise for as long as I live."

Bella's hand found mine, and she squeezed.

"I still don't think I've done enough good in this life to deserve this," I continued. "But I won't ever let you down. I'll protect this gift and make sure your daughter grows up happy and healthy. Trust me, just this last time. *Please*."

My throat clogged. Juliette's hand rubbed my back.

"You're doing great, Lux."

"Yeah, Auntie Lux, you sucked at first, but you're better now."

I couldn't help but laugh at Bella's bluntness.

"Thank you both. Just a few more minutes and we can go."

"Just a few," Bella mumbled and buried her head into my side, where she stayed for far longer than a few minutes.

Thank you. My sister. My other half. The only person in this world who saw me.

I turned to catch Juliette's tearful gaze. *Until her.*

I think we will be just fine.

Chapter 34
Lux
One Year Later

"Remember what we talked about, okay?" I whispered as Bella gripped the tray with two hands.

"I'm not stupid, Auntie Lux," she whispered back.

"I know, I know," I said, and patted her back. "I have to get in place, but remember you go after the bridesmaids—"

"*I know,*" she hissed like I was exhausting her. Her hair was done in a half-up, half-down style with two pigtails in the back. She had picked out two small white braids that matched her white and light pink dress. In her hand, she had a bucket of pink and red flower petals. "Now get in place before Juliette thinks better of it and decides not to marry you after all."

"Right," I said and quickly fixed my hair and suit. I took a deep breath, giving Bella one last look before I went to the sliding glass door.

"Auntie Lux," Bella called, stopping me.

I turned back to look at my niece. She looked so much like my sister it hurt. But it was a good kind of hurt, unlike almost

two years ago. It warmed my soul to see a piece of my sister still alive on this planet.

Bella might not be my daughter, but she was the best gift I could've ever been given. She stood straight and confident, all the anxiety and fear that had once filled her gone. She was slowly blossoming into a woman I knew my sister would be proud of.

"You got this," she assured me, giving me a smile. "I love you. And thank you for bringing Juliette into my life. *Our* life."

Tears welled in my eyes. *Fuck.* "I love you too, sweetheart."

Then she motioned for me to get out of there with a scowl, the sweet moment over just as quickly as it began.

Her teenage years will be... interesting.

I let out a choked laugh and ran out to the backyard.

The vast green yard had been completely transformed. There were white and pink chairs to my right and left, and a long aisle at the end of a gazebo peppered with hundreds of wildflowers. Harmony, Juliet's ex-roommate, stood there in a pink dress that matched the color themes.

I got in place beside her, and she gave me a reassuring wink, obviously feeling the nerves running through me.

She motioned to Marci, who was off to the side at the DJ booth, to start the music. My heart pounded in my chest as a modernized version of the traditional wedding song played through the speakers.

All eyes were on me.

At first, I didn't know who to invite to the wedding, but after some thinking, the chairs started filling up faster than I expected.

Mia, Laura, and Gina all said yes. Juliette didn't extend the invite to any of her extended family, for good reason. As the good person she was, she floated around with the idea of inviting them, but I could see in her eyes she didn't truly want them to be here.

They didn't need to be. This was *ours*. We didn't need them ruining what was supposed to be one of the best moments in our lives.

I sent an invite to Sloan as a thank you since it was because of her invitation to Club Pétale that Juliette and I had met in the first place. I told her to invite her partner, who currently sat in the second row, and when she asked if she could bring her friend and their partner, I didn't expect it to be Nyx, who brought Ax, who happened to be the owner of the club.

That's how somehow our wedding became the talk of the club, so when Lillian asked if she could bring more people, of course I said yes. As such, there were five more people there that I'd never met before, all of them sitting together in the second and third rows, looking happy as ever to be there. Except for one girl with black hair and blue eyes who looked like she wanted to be nowhere near a crowd. Her partner, though, seemed to be pretty excited.

When I extended an invite to my work family, we were at full capacity. And even though it was a small event, for once I was feeling a little bit of performance anxiety.

There was one person in the far right corner, his eyes on me and a heartbreaking smile on his face. A person I never thought would show up, or, until a short while ago, knew still existed.

My father.

I met his gaze, and he gave me a small nod. He hadn't been around for my entire life, but that small gesture meant everything. I had no one to rely on. No one to look to for help, but he showed. *Finally.*

I took a deep breath, my hands coming to tug at my clothes. Anxiety was reaching its peak.

But all that melted away when the best man made his way down the aisle.

Lucas walked with a confident swagger that only he could pull off and came to stand beside me. He gave me a pat on the back and smiled before saying, "If you hurt my sister, I will hunt you down."

He'd been saying that ever since I proposed, and I didn't hold it against him. I was in no danger. I'd never hurt Juliette.

My heart squeezed when the bridesmaids started walking down the aisle because I knew Juliette was just that much closer.

It was April, her ex-roommate, followed by Erin, and then Gina. Harmony would've been in there too if she hadn't decided that she randomly wanted to become a wedding officiant just for Juliette's wedding.

When Bella came next in her pretty dress, I was smiling wide. She took her job as flower girl very seriously and made sure to walk in pace with the music as she spread her petals.

She met my eyes and stopped in front of me, her hand reaching out to grab mine. I gave it a squeeze, and she was off to stand at the end of the bridesmaids' line.

There was a pause, and I swear I wasn't breathing as I watched Lucas loop around to wait for my bride at the sliding glass door.

I was annoyed at first that he insisted on being both the best man and walking Juliette down the aisle, but I knew it had to be him. And seeing both their smiles as she reached for his arm had all of the annoyance washing away.

Butterflies swarmed in my stomach. My heart hammered in my chest, and my skin heated unbearably. I had been successful in holding back the tears until that very moment.

Juliette coming out of the house in a wedding dress was

hands down the single most beautiful thing I'd ever seen in my life.

Her blonde hair was pulled up into a half-up, half-down hairdo that resembled Bella's—not by accident, I was sure. She had a lacey veil on with pink flower petals sewn into it. The dress itself had puffed-out long sleeves and a crystal bodice, and the puffy skirt bounced elegantly behind her as she walked.

When she met my eyes, the world fell away.

She was perfect, and I couldn't believe she was *finally* going to be mine in every sense of the word.

Her brother placed a kiss on her palm. Juliette's eyes were already watery, but a single tear fell when he whispered something that sounded a lot like "our parents would be proud" to her.

He handed me her hand with the utmost care, and I took it, giving him a smile as he went back to his position.

Harmony addressed the crowd and gave the normal spiel, but I didn't hear a word. I was too obsessed with Juliette.

I pushed back her veil so I could get an unobstructed look at her face.

"Hi," she whispered with a smile.

"Hello, beautiful," I whispered back.

I didn't care about the crowd. I was barely able to follow Harmony's prompts, but I did because I knew at the end I would finally be able to kiss my wife.

Those two words sounded so beautiful swirling around my head, and I couldn't wait to use them.

"Juliette, do you take Lux as your lawfully wedded wife?"

"I do," Juliette replied, her voice shaky.

"And do you, Lux, take Juliette as your lawfully wedd—"

"I do." My hurry had a few people chuckling, including Harmony.

I put the ring on Juliette's finger, a gold band with a mix of different-cut diamonds that I had found at an antique shop. Something I knew would fit Juliette perfectly. She had all but collapsed when I pulled it out on a weekend getaway to the Hamptons.

She put a simple diamond band on mine.

"By the authority vested in me by the state of New York, I now pronounce you wife and wife!"

I grabbed Juliette, kissing her like there was no crowd. The hoots and hollers did their best to remind me there was, but I didn't care.

"My wife," I whispered against her lips. Her hands grabbed my shoulders, and she kissed me with a passion that threatened to make me blush.

They were just about to pull us apart when I finally brought us up for air.

Juliette's eyes were sparkling, and she met me with a devious smile.

"Mrs. Sterling," I whispered. "All mine."

"You did say you always got what you wanted," she said with a light laugh.

Bella ran to us, her arms wrapping around us.

"Congratulations!"

We laughed and pulled her into a hug. The perfect family. Just the way we were.

I had the angel the universe had sent me. I had my niece, who made me grow in ways that I never knew were possible.

Both had taught me how to love and be loved. And I could never imagine a world without them.

"I love you both," I whispered, and both my girls looked up at me with a smile.

"And we love you, Lux. Forever."

Epilogue

We decided our honeymoon was going to be *nontraditional*.

My back arched, and I tried to move my hands, but they were tied to the metal headboard behind me.

"Fuck, Lux!"

I cried as another orgasm slammed into me like a freight train. Black spots flashed across my vision, and my body was convulsing with just how strong the waves of pleasure were.

My legs were tied to the end of the bed. Lux was between them. A large bulbous vibrator was placed over my clit, its long cord plugged into the wall.

"My wife. My beautiful, sensitive *wife*."

Lux couldn't get enough of saying it, and I couldn't get enough of hearing it. The word alone sent a flutter through me.

My eyes locked in on the mirror right above the bed. Seeing myself spread out, panting and naked was erotic. So was seeing the obscene amount of wetness that stained the bed below me.

Toys lay around me, ranging from large, fake cocks to small

vibrators to whips. If I thought Lux was ravenous before, she was a straight-up demon now.

She had taken the liberty of getting us a room back at the place where we first met.

Club Pétale.

When we entered the club, we didn't linger for long. Lux took me straight back to the room, the same one where we spent our first night together, where she undressed me as quickly as possible and forced me onto the bed just like back then.

She couldn't keep her hands off of me. At first, I tried to touch her but quickly figured out that she wanted nothing more than to hear my cries as she made me come over and over again while using her new favorite title for me.

My wife.

That was fine. I had the rest of her life to make her come. I could be patient.

"Tell me the safe word again," she demanded, taking the vibrator off my clit.

"Bubblegum. Bubblegum. Bubbleg—"

I groaned as the vibrator was placed back against my clit as she slowly pushed one of the fake cocks to my entrance. We had worked our way up, and now she was inching an even bigger one into me.

The stretch felt so sinful, I almost came right then and there.

And then, when it was fully seated, the head brushing up against my cervix, I let out a choked gasp.

"More, sir. Please. More."

"More what, my beautiful wife? Use your words."

"Fuck me, please, sir. Please, fuck me."

I let out another loud groan as she slowly started to pump the cock in and out of me.

"No," I gasped.

She looked at me, raising a brow.

"No?"

"Harder, faster," I commanded. "Please, sir."

I was silenced as her slow pumping turned into something animalistic in a split second. She fucked me hard and fast, each thrust hitting my cervix and sending my eyes rolling to the back of my head. I tried to spread my legs further for her. I tried to take more. I wanted more.

"Oh God, Lux... Yes, just like that!"

"You're going to come for me, aren't you, Angel?"

I couldn't answer her because I was already coming again. I was so sensitive, so overstimulated.

Pleasure rocked through me in waves, starting from my core and working outward.

I was stuck there, motionless as she continued to fuck me, sending me over the edge again. I thrashed and flailed, unable to keep still.

"I need to taste you," I panted as she finally let me come down.

Lux sent me a wicked grin.

"Anything for my angel."

"No. Anything for your *wife*."

She grinned wider as she took the vibrator away but left the cock in while she undressed. Lux never untied me, and I was fine with that.

When she finally got her pants off, she maneuvered herself so her cunt was right over my lips. She leaned over, her lips placing a small kiss on my clit as she grabbed the dildo, slowly pumping it in and out of me again as her tongue ran circles around the swollen bundle of nerves.

I pushed up, grabbing her hips and bringing her cunt into my mouth. She let out a moan, and I took it as the go-ahead to spear her with my tongue before pulling her clit into my mouth and sucking hard the way I knew she liked.

"Fuck, if you keep that up, I'm going to come too fast."

"Give it to me," I commanded and kept going, sucking first, spearing second, alternating and exploring her thoroughly as I paid attention to what made her jerk. All the while, she never stopped pumping that dildo, bringing me to a slow orgasm.

She was right about coming fast. Wetness exploded from her, and I licked it up greedily as I continued fucking her with my mouth until she stopped shaking against me.

"Again," I commanded.

She chuckled but let me continue to bring her to another orgasm with my mouth.

"My wife," she whispered and kissed my clit.

"*My* wife," I whispered back. "I love you."

I raked my teeth against the inside of her thigh, and she cursed again, bringing her cunt down to my mouth. She was all but riding my face at that point.

"Fuck, I love you so much, Juliette. I love you. I love you. I lov—"

She came in with an explosive cry before moving off me, her lips coming to mine. Her tongue glided across mine, mixing our orgasms.

We tasted delicious.

"If we keep this up, we're never going to leave," I said with a laugh.

"Good thing I signed up for memberships and already scheduled Harmony to babysit every Friday for the next three months," Lux replied.

I pulled her into another kiss and gasped when the vibrator connected with my clit.

She was ravenous and unforgiving, but I wouldn't want it

any other way. She introduced me to a part of myself that I never knew existed, and there was no going back.

"Was a million dollars worth it?" I asked.

She smiled against my lips.

"Best investment I've ever made."

Thank you for reading LOVE ME NOT, if you want more... consider preordering the next book...

HATE ME NOT

An auction seemed like the perfect way to have some fun and make a little extra cash.
Until my anxiety whispered that no one would ever want to buy *someone like me.*
But even my inner critic couldn't have predicted who would actually *win* me.
One million dollars. One night.
With the girl who tormented me throughout high school.
This time, let's just hope *I don't fall in love again*

Want to be in the know? Join my newsletter for publishing updates and free shorts!

Join my Patreon and you will get access to all stories BEFORE they are published.

If you join now you will get free stories and deleted chapters!

There is also a tier for NSFW art that is exclusive for my Patreon members where you can see THIS

But naked ;)

Check it out here or go to https://www.patreon.com/elle maebooks

If you liked this, please review!

Reviews really help indie authors get their books out there so, please make sure to share your thoughts!

About the Author

Elle/Eden is a native Californian who has lived in Los Angeles for most of her life. From the very start, she has been in love with all things fantasy and reading. As soon as Elle found out that writing books could be a career, she picked up a pen and paper. While the first ones were about scorned love and missed opportunities of lunchtime love, she has grown to love the fantasy genre and looks forward to making a difference in the world with her stories.

Loved this book? Please leave a review!

For more behind the scene content, check out my Patreon!

X x.com/mae_books

instagram.com/ellemaebooks

goodreads.com/ellemae

patreon.com/ellemaebooks

tiktok.com/@ellemaebooks